CANINE
CRIMES

Presented by Jeffrey Marks
Published by Ballantine Books:

CANINE CRIMES

Books published by The Ballantine Publishing Group are available at quantity discounts on bulk purchases for premium, educational, fund-raising, and special sales use. For details, please call 1-800-733-3000.

CANINE CRIMES

Presented by
Jeffrey Marks

BALLANTINE BOOKS • NEW YORK

A Ballantine Book
Published by The Ballantine Publishing Group
Compilation and introduction copyright © 1998 by Jeffrey Marks

"Eric, the Family Savior" copyright © 1998 by Brendan DuBois
"Peanut and Shadow" copyright © 1998 by Carolyn G. Heilbrun
"Building Herbert" copyright © 1998 by Deborah Adams
"The Invisible Sky" copyright © 1998 by Polly Whitney
"Doggone" copyright © 1998 by Jonnie Jacobs
"Sleeping Dogs Lie" copyright © 1998 by Laurien Berenson
"Manor Beast" copyright © 1998 by Lillian M. Roberts
"Foolproof" copyright © 1998 by Taylor McCafferty
"Nosing Around for a Clue" copyright © 1998 by Valerie Wolzien
"Cooking the Hounds" copyright © 1998 by S. J. Rozan
"Daisy and the Archaeologists" copyright © 1998 by Anne Perry
"The Long Arm of the Paw" copyright © 1998 by Jeffrey Marks
"Best Served Cold" copyright © 1998 by Dean James
"Like Alpo for Chocolate: A Short Story in Fragrances" copyright © 1998 by Steven Womack
"You'll Never Bark in this Town Again" copyright © 1998 by Melissa Cleary

http://www.randomhouse.com

Library of Congress Catalog Card Number: 98-96401

ISBN 0-345-42411-5

Manufactured in the United States of America

First Edition: November 1998

10   9   8   7   6   5   4   3   2   1

Contents

Introduction

Jeffrey Marks

"Mr. Holmes, they were the footprints of a gigantic hound." Even when I read those words today, my heart races with excitement at a mystery to be solved. *The Hound of the Baskervilles* sent Sherlock Holmes from 221 B Baker Street to Dartmoor to locate the source of a family curse and a deadly killer. Visions of the monstrous, glowing dog galloping the moors at night have thrilled audiences for over a century. As a result, big dogs were given a homicidal reputation.

Yet if dogs match the personality of their owners, we should determine the villains by their packs of hungry Dobermans or snapping pit bulls. They might as well wear black hats and twirl their mustaches. Lillian M. Roberts's story in this book, "Manor Beasts," wouldn't work with chihuahuas, nor would S. J. Rozan's tale, "Cooking the Hounds," with poodles. Good guys have kept to terriers and smaller domesticated dogs, or perhaps the dogs have trained them. Laurien Berenson's Jack Russell terrier can be mischievous but is never dangerous. No one envisions the drooling jaws of a mastiff following gently behind the hero.

Nor can readers imagine a dangerous housecat. Instead, the feline species have long been associated with libraries and whodunits in particular, in their roles as the witch's familiar and as the icon of the cozy mystery. While notable exceptions exist, man's best friend occupies a less prominent place in mystery.

Agatha Christie often compared Inspector Japp, the inept police foil, to a bloodhound with his nose to the ground, sniffing things men weren't supposed to inhale. Several of the stories in this anthology recognize that attribute and use the dog's keen sense of smell to their advantage. In Valerie Wolzien's story, a dog finds a body based on smell.

However, the dog's role is not limited to its olfactory sense. In *Poirot Loses a Client*, Christie provides a more benign canine companion. Poirot is called upon to indirectly clear a dog of harming his mistress. While he doesn't stand trial at the Old Bailey, Bob, Emily Arundell's wire-hair terrier, was fingered for one of a number of close calls with death. The playful act of bouncing a ball down a flight of stairs in their home had injurious consequences. The accident causes the older woman to alter her will as she prepares for death. Yet the victim visited Poirot only days before her impending demise, suspecting a two-legged member of her household of staging the crimes. While he dog-sits, the detective's little gray cells look for a more human killer.

Hardboiled Dashiell Hammett wrote about Nick and

Nora Charles, wisecracking socialites, and their dog Asta. Although the couple rarely turns up sober, the novel has a light, humorous tone missing from most of his other work. The Schnauzer who was often mistaken for a mix between a Scottie and an Irish terrier only made a brief appearance in *The Thin Man*, but the debonair dog took a more active role in solving crimes in William Powell/Myrna Loy movies.

Additionally, S. S. Van Dine wrote *The Kennel Murder Case*. The author of the Philo Vance series bred dogs as a hobby and wanted to pontificate on the subject. The accessibility of the canine antics proved a welcome respite from Vance's normal arcane banter. Other real dogs appear in fiction. Taylor McCafferty's creation Haskell Blevins has a dog, RIP, modeled after her own pet, and Anne Perry's nonfictional dog, Daisy, appears in her story for this book.

In the past few years, dogs have taken a more prominent place in the world of mystery. Where would the world of detection be without Susan Conant's dogs or David Handler's Lulu? Hoagy would be a different man with a Yorkie. Dogs add spice to stories, sniffing where humans wouldn't and actively participating in the solution of crimes. They are not only man's best friend, but also a detective's as well.

This anthology contains fifteen brand-new stories from some of the brightest talents in mystery writing today, all dog lovers who will gladly regale you with anecdotes about their personal pets. Curl up with your favorite canine and enjoy a good read.

Eric, The Family Savior

Brendan DuBois

BRENDAN DUBOIS, a former newspaper reporter, is a lifelong resident of the New Hampshire seacoast. An acclaimed novelist, he has also published over thirty short stories in such magazines as *Playboy*, *Ellery Queen's Mystery Magazine*, and *Alfred Hitchcock Mystery Magazine*. DuBois's first published story in 1986 was a finalist for the Robert L. Fish Memorial Award; his subsequent stories have been nominated numerous times for the Edgar Award.

On a Saturday in September, after the tourists had fled back to their cities and suburbs, Gil Donahue stood on a little point of land that jutted into the waters of Lake Hanrattey and looked out across the water into the northern woods of Maine. A stiff breeze had come across the lake, making the gray water choppy, and up on the mountains and hills that surrounded the lake, the colors of the fall foliage had already begun their annual riot of orange, red, and yellow.

He turned and glanced back at his house. It was two-story, with a dock that jutted out into the water. On the near steps of the house a yellow Labrador retriever sat, tail wagging slowly and expectantly. Gil put his hands in his coat pocket. This place had been a refuge once, for him and Terri and for Terri's daughter Melanie, and even for the dog, Eric. A great place to live, left well enough alone by the neighbors and tourists and even by the people in the nearest town of Lincoln.

But then in a cold spring two years ago, a drunken truck driver hauling a load of logs for a pulp mill had taken Terri away from them, and after a long and empty summer, and an even colder winter, they had regrouped and survived. He had thought the family was going to make it, until last week when they came and took Melanie away from him.

It had been a warm day for mid-September, and he had let Melanie go out by herself in a small sailboat. She had on a lifejacket that almost swallowed up her nine-year-old body, and her eyes had been wide and serious. She half jokingly asked if Eric could come along.

"He's a great swimmer, you know," she said, tugging at her blonde ponytail with one hand and rubbing Eric's head with the other.

"I know, but he can get excited when the sails start flapping," he replied. "You go and have fun. But don't go beyond the birches. All right?"

"All right," she said, and in a few minutes he stood at the end of the dock, watching her handle the sails with ease. The wind was slight enough to give her some movement, but not enough to cause the boat to tip over. To the right the lakefront curved around, on which a stand of white birches made a barrier to going out on the lake any further. His own outboard motorboat was tied to the dock. If she got into trouble at all, he could be there in a minute.

Later that morning, sixty seconds would prove to be too long.

He was working by the side of the house, tearing away a set of rotted porch steps. Eric was bounding in and out of the brush and small trees near the woods, chasing after squirrels. And then came the gurgling sound of a motorboat, the sound getting louder and louder, and he dropped the hammer and started running at the sounds of Melanie's screams.

He pounded his way to the dock, just in time to see the events unfold in slow motion, as if everything were moving through clear amber: a large and powerful-looking black motorboat, approaching the sailboat, barely slowing down . . . Melanie screaming as the sailboat almost founders, sails flapping. . . . Three men in the motorboat, two of them reaching over and grabbing Melanie and hauling her in. . . . And then the motorboat making a quick turn, its stern almost contemptuously swamping the small sailboat, as one of the men tosses something bright and orange overboard.

By the time he had gotten his own boat untied and the motor started, the powerful motorboat had made good distance, the spume raising up like a rooster's tail as it boomed its way north up the lake. His own boat's motor sounded feeble as he made his way to the swamped sailboat, and when he had retrieved a small orange buoy that had his name written on the outside, the motorboat was gone, having headed to the east where there was a maze of coves and islands.

The buoy was bright orange and made of hollow plastic, and inside was a note. He switched off the motor's engine and sat there in the bobbing swells, his shaking hands causing the notepaper to rattle:

Hello, Gil—

This is from an old acquaintance from your past—Jean-Paul. Remember?

This is also to inform you that we have your stepdaughter. She is safe and will be safe and returned to you once you have turned over $500,000 to me and my associates. I do hate to insult your intelligence so, but please do not go to the police or any other authorities.

We have your home, your truck, your property, and your telephone lines under constant surveillance to ensure just that. Need some proof?

Two days ago you called Kym's Video, looking for the latest Disney release for your stepdaughter. When you went to get groceries a week ago, you listened to talk radio from Portland in your truck. Last night Melanie asked you in the living room to stay up an extra half hour to listen to the loons. You said yes (such a softy!). And yesterday morning, when you were chopping wood, you relieved yourself against a dead oak, when you thought no one was looking. But we were.

And another insult to your intelligence (sorry!), but if you attempt to locate our surveillance devices, you will never see your stepdaughter again.

Here is the deal with no negotiations allowed. You have five days to contact your banker in Lincoln to arrange the liquidation of your funds. (And trust me, I know you've done quite well, while I've been rotting in prison in Brussels.) During that time you will not leave your property, except to go in and out of town to get the money.

On Sunday next, at nine A.M., we will come to your property for the exchange. You will show us the money in a plain office briefcase. Despite the cold weather, you will be barefoot, wearing just briefs—sorry, I know how deadly you can be when irritated, and I don't want any mistakes with concealed weapons on your part!

And once I am happy, you will get your stepdaughter back.

And by making me happy, I will begin the very long road of finally forgiving you for betraying me and the others, all those years ago.

Au revoir,
Jean-Paul

At first he crumpled the note in rage, ready to toss it over, but he forced himself to think. He had to, for Melanie—now terrified and scared and wondering what in hell was going on with her young life—was now counting on him. He restarted the small boat's engine and tied off a line to the swamped sailboat, and he towed the vessel back to the dock, the soggy sails flapping in the breeze like the banners of a defeated army.

He blinked hard and looked again over at the lake. Difficult to believe it had been less than a week. He had hardly slept in that time, wondering who was watching and who was listening. Even Eric seemed affected; the yellow Lab sulked in the house and would whine at times, as if wondering where Melanie had gone.

Gil turned, looked back at the house. Eric was still sitting expectantly on the side doorstep. The dog had been Terri's and had quickly bonded to him when he had joined with her. Gil had never been much of a dog person, but Eric was a boon companion, especially during walks out in the woods or when he had work to do around the property. A Lab—complete with webbed feet—he enjoyed playing in the lake and could spend hours racing in and out of the water, retrieving rubber balls that either he or Melanie had tossed out. At night he would scramble out in the woods, chasing God knows what, and then he'd come back, covered with dirt and brambles, breathing hard, his brown eyes shining with the excitement of whatever chase he had performed.

Gil slapped the side of his leg twice and Eric bounded away from the steps and was at his side in a matter of seconds. The dog flopped down at his feet and rolled over on his back, and Gil reached down and scratched the dog's belly.

"Just one more day, pal," he said quietly. "Just one more day."

Some distance away, Jean-Paul Cloutier talked to another man who was looking across the lake with a set of high-powered binoculars. They both wore camouflaged clothing and Jean-Paul said, "Nate, what is going on over there?"

Nate kept the binoculars up to his face. "The guy was standing by his house, and the dog came over to him to get scratched. Just like yesterday, and the day before. He's following your instructions, that's for sure. Only time he left was yesterday, when he went to the bank to get the money."

"Ah, that is good," Jean-Paul said, crossing his arms. Gil, he thought, I have finally caught up with you, after all these years. And it was almost spooky, because Nate spoke up, just like he was reading his mind.

"A question, if you don't mind," Nate said.

"Go ahead."

The binoculars came down. Nate was beefy, an ex-soldier who had been drummed out for being too enthusiastic in certain training sessions. "Are you sure this guy betrayed you and your friends? Are you sure?"

Jean-Paul closed his eyes for a moment and was back in the stinking cell, water dripping down, no sunlight, no fresh air, nothing green and alive. "We were a small group, a contract force that went here and there, doing special tasks that needed to be done, privately and securely and without a lot of publicity. Gil was part of this group. We were all cross-trained in various skills but Gil was our computer expert. One day he resigned. Said he wanted to do something different with his life. Very well. Who could argue with that?"

And once again, the memory of what happened made his fists clench at his side. "Then, a few months later, there were arrests. In five different countries. All of us in this contract force, all of us were arrested. Except for Gil. He had disappeared. And I knew what had happened. He had betrayed us for money, and I knew that someday, I would return and get my vengeance."

Nate grunted. "So, tomorrow you get your money and you get your vengeance. And then we leave?"

Jean-Paul tried to keep his voice in check. "No, tomorrow there will be more than money. We will take the girl back, as promised, and when the money is exchanged, he will have her, as promised. But I didn't promise that she would live for very long after that."

Nate brought the binoculars back up to his face. "I don't do kids."

"Good for you," Jean-Paul said, slapping him lightly on the back. "It must be nice to have a conscience. One of these days you will have to tell me what it's like."

Later that night Gil was in the darkened living room, a small fire crackling away in the fireplace, looking over the briefcase and the carefully banded groups of bills inside. He kept quiet just like the day before and the day before that. He had searched the house thoroughly and had found the listening devices that had been put in—probably when he was in town with Melanie, running errands or doing shopping—and had left them alone.

He touched the money, his entire life's saving and investments. Earlier he had experienced elaborate fantasies of how he would retaliate. He could go out in the woods at night with his weapons and hunt down the kidnappers—if he was being watched, they had to be close by. Or he could try to find out where they might be hiding—that power-boat was too conspicuous not to have been noticed by other people on the lake. Or he could rig the briefcase to explode in Jean-Paul's face.

Sure. Fantasies all and they made him feel better for a few minutes, but he did what he had to do. He left those fantasies alone. He closed the briefcase and then went out to the enclosed porch. Eric, who had been warming himself in front of the fireplace, got up and followed him, flopping down at his feet as Gil sat down on the couch and looked out over the dark lake.

He reached down and gently stroked the dog's fur. It was on a night like this, over three years ago, that he had met Terri, and later, her daughter and their dog. He had been driving through this part of rural Maine in a fierce rainstorm when his pickup truck had broken down. He had been working under the open hood, getting soaked, when Terri stopped and offered him a lift into town. She had long brown hair tied up in a ponytail and an infectious laugh, and when they found the town's sole service station was closed, she offered him a place to stay for the night.

Repairs to the truck took a couple of days, but when those repairs were finished, he didn't leave. Eventually they were married on the dock by a local justice of the peace, and one night, on this very porch, he had asked her why she had stopped, that first time in the rain.

"Because you needed help, silly," she said.

"But isn't that dangerous, picking up strange men?"

Terry gently poked him in the shoulder. "Dear, you're odd, but not strange. And I have a way with people. I felt good about you, the minute I talked to you. If I hadn't—well, I would have driven you over to Gerrish and would have dropped you off at the Pine Tree Motel and would have wished you luck, and that would have been it."

It was on this porch, too, before they were married, that he had tried to explain to her what he had done before coming to Maine. Terri worked as a children's book illustrator— and was quite good at what she did—and at first, Gil only expained that he was retired and living off his investments. One night he told her more.

"I used to work for the government, in . . . security matters," he said. "I was good with a computer and was good with a gun, but my group's budget got cut and a number of us were laid off."

Terri had nodded, sipping from a glass of wine. "Downsizing. Ain't it grand."

"Sure," he said. "So there I was, with some unique skills and not much opportunity to use them, when I was contacted by a firm that said it did contract work with the government. I'd be doing similar things but at a higher rate of pay. It sounded pretty good. And it was, at first."

She eyed him strangely over her wineglass. "Did you ever shoot anybody?"

He swallowed. "Yes."

"Was it necessary?"

"Yes."

"Do you still have firearms?"

Gil said, "I do. But I'll get rid of them if that bothers you."

She shook her head. "I'm a Maine girl, through and through. Guns don't bother me. All right, go on."

He took a deep breath. "Then one day, I found out that this particular group was expanding . . . was expanding its option of services. This particular service involved a civil war in Africa, a civilian airliner, and a surface-to-air missile. One day later I quit . . . and a couple of weeks later, I gave them all up. Last I heard, they're all serving very long prison terms."

She was eyeing him oddly. "Good for you."

He shrugged. "I didn't feel particularly good at the time."

She put down her wineglass and came over and sat on his lap.

"How do you feel now?" she asked, nuzzling his neck.

"I feel great."

The room was dark and she had a cloth tied over her eyes, and Melanie was saying her prayers, over and over again. She would start with "Hail Mary," go into "Our Father," and then finish with "Now I Lay Me Down to Sleep." Then she would start all over again. Every time she stopped, she'd start crying, and she didn't want to do that so she kept on with her prayers. She prayed to God and the angels and to Mom, up there in Heaven, hoping they would all work together to get her out of this dark place. She thought of her dad—she knew that he was really only her stepdad, but her real dad in California was a real loser, as Mom said—and thought of Eric, and she cried some more and started saying the prayers again.

Eric and her dad Gil were her only family, and she wanted to be back home so badly.

It was chilly in the cabin as Gil got up from a bad night's sleep. He was too wired to do anything but brush his teeth and wash his face. He went to his closet to get his clothes for the morning. He frowned as he opened the door, remembering Jean-Paul's instructions. Not many clothing options for today. He looked up at the top shelf of the closet, at his holstered 9 mm. Right, he thought. He raised his hand and took down a yellow belt, then a pair of shorts, and then he got dressed.

* * *

Jean-Paul felt like whistling as he walked through the woods. Nate and Jerry—who had driven the boat so well earlier this week in picking up their booty—were in front of him, holding the girl between them, her eyes still blindfolded. Their weapons were slung over their backs, and Jean-Paul carried his own pistol in a holster at his side. The air was cold and the ground was wet from a brief overnight shower, and in a few minutes it would all be over. Five hundred thousand dollars for a week's work. Not bad at all. Nate and Jerry would get half and he'd get the other half, and at long last he could start having fun again in this man's world.

And he grinned, thinking that with every dollar he spent of Gil Donahue's money, Gil and the little girl would be slumbering in a very long sleep indeed in this rocky soil.

Gil stepped out of the cabin, wearing just the shorts and carrying the briefcase. He started shivering and was embarrassed. Jean-Paul and his crew would probably think it was fear instead of the cold that made him tremble so, and that thought bothered him. Eric had come along with him and he said, "Lie down, Eric," and after the dog briefly licked his hand, the yellow Lab stretched out on the wooden steps, his soft brown eyes taking everything in.

He winced as he walked across the rough ground and grass, the dirt cold against his bare feet, and he didn't have long to wait. He saw movement in the woods and then three men came out, with Melanie among them, blindfolded and stumbling as she walked. The sight made his heart ache, and, for the thousandth time this week, he apologized to the memory of Terri for letting this awfulness happen.

He remembered the day after Terri's funeral, sitting on the front porch, just staring out at the dark waters of the lake. The house was empty of friends and relatives and Melanie had come in and had climbed up in his lap. From the very beginning the little girl had accepted him as part of the family, and after he and Terri got married, she had shyly asked him if she could call him Dad. He could not say a word in reply, could only nod, and that had been bliss.

Now, with Terri gone, Melanie put her arms around his neck and said, "Are we still a family?"

"Sure we are," he said, gently stroking her hair. "You and me, we're still a family. That's how your mom would have wanted it."

"And Eric, too?" she asked, and the Lab looked up at hearing his name and thumped his tail on the floor.

"Yep," he had said, still staring out at the lake. "You and me and Eric. We're a family. We'll take care of each other."

"Sure," Melanie said. "You and I will take care of each other, and Eric, he'll take care of us. Right?"

Another thumping sound from the dog's tail striking the floor.

He gave her a little squeeze. "That's right, hon. Eric will always take care of us."

So there he was, Jean-Paul thought. The man who had betrayed him and the others, all for some old-fashioned sense of morality. There he was, with his life's savings in a briefcase, standing there and shivering in a brief pair of shorts that disguised nothing. Poor little man, he thought. He thinks today will be the end, that he will be able to recover all after the girl is returned to him, and he doesn't know that, in a few minutes, he and the girl will be cast into the dark.

He stopped the group about ten feet away, and he bowed in the direction of Gil.

"Bonjour, mon ami," Jean-Paul said, enjoying the sight of seeing his betrayer trembling this cool morning. "It is good to see you, and it is even better to see you holding that briefcase."

"Let's get this over with," Gil said, opening the briefcase and holding it up to him. Jean-Paul heard little gasps of pleasure from Nate and Jerry, and even he couldn't hold back a grin. The briefcase was stuffed with money, banded groups of bills. That's all there is in life, Jean-Paul thought. Getting money—either making it or stealing it— and spending it right away on those many pleasures out there. And this was going to serve him for quite a while.

"Very good," Jean-Paul said. "And now, here is my side of the bargain. Gentlemen, if you please."

Nate and Jerry let go of the girl and stepped back as Gil snapped the briefcase shut. Jean-Paul brought his hand down to his side. Just a couple of shots, that's all, and we'll be out of here.

And then Gil slapped the side of his leg twice, and a dog bounded off the porch and ran to him.

Just like yesterday, Jean-Paul thought. What a silly man.

The dog raced over to Gil and then flopped over on his back, revealing his belly, just like yesterday, and the day before that, and the day before that—

But this time was different, the dog's belly was dirty, no, there was something there, something was wrong, something was wrong—

A holstered 9 mm, kept in place by a yellow belt, cinched around the dog's fur.

And his hand raced to his side, reaching for the holster, and he opened his mouth to shout a warning to Nate and Jerry.

"Melanie, get down!" Gil yelled, and he grabbed the pistol and brought it up and snapped off three shots, the loud reports echoing across the lake, saw everything as if in slow motion, the closer two men falling and then Jean-Paul, and Gil hated himself for enjoying the look of surprise on Jean-Paul's face.

And then all he heard was the sound of Eric barking and Melanie crying. He raced forward, grabbing her and pulling her back, whispering, "It's okay, it's okay, don't look hon, just don't look, everything's okay."

And when he ran with her into the cabin, Eric barked and pranced at their heels.

Later that night, his hands were dirty and sore from all the digging he had to do. He knew that eventually he would have to search the shores of the lake to find the black powerboat and the place that Melanie had been kept and take care of any evidence, but that could wait. Right now all the doors were locked in the cabin and a fire was burning and they were all cuddled on a couch on the porch, a comforter over them, Gil and Melanie and even Eric, who every now and then would lick Melanie's face in pure joy at having her back.

"I knew you'd get me back," Melanie said. "I just knew it, I just knew it."

"I'm glad you're right," he said, still wired up after what had happened.

"And the bad men, you don't think they'll come back, do you?" she said, her voice more serious. "I know you said you scared them off with your gun, but don't you think they'll be back?"

"No, I don't," he said, grateful that she could accept the lie that the bad men had just run away. "I can promise you that they'll never come back."

She snuggled in deeper in the comforter and said, "I bet you I know why they won't come back."

"And why's that?"

She smiled. "It's because of Eric. I bet you they were scared of Eric. He can be scary when he wants to be. He saved our family, right?"

Gil nodded and reached over and scratched the Lab's head. "Your absolutely right, hon. Eric saved our family."

Peanut and Shadow

Amanda Cross

AMANDA CROSS has been writing mystery novels since 1964 when she had to hide her true identity (Columbia University English professor Carolyn G. Heilbrun) behind a pseudonym. Her detective, Professor Kate Fansler, introduced in the Edgar Award–nominated *In the Last Analysis*, is one of the most literate characters since Lord Peter Wimsey. The author's own love of dogs comes through in her recent novel, *The Puzzled Heart*, and in *The Collected Stories*.

Dog walkers with similar schedules are likely to pass each other with almost daily regularity, although with different responses to such encounters. Some nod a formal greeting; some suddenly determine to avoid the daily meeting by choosing alternate routes through the park; some smile and chat for a moment, the dogs, after a perfunctory sniff, regarding one another with practiced indifference. A few dog owners, a very few, fall into conversation, short at first, never lengthy or personal, but over the years expected and even anticipated.

So it was with Georgia and Ophelia. They had, in the fullness of time, by now a matter of years, exchanged first names, commenting on the slightly unusual quality of both, but never moving further into private territory. Rather like travelers who meet on airplanes, they spoke of general matters, occasionally offering something personal, but nothing as particular as a last name or address. It sometimes occurred to Ophelia that she and Georgia might run out of things to mention, as they stopped for their almost daily chats, but Georgia no more than Ophelia showed any inclination to pass on without pausing for their regular exchange of pleasantries. Neither knew the other's profession, if any, but they had long since determined that their morning schedules were similar. Rain or shine, heat or cold, these two met.

Perhaps they had been so willing at first to pause because their dogs, unlike themselves, were remarkably similar. Both dogs were large, with light brown short hair, dropped ears, black masks, and with what the two ladies were amused to discover they both referred to as black eye makeup. Georgia's was male, Ophelia's female. Both were neutered—rather like us, Ophelia sometimes thought but did not mention to Georgia. Once Ophelia had met Georgia's dog being walked by a man, and could not resist stopping to inquire. The young man, friendly and clearly fond of the dog, said he was Georgia's nephew and godson on a visit. He lived in California and liked Peanut, Georgia's dog, particularly because he was not able to have a dog of his own. He had reached out to pet Ophelia's dog Shadow—a nice name, he had said. Ophelia had explained that the name came from a poem by Robert Louis Stevenson, beginning "I have a little shadow that goes in and out with me."

"Very appropriate," the man said. "Peanut was named for his puppy color; now he's a darker Peanut."

The following day, Georgia had said yes, he was a lovely young man, and Peanut was very fond of him. She offered no more information about the nephew or any other part of her family, and Ophelia did not like to inquire, herself not liking direct, personal questions. Perhaps the only extended subject on which they had spent some time and frequently returned to was their sense, at the ages of seventy and seventy-one, that they were not granted by the world around them their sufficiency of energy, resources, and ability. Clearly, both had retired, though neither asked the other from what.

Ophelia had worked her entire life for a lawyer who was also an accountant; he had been in business for himself and had made a handsome income working for several large firms and some individuals, who trusted him to run their financial and, when necessary, legal affairs. Ophelia knew as much about these clients as her boss did, a fact he both welcomed and appreciated. He had long ago established a pension fund for Ophelia, and when he retired he saw to it that she was generously provided for. He and his wife had moved to Florida, whence came a card at Christmas with family news and, on her birthday, a handsome gift. Many of her friends had supposed Ophelia to be in love with her boss, but she responded that they had seen too many movies and read too many romantic novels. She liked the job, the challenge of being solely in charge of the office's business, and she especially liked working for an individual person, who played no office politics and held no ill feelings.

When work became heavy, at income tax time, for example, Ophelia would hire a temporary typist, later a computer worker, in addition to her own assistants, a

changing brigade of young women who left when the un-
likelihood of meeting young men, or even other young
women, was borne in upon them. The shifting staff was
fine with Ophelia, who needed only what she called the
"dogsbody" kind of help, and who did not want the burden
of some extended relationship.

To Ophelia, solitude was bliss, and the autonomy her
job offered very much heaven. She had been the oldest in a
poor family, left in charge when her mother, worn out with
childbirth and endless domesticity, died. Ophelia worked
hard to give the younger children a good upbringing and in
actuality served them better than their mother had been
able to do. When the last child was out of the home, or
rather, rushed out, if Ophelia were forced to tell the truth,
her father fell ill and into her sole care. Awaiting his sadly
prolonged death, she yearned constantly for her own
space, for uninterrupted solitude in her own domain, for
time and privacy that was hers alone, unassailable, subject
to no one's demands. Once she had attained this coveted
state, which unlike many objects of longing had not turned
out, in reality, to be a disappointment, she was a happy
woman and would have spurned marriage had it been offered to her. But she gave no opportunities for such an
offer to occur.

Ophelia spoke of none of this to Georgia. She would
have liked, because it was the sort of information that told
you much about a person, to know the woman's former
profession or job—Georgia had made it clear that she had
retired at her own wish, but not from what. And so they
contented themselves with clicking their tongues imper-
sonally over murders in their beloved park, and with
jointly worrying about the litter and the bicyclists who,

with the whole road at their disposal every day from ten in the morning until three in the afternoon, insisted upon riding on the paths to the endangerment of dogs and pedestrians. But they were good-natured, not given to speaking of former times as better, and shared their delight in welcoming the workfare people who kept the park neater than it had been in years.

And then one day, as the fall was edging itself into winter, when all the trees except for the oaks were quite bare and an occasional blast of wind sharpened the senses, Georgia and Peanut did not appear. Well, Ophelia thought, something has come up, or she has flu, and of course there was no way they could let each other know of an unanticipated absence. When she did not appear the next day, or the next, or for the entire next week, Ophelia found herself troubled and a little sad. Still, unforeseen events occur even in the best-managed lives, which Georgia's certainly seemed to be to judge from appearances and previous regularity, and obviously there was nothing to be done. Ophelia kept to the same path, that week and the next, not wanting to miss Georgia should she return, but there was no Georgia.

Ophelia was astonished at how bereft she felt. This is ridiculous, she told herself. We aren't related; we aren't even friends in any accepted meaning of the word. The woman has decided not to walk in the park anymore, or she has broken a leg, or she has just decided meeting me in this regular way is too tedious for words. Forget it. But her mind would not settle to a calm acceptance of this sudden rejection—for that, after all, was what it was. Georgia had seemed, had been, a mannerly person, who would not simply drop someone without a word.

But how could she drop me a word, Ophelia argued with herself. She no more knows my address than I know hers. Why did we have to be so private, so careful not to intrude? And as the days passed, Ophelia, taking each time the route on which she had encountered Georgia and Peanut, could not dispell the worry that seized her. No lectures to herself about the irrationality of her anxiety served to quiet emotion. Daily, having returned from her walk with Shadow, Ophelia would slip back into her own life and thoughts of Georgia would sink below the surface of consciousness. But the next morning they would be back, as hope was again defeated.

And then, one day, there was Peanut. Ophelia was sure it was Peanut—of that there could be no doubt once he had spotted her and Shadow and rushed to greet them. Peanut was in a sad state. He must have gone into the lake, which neither dog had hitherto shown the smallest interest in doing; his fur was matted and spattered with mud; his collar was gone, together with all identification. But ragged, filthy, unlabeled, it was still Peanut. Ophelia was visited with a rush of emotions coming one on top of the other, and all required postponement until she had time to think. She took off Shadow's leash, which was never necessary, Shadow being well-named, but used because the law demanded it. She fastened it around Peanut's neck, pulling the length of the leash through the handle to make a collar. Peanut seemed relieved to have a collar again, even a makeshift one, and without allowing her feelings the scope they clearly demanded, Ophelia set off with both of the dogs for home—Ophelia's home.

Peanut seemed to have decided—so Ophelia perceived it—that he had found his new and permanent home. After he was fed and bathed, Ophelia fastened an old collar of Shadow's around his neck, an event he clearly found satisfying, standing quite still while Ophelia buckled the collar into place. Then he lay down next to Shadow's bed. Within the day, Shadow had decided to welcome Peanut, allowing him to rest first part of himself, then all of himself, on Shadow's bed. Ophelia found Shadow's identification tag from the ASPCA, and attached it to Peanut's collar. At least if he were lost and found again, they would know he belonged to someone. (Shadow wore a tag with her name, address, and telephone number on it: a form of ID Ophelia considered more practical and less reliant on the overworked ASPCA.)

Those tasks completed, it remained only to wonder about Georgia, and to speculate on how she might be found. That Peanut had been lost certainly suggested that some ill fortune had befallen Georgia; whatever had happened, Georgia had to be located. It never occurred to Ophelia to question for a moment the absolute necessity of her undertaking this difficult task. Apart from all her natural humanitarian impulses, Ophelia's detective instincts had been aroused: no one who has long run an office is without detective instincts. But just how difficult her task would be Ophelia did not actually admit to herself until some time had passed.

Her first idea was to take Peanut out alone and encourage him to lead her to his former home. Admittedly, this was long shot, Ophelia having no idea whether Georgia had lived on the East or West Side, near the park or distant from it. They had always met coming from opposite directions and, similarly, parted heading away from one another.

A few days after Peanut's arrival, Ophelia took him, wearing his new collar, out alone, leaving Shadow behind, an action Shadow could hardly believe, barking after them as though to say, "Hey, you forgot me." Even Peanut acted concerned at their exclusive departure. Ophelia led him to the path in the park on which she and Georgia had always met. Arriving there, Ophelia unhooked Peanut's leash, and said: "Home, boy, home." Peanut looked worried at this command (anyone who has ever owned a dog knows worry to be one of their most conspicuous facial expressions), but, at Ophelia's urging, he set off slowly toward the West Side, from which they had come, looking back constantly to be sure his new owner was with him.

Not only was she with him but it was to her home that Peanut headed, never swerving. Ophelia sighed. This was his new home, he seemed to say and, being a dog, did not wonder why suddenly she could not find it without his help. He greeted Shadow joyfully as Shadow did him, and Ophelia, shrugging at that failed attempt at detection, fixed lunch.

Her next foray was into the Manhattan telephone book, in search of people with the first name of Georgia or even just the initial G. This, of course, turned out to be hopeless. There was a Georgia somebody, who was very annoyed at being disturbed, responded to questions with the abrupt information that she loathed dogs, all in a high register and with a French accent.

Certainly, Ophelia had no objection to keeping Peanut, who had settled into the household without a hitch. Shadow, Ophelia rather thought, acted like an adolescent girl who had at last been allowed to bring a friend home for a sleepover. But what of Georgia? Could she have simply taken off, abandoning Peanut in the process? Ophelia could not believe it. But what if she had been taken ill, in the park, say, and Peanut had been for a while ignored? Surely, unless she was dead, Georgia would have tried to get him back. Of course, Ophelia thought, striking her forehead, impatient with herself: Georgia would have advertised.

The thought of going through back copies of all the New York papers and magazines, or even the *New York Times* alone, was too overwhelming. Even if Peanut had been on his own for only a week, the job might prove endless. But Ophelia bethought herself of all the part-timers and temps, always hard-up and in need of funds, whom she had hired in her working life; within hours she had set two such people searching their way through the classified ads in New York papers and magazines.

Days later, it was clear that Georgia had not advertised. Dogs had been lost, but dogs utterly unlike Peanut. So be it. The answer to that dead end was to advertise herself: *Brown dog named Peanut found in Central Park on path around the Great Lawn.* That should do it. She would place it in every New York paper, for who knew what paper the finder might read. The use of the name would help to identify the caller's honesty, for its provenance would be asked, as well as knowledge of the dog's size. Ophelia called up all the papers and magazines, including those in foreign languages, and settled back to wait for as long as necessary.

Long it was, for the answers were many, but none that survived the most superficial questioning. What on earth were such people looking for? Not a dog, surely, for there were many dogs available for adoption everywhere. Probably they were hideous people who sold dogs to laboratories for purposes Ophelia chose not to dwell on. Nor, as she came to realize, did her failure in this method necessarily prove that the dog's owner was still not searching. Perhaps, like Ophelia, Georgia was not a reader of classified ads.

During all this time, Ophelia and the two dogs took their daily walks, part of a new household, a new set of walking companions, content enough, were it not for the nagging sense that something horrible, well at any rate unusual, had happened to Georgia. Ophelia was racking her brain for other fields of investigation when fate dropped an answer into her lap. Ophelia smiled—her employer, a man of several oddly endearing convictions, used to say that when you have exhausted everything in your power, when you have really tried, fate is very likely to offer a wholly unanticipated stroke of luck.

Ophelia lived in a small apartment house on the Upper West Side, quietly elegant but in no way pretentious. The tenants knew one another by sight, some better than that, but Ophelia, as always, had kept to herself. On this particular day, however, she, together with Shadow and Peanut, descended in the elevator with an odd, youngish man, mid-thirties Ophelia thought, whom she had encountered only occasionally before since their daily schedules rarely coincided. He was a serious young man, with a long thin face and a long beard, who reminded her of photographs she had seen of English writer Lytton Strachey. He had always, when they met, patted Shadow, remarking that he liked dogs and wished he could have one, but circumstances did not permit. It dawned upon Ophelia how many people claimed to want dogs but felt unable to have them. Rather, she thought, like those people who always wanted to read the great novels but never had the leisure to do so.

Now, meeting Ophelia for the first time since Peanut's arrival, the youngish man congratulated her on having acquired a second dog. He actually stopped to welcome Peanut, and to assure Shadow that she would be loved no less. "But I didn't *acquire* Peanut," Ophelia said. The young man looked at her with interest and only a hint of trepidation, for Ophelia was old, and the old are notorious for launching into long, rather pointless stories. Ophelia, reading his expression, merely said, "He belonged to someone, but I've been unable to find her. She's disappeared. I've tried newspaper ads and everything. I worry." She stopped talking, and the young man said, "You must try the Internet. Look, I'll help you when I get home. Come up to my apartment this evening—nine-A— anytime after eight. I'm quite harmless really; I like to fool around with computers. We'll have a go at it. See you then." And he was off.

The doorman, having observed this consultation, seemed to sense Ophelia's skepticism. "A nice fellow," the doorman said. "He's always doing things with computers. Funny that; people either can't figure computers out, or don't do anything else. Have you noticed? I have. It's something new in the air, or maybe in the water."

Ophelia thanked him and departed for her walk, bemused. Well, nothing ventured, nothing gained, and it was then that she recalled her employer's counsel of hope. She would descend to the lobby this evening, ask the doorman for the computer fellow's name and apartment, pretending she had fortotten it was 9A. Should she, in her turn, then vanish, at least the doorman would know where she had, when last seen, been headed, which was more than could be said for Georgia.

"How much do you know about the Internet?" the young man asked that evening as she obediently sat down, facing the computer but not able to see the screen very well from that angle, on a chair he had pulled up for her. "Do you use it much?"

"Never," Ophelia answered firmly. "Word processing only; no Windows."

The young man made clicking noises of regret. "If all you people afraid of computers knew what you're missing," he moaned. "Well, here we go. We'll ask our query of the Internet and see where that gets us, if anywhere; it depends on who responds. The question is, what is the query? A dog, a person, the whole tale, what information are you asking for? Shall we describe Peanut, his former owner? I suggest we do not use the word *Peanut* alone. We'll get everyone from admirers of George Washington Carver to sufferers from peanut alergies."

"How many words can we have?" Ophelia asked.

"Counting words doesn't come into it," he answered. "You can just go on and on as long as you like, offering anything from poems to warnings about international conspiracies. Where do you want to start?"

"Is there a dog chat room? I have heard of chat rooms."

"Probably. But let's get into where people might be on the outlook for other people similarly circumstanced. How about: 'Searching for woman named . . .' " He paused.

"Georgia," Ophelia said. "I don't know her last name."

" 'Georgia, former owner of dog named Peanut. All and any information welcome.' I think we better describe her a bit. Age?"

"Seventies. Vigorous woman, gray hair, glasses, blue eyes—very blue. Wears sneakers when walking her dog."

"Good description," the young man said, "but let's keep most of that up our sleeve until we get some sort of response."

"Do you think we'll get any responses?" Ophelia asked, amazed at his expectations.

"My dear madam, the problem will be to sift through the hundreds we get; welcome to the Internet." He began moving the mouse around, clicking on what he told her were icons, mumbling to himself, swearing at the refusal of the machine to respond instantly. He typed for a while. "Okay, we've done that; I've said that she lived in Manhattan when last seen. Anything else you know about her for future reference?"

Georgia was shaking her head when she remembered. "She has a nephew in California, her godson. He walked Peanut for her one day; like you, he was unable to have a dog of his own. That's absolutely all I know about him. Should I try to describe him?"

"No, let's keep that to ourselves for now also, in the event we need further identification in the future. I'll put in another plea to learn more about the nephew from California. I'll let you know if anything turns up."

Ophelia rose to go, eager to assure him that she would not take up his time unnecessarily. She longed to ask him if he worked at computers all day, but restrained her curiosity. Yet he seemed to guess her question. "I'm a epidemiologist," he said. "I take the data researchers give me and try to develop a program that can make decent use of it. I hope we make faster progress with your search." He wrote down her telephone number. If anything did turn up he would let her know, and he walked with her to the door.

The progress he made with her search was faster than either of them had supposed possible, Ophelia because she had little hope now of results from any method of investigation, and the young man because the search seemed hopelessly unspecific. But two evenings later he was on the telephone.

"I've had an answer from the nephew," he told her. "Apparently someone saw my notice and, knowing he had an aunt in New York or whatever, got in touch with the guy. His name is Edmund, Frank Edmund. He asked for your telephone number, and I've given it to him. He'll call you about ten-thirty tonight, your time. I hope that's not too late. I did have one or two minor worries about giving him your number, but I thought if the worst happens, you can always change it. He doesn't know anything else about you."

But Frank Edmund, when he called, knew as much about her as she about him: he knew Peanut and remembered meeting Shadow. "I'm sorry I couldn't let you know about my aunt," he said. "And I'm afraid I don't know what's happened to Peanut. The truth is, my aunt died. She took too many sleeping pills after a drink or two. I'm told that's how it often happens. Insomniacs wake up, don't remember how many pills they've had, and take more." Here, Ophelia interrupted to tell him she had found and adopted Peanut. "That is a relief," he said. "I'm so sorry to be the bearer of such sad news, but I am glad about Peanut.

Perhaps we can meet in the park when I'm next in New York, although I've no idea when that might be. I used to come mainly to visit my aunt Georgia." They exchanged a few more pleasantries and condolences, and the conversation ended. He left her his telephone number in case she wanted to reach him for any reason.

Ophelia lay down on her bed after hanging up the telephone. She was dizzy with shock, and lying there as the room slowly stopped spinning, she asked herself, Why? Wherefore the shock? Because Georgia, whom she hardly had known, whose last name she did not know, was dead? Had perhaps killed herself instead of mistaking the number of sleeping pills she had consumed? And whence the sleeping pills? They were not easily come by these days, when milder forms of soporifics that did not interfere with REM sleep were widely prescribed; she knew this from tales told in the office by temps and part-timers whose friends had AIDS and were desperate for release.

No, she wasn't shocked because of Georgia's possible suicide, or even because of her death. Ophelia was ruthlessly honest with herself, and knew her shock came from profound disappointment, disappointment not even at the loss of Georgia, but at the loss of the fantasy she had conjured up and come to believe in. It was *quite* a fantasy in fact, with several versions, all dramatic and exciting. Perhaps Georgia had been a spy, now suddenly needed and wafted off by the CIA, or the FBI, or a foreign country. Perhaps she had been the only person fluent in some obscure language in which, all unexpectedly, such proficiency was essential. Perhaps she had been kidnapped or even murdered by her nephew, or supposed nephew as he would have to have been, craving her money, her apartment, her possessions.

It had been none of those. Whether or not she had killed herself, Georgia was only the sort of person who took sleeping pills, accompanying them with liquor to induce unconsciousness; she was no more than that, an ordinary old woman, ill perhaps, who couldn't face up to whatever it was that had frightened her. Peanut was all that was left of what might have been an adventure for Ophelia, a chance to practice detection on a large scale. She tried to laugh at herself, tried not to care, but tears ran down her face and onto the pillow. Pull yourself together, she told herself sternly. It's not what anyone could call a personal tragedy, as far as you yourself are concerned.

Two days later, Ophelia called the nephew and asked for his aunt's last name, which neither of them had got around to mentioning in their first conversation, and her address. He was not yet home when she called, but she left a message requesting that he leave one in his turn with the information she had requested. He probably didn't want to engage in further conversations, and she definitely did not. Her preposterous disillusionment might have somehow revealed itself in her tone; she was adamant no one would ever guess at that.

He left the information she had asked, without questions or offers of help, for which she was grateful. Georgia had lived on the West Side after all, in a brownstone apartment. On the next day, Ophelia decided to walk there with the dogs.

Once recovered from the first blow of regret that her fantasy had resolved itself into so mundane an explanation,

Ophelia had begun to wonder about the ease with which Peanut had found her and Shadow, particularly after what must have been some days in the park, to judge from his condition. How had he happened upon them, and why hadn't the park patrols or the ASPCA picked him up? She remembered Peanut's first meal, offered him on their return to her apartment in the belief that he must be hungry. Like any healthy dog, he was happy to eat, but he had not eaten like a starved animal; indeed, he had let Shadow share the meal, which no ravenous dog, however tame, would be likely to have done without at least a warning growl.

He hadn't been ravenous, of course. Ophelia wondered why she had not thought of this before. Georgia, she now understood, must have messed him up, induced him into the lake, rubbed mud into his coat; she had not, of course, left him to his fate. She had watched as Ophelia and Shadow took him in charge; she had made sure he was safe. You didn't think of all this, Ophelia now told herself, because you liked the chance of it, you liked the idea that luck or fate seemed to have taken a hand, you wanted the meeting with Peanut to be adventure as the odd disappearance of his owner would turn out to be adventure.

Ophelia, with the dogs, found the brownstone easily enough. It was well kept. Even the garbage was in orderly cans, the entranceway clean. She pressed the button for the superintendent and waited, doubting if he would come, guessing that he would not be receptive to her questions, prepared for rejection.

But in this at least she was not to be disappointed. He appeared from a door in the areaway and recognized Peanut, whose furiously wagging tail confirmed their long acquaintance. "I was wondering," Ophelia began, "if you

could tell me anything about my friend, Georgia Zorn?"
(And I would have had to make it all the way to the Z's in
the phone book, Ophelia suddenly thought as she said the
name.)

"She lived here a long time," the man said. "She was
a good tenant, and we used to meet when she took the
dog out. I'm glad to see he's fine. How are you, fellow?
Missing your lady?" He seemed to think for a moment.
"Your name is Ophelia, right? Dog named Shadow?"
Ophelia nodded. "Okay," he said. "She left a letter for you,
just in case you ever came by. She said it might be a long
time or never, but I said I'd hang on to it while me and the
building were here. I'll get it."

He went inside and returned with an envelope. *Georgia
and Shadow* was clearly printed on the front. "Nice to
have met you," he said.

"Have you rented the apartment, her apartment?"
Ophelia asked.

"Oh, yes; had to, of course. All her stuff went into
storage for her nephew. He doesn't need it yet. She left me
plenty of money to take care of all that. A good lady. She
trusted me and I trusted her. Goodbye, Peanut."

Ophelia went into the park with her letter, and, after the
dogs had had a good walk, sat down on a bench to read it.
The dogs lay on either side of her feet. It was winter now,
but one of those cold, windless, sunny New York days that
Ophelia loved best.

My dear Ophelia,
    You may never read this letter, since you know
nothing about me, but I have a hunch that you may be

able to seek me out and that kind Mr. O'Hara will have kept it for you.

I have decided to end my life now, when I choose and on my own terms. The cancer I had fought off ten years ago is returning, and I don't want to go through any of those treatments again. What possible reason could I have for such torture with such uncertain results? Most people, as I know from my last hospital stay, will do anything to go on living, even when they are older than I. One must decide for oneself. Perhaps if I had had a family—which I never wanted, nor, I suspect, did you—or dear friends I would have felt differently; but I was without a connection in a world that obligated me to remain in it.

I did wonder for a time if you and I might have become friends, might have discovered the sort of friendship that can be a gift at any time of life, and especially at ours. But I dared not risk either your rejection at a gesture on my part toward intimacy, nor my regret if you turned out to be, after all, an unoriginal, conventional sort of person. I doubted you were, but that doubt might well have reflected my hope rather than a realistic expectation.

Once the decision was made, I had only Peanut to think about. I messed him up—rather to his bewilderment, poor chap—and deserted him by hopping into a waiting horse-drawn carriage when I saw you and Shadow approaching. Nor did I leave it at that. I lurked in another carriage in the park on a day soon after until you and the two dogs appeared, so that I could know for certain you had claimed Peanut.

Have I been depressed? I dare say I may have been,

in a manner of speaking. But mine has been a good life; I was a doctor and missed that life when I, from fear that I might have grown inattentive, abandoned it. You, I would guess, unlike me, relished your retirement, whatever it was from.

Thank you for taking on Peanut, and for being someone, however unfamiliar, on whose generosity I could count.

Georgia

Building Herbert

Deborah Adams

DEBORAH ADAMS agreed to a blind date with a man who later became her husband *only* because he had a Saint Bernard. Adams is a Macavity Award–winning short story writer who also creates the series of novels known as the Jesus Creek mysteries. (The first one, *All the Great Pretenders*, was an Agatha Award nominee.) She currently plays mom to Clifford, a shaggy black stray who wandered into the yard and forgot to leave; Data, an abused mongrel who was abandoned near the Adams home; and an assortment of cats and tropical fish.

The cadaver on the bed had no personality to speak of, but Rhonda felt that was partially *her* fault. After all, the dead one (male, female, whatever—it was a mixed bag of bones) couldn't contribute much to a conversation and Rhonda hadn't really tried to draw out the corpse.

"Now, Fletcher," she patted the sleek retriever beside her, "first thing we should've done is give it a name."

Fletcher stared intently at his mistress, flicked his tail twice, and waited to be let outside where he could indulge his passion for fetching. He lived to fetch—sticks, rocks, stray tennis balls, shoes, the occasional tailpipe. But mostly he liked to fetch bones, which he traded in for Rhonda's homebaked goodies.

"Herbert?" Rhonda said. "Do you really think it looks like a Herbert?" She'd been hoping for a girlfriend, somebody to share secrets with. Rhonda had always yearned for a sister, but it looked like she'd have to keep on yearning.

She waited for Fletcher to offer another, less gender-specific name, but the dog remained firm. Rhonda sighed. She'd gotten used to Fletcher's stubborn nature and knew the futility of argument. Sometimes she thought letting a dog sway her to his convictions might be a sign of weakness. On the other hand, Fletcher was almost always right; that's why Daddy had trusted him.

"Fletcher," she cooed, "show me where you found Herbert and I'll give you a special treat."

The bribe hadn't worked in the past, either. Fletcher used the location of the bone cache to manipulate her; he brought home little bits of Herbert, doling them out like Halloween candy, but never allowed her to know where they came from.

Rhonda should have been angry, but what could she do? She loved the mutt.

"Do you think Herbert is comfortable?" She gave her attention to the neatly arranged bone collection, momentarily forgetting to stroke Fletcher's head.

Fletcher perked his ears. Was he dismissed?

"Oh, come on!" Rhonda protested. "The pillow is just fine. It's not like he needs a good night's sleep. He never *does* anything."

Fletcher inched toward the door, signaling his desire for a foray into the great outdoors.

"Sure he's a guest, but—I am *not* being selfish!" Rhonda looked into the skull's empty sockets. "Am I being selfish, Herbert?"

Fletcher licked her hand, whining just a little to emphasize his point.

"I should've known you men would stick together." She sighed. "He can have Daddy's pillow. Come on, Fletcher. I'll make dinner while you go out and look for more Herbert."

While the noodles boiled, Rhonda watched Fletcher through the window. The dog seldom wandered far, trained as he was to guard the immediate property. He knew it wasn't safe to leave the compound, even though he'd helped Daddy set the warning devices around the perimeter of the farm. Now and again a wild animal would trip a wire and—voila!—fresh venison for dinner. It was a nice change from the usual freeze-dried and home-preserved meals, but she certainly didn't want anything like that to happen to Fletcher!

Rhonda had suspected Daddy was a little mad when the county people called her home. They'd tried talking to him—threatening him, she suspected—but he ran them off with a few shots fired from his rooftop fort. He'd even trained the gun on Rhonda when she'd first stepped out of the sheriff's car, but it didn't take long for him to recognize his little girl and welcome her back home. They got really close after that, and Daddy told her the truth about what those county people had in mind. It was scary at first, but it all made sense and Rhonda was glad to have Fletcher there to help carry the burden now that Daddy was gone.

She glanced through the open door into the bedroom where Herbert reclined. "Maybe we'll get you some clothes later on. When you're more . . . complete," she said. "I kept all of Daddy's things. Takes up a lot of space, but Daddy always said you never know what might come in handy."

Outside Fletcher surveyed the yard, picking up the odd stick and adding it to the pile near the front door. Rhonda was grateful for a dog that distinguished between kindling and Herbert. It saved her the trouble of sorting.

While dinner cooked, she readied the plates and utensils. It wasn't likely that Herbert would eat much, but Fletcher could have the leftovers. She never threw out food. Daddy had reminded her over and over—if you waste not, you'll want not.

That was why Daddy had moved to the roof in the first place. He'd been sure it was the only way to ward off an attack by the county people who wanted to take the farm and turn it into God knows what. A parking lot, maybe, or a trailer park. Daddy had worked all his life for that land; he wasn't about to give it up, to waste all those years and all that effort.

Fletcher's barking drew her to the window, her heart racing. It had been months since he'd alerted her to possible invasion, and she'd hoped the county people had given up. They'd turned off the electricity a long time ago, but Daddy had already planned around what turned out to be a minor inconvenience. Then they'd tried blocking off all the roads around the farm, but Rhonda didn't care. She didn't have anywhere to go anyway. She just ignored the county people and pretty soon they got tired of the whole thing and went away, the time and manpower they'd put into that pitiful excuse for a siege wasted.

Once in a while some deputy or other would come by, but she'd send Fletcher out to deal with that. It hardly bothered her anymore. Just a minor nuisance in her otherwise ordinary existence.

"Stay where you are, Herbert!" she ordered. "I'll take care of this."

Rhonda wiped her hands on a dish towel and stepped onto the front porch just as a shiny Ford Taurus pulled into the yard. It didn't look like the usual county car, but she knew full-well how sneaky they could be.

Fletcher barked and bounced back and forth between her and the intruder. For the moment he'd forgotten all about fetching, which worried Rhonda just a tad. She stood with arms folded across her chest, waiting for the enemy to make a move.

The lone figure seemed reluctant to get out of his car, no doubt because of Fletcher's manic behavior. Rhonda did nothing to settle the dog; he was only doing his job, after all, and uninvited guests shouldn't expect better.

At last the driver's door opened and a pudgy-cheeked man in a dark suit stepped out onto Daddy's property. "Evenin'!" he called, nervously jolly. "I'm Brother Hadley from the First Community Church. Just wanted to stop by and see how you're doing."

"Why?" Rhonda asked.

Fletcher stopped barking and planted himself like a protective boulder in front of his mistress.

"Well, because . . ." Brother Hadley paused to pull a big red handkerchief from his back pocket. He rubbed it across his face and the back of his neck before stuffing it into his pants again. "Like all of us, you're a child of God. I've just come to the congregation here and when I heard you lived out here all by yourself, I thought I ought to offer up an invitation. We'd sure like to have you come worship with us this Sunday."

"I don't leave the farm," she informed him, "but I expect you knew that. I expect you've been sent to try and lure me away."

His broad grin didn't cover the guilt in his eyes. "Now, ma'am, I don't want to lure you anywhere except into the welcoming arms of Jesus."

Fletcher turned his head to look at her, then fixed the preacher in his gaze again.

"Fletcher says they sent you out here," Rhonda told him, "and he always knows. You're not the first, but you're the first to come without a badge. All the same, my answer's no. I'll not give Daddy's land over for them to throw away."

Brother Hadley's expression grew serious. "Now from what I'm told, your daddy's been dead a long time—"

"Three years," she informed him, "next month."

"Well, and is it right that he never had a proper burial?"

If there'd been any doubt in her mind, this confirmed Rhonda's and Fletcher's assessment of the man. He was changing tracks, trying to come up with an argument that would persuade her over to their side. Fortunately she was familiar with this tactic, having used it herself on Daddy back when she'd thought he needed saving. She had answers ready because she'd listened and remembered Daddy's logical explanations.

"He's buried just fine," she said, "I took care of it myself." It had taken her two days to dig a shallow pit in the packed clay soil of the cellar, but that had been the best, the safest place to put Daddy. She couldn't bury him out in the open; he'd told her this himself. The county people might get to him there and use his remains for all kinds of weird experiments. Rhonda hadn't thought it likely, but she figured Daddy deserved an eternal cover over his head after all those years of living in a tent on the roof.

"But don't you wish he could be in consecrated ground?" Brother Hadley pushed. "So his immortal soul can go to the Lord?"

Rhonda almost laughed. "They must be getting hard up if you're the best they've got to offer. Or didn't anybody tell you how many have tried to take this land? Didn't they tell you how crazy I am? How my Daddy used to shoot at 'em when they came here to bother him? Didn't they tell you the gun's still here?"

Fletcher stood at attention, eager to do something but obediently awaiting a command.

Brother Hadley went pale and pulled out his handkerchief again. "Now, now." He giggled for no apparent reason. "I don't see a six-shooter on you and I can tell you're too good-hearted for that kind of behavior. If I could just come inside for a friendly chat."

"Friendly?" she asked. "You're all trying to steal everything my Daddy loved and you call any of it friendly? I've got news for the lot of you. It's my land now. It's *my* house and maybe I *am* crazy, but that's how it is. Now go back and tell the rest of the robbers to leave us alone."

"Look, ma'am." Brother Hadley's confidence in his Christian charisma was slipping away. "It's the truth what I've told you. I heard about your situation out here and I've come to offer help and comfort. I don't have anything to do with tax collection or that warrant, and I sure didn't come on behalf of the county—"

Daddy had trained Fletcher himself. He'd read somewhere that you should always teach your dog to respond to commands nobody else would guess. Kept intruders from countermanding orders you'd already given the animal, he'd said.

Naturally, given his constant expectation of invasion, Daddy had taught Fletcher to attack whenever he heard a cry of "County!"

Brother Hadley's eyes bulged out so much it turned Rhonda's stomach. She used his red handkerchief to cover his face. Then she grabbed him by the ankles and pulled him up the steps and into the house. Fletcher was an efficient killer. There was hardly any damage except right there at the throat.

The underwear was too far gone, so Rhonda threw that into the cookstove to burn. Then she stripped off the preacher's suit, shirt, tie, socks, and shoes. She carried it all into the bedroom and added it to the pile of county uniforms—what was left of them by the time Fletcher had got through. She figured some of it probably belonged to Herbert, but she wasn't about to put him in an enemy uniform while he lived in *her* house. "You won't have to wear Daddy's old work clothes after all, Herbert," she said cheerfully.

Fletcher was still standing guard over Brother Hadley when she returned, remorse and regret written on his furry face.

"Well, I guess you are sorry," Rhonda said. "I don't have to depend on your little offerings anymore, do I?

I've got enough here to finish up Herbert with plenty left over to make Christmas decorations."

Fletcher whined, and Rhonda scratched his head affectionately. "Silly thing," she said gently. "Of course I'll share with you. But first I've got to clear out a space in the smokehouse before he spoils. Don't want him to go to waste. You know what Daddy always said. . . ."

The Invisible Sky

Polly Whitney

POLLY WHITNEY is the author of the Until series of mystery novels, which began with *Until Death* (an Agatha Award nominee). Whitney also writes short stories for a variety of mystery publications and has a regular column on writing and researching the mystery novel. When not living in the sunny climes of Florida, she hangs out in cyberspace, where she commits humor on Dorothy L.

Capote carries a license entitling him to be a legal beggar. Most panhandlers in New York City just go out on the street with cardboard cups and do their thing. Capote went to City Hall before he established himself—almost as a landmark—on Fifth Avenue, with other notable monuments such as Tiffany's, The Trump Tower, St. Patrick's Cathedral.

Capote almost certainly isn't his real name. He sets up for the day much earlier than anyone else who works on that high-priced strip of real estate, and the neighborhood has somehow linked him in the parochial collective consciousness with *Breakfast at Tiffany's*. They named him after its author.

Down at City Hall someone must have a record of Capote's vital statistics, but the locals are satisfied with their own version of what little they know about this man. Everybody loves that movie.

It's Capote's dog, however, that makes him special to Fifth Avenue and that originally suggested affection to the regulars who stop and give a little change to the beggar. Lucy is a sweet-tempered, patient, utterly loyal, big-shouldered animal with the heart of a lion, who dares to lie down before the packed and onrushing crush of pedestrians, without ever flinching. She is well trained, a good worker who acts as Capote's pathfinder and escort and protector. Her harness rests lightly on her well-groomed back, where gray hair has begun to shine among the pale yellow, and Capote only takes up her leash when it's time to move along.

Everyone knows the guide dog's name. If you ask Capote about the mixed golden lab/husky, he says, "That's Lucy." Capote's a man of few words. "That's Lucy." Very few words, indeed. In fact, two.

And if the passerby offers to feed Lucy a bite of a hot dog or a pretzel, Capote only says, "If she wants." Very few words. Three, to be precise.

Capote rarely says anything else, not even "thank you" when he hears the clink of a coin dropped into his tin cup or the rustle of paper money among the coins. He does wear a small sign pinned to his jacket, bearing a simple legend. I'M BLIND. PLEASE HELP. GOD BLESS YOU.

Lucy seems to have the task of communicating for both of them. She never forgets a face, never forgets the people who come up and put something in Capote's cup. Somebody in Gucci's started the joke that the beggar's cup is the box office, where you pay the price of admission so you can pet the sweet dog. There probably never was a friendlier dog, at least not in New York City.

Capote stands there with Lucy every weekday, in all kinds of weather, his big right hand around his little tin cup, where he keeps several no. 2 pencils, which nobody accepts in exchange for their donations. Petting Lucy, or smiling at her, or saying her name—those seem to be all anyone wants in return for a small donation.

Still, Capote always keeps new pencils in his cup, as if he is loath to offer inferior goods and somehow compromise his status on Fifth Avenue. Or his dog's.

Lucy's friendly, but she never wanders more than a couple of feet from her master. She sits beside Capote on the sidewalk, on a thickly padded rug that protects her from the dead cold of the pavement, or the radiant heat, or whatever condition it is that nature has laid down at Lucy's place by Capote's side.

The man is tall and so black he shines and it's nearly impossible to see his eyes, because he always stands quietly, unmoving, looking up at the invisible sky. Capote's thick black neck—its stiff veins, the tired Adam's apple—is arched away from those who stuff money in his cup. He isn't facing the crowds on Fifth Avenue.

Somebody at Cartier's says that Capote is looking up at the sky because he's praying for a big diamond solitaire ring and the ability to see his hand in front of his face.

The manager of Steuben's thinks Capote is looking up at the sky because he knows he doesn't belong on this planet and he's waiting for the mother ship.

The doorman at the Plaza Hotel says it doesn't matter why Capote is looking up at the sky, he can't see. He's blind, for God's sake. Who cares what he's looking at?

Capote wouldn't notice Bette Midler in a red raincoat if she came up and waved her hand in his face. That's what the doorman says.

Lucy, unlike her master, notices everything, or seems to. It's difficult to guess her age, but surely she's well past her prime. No one can remember a time when Capote was without her, and he's been begging on Fifth Avenue for a long, long while. The dog lies on the little rug, her chin resting on her paws, her brown eyes gazing alertly at people who approach Capote. New York may well be a kinder, more caring place than the stereotype would dictate, for there is no sign on the dog of any injury, deliberate or accidental. Most people think she has a good life, and they admire her poise.

The blind man and his dog leave their post on Fifty-sixth Street and Fifth Avenue only once during the workday, when they go have their lunch, like hundreds of other New Yorkers, on the steps of St. Patrick's Cathedral, down on Fifty-first.

Such regular habits, such a predictable existence, the utter inevitability of that dog and that man—these were the things that gave Craig McBroom his burst of desperate insight into how to fix a big problem in his life.

Twenty-four stories above Capote's spot on the Avenue, McBroom had been thinking and wondering and praying about the crushing vise of brilliant blackmail that was about to cut him and his life into little pieces.

His partner in the investment firm of Beale & McBroom had all the weapons. Joseph Beale's smiling face was killing McBroom. Beale had hard evidence on a computer disk, tucked away in his safety deposit box at Chase Manhattan, showing that McBroom was guilty of enough insider trading to shock even the post–Milken Securities and Exchange Commission, as well as net McBroom probably twenty years in jail.

Oh, it would be a nice jail. But *jail is jail*, McBroom thought.

Beale had given McBroom five days to accept a buy-out offer of two million dollars for McBroom's half of the company. If McBroom failed to comply, Beale would go to the authorities. Beale smiled when he made the ludicrous offer. McBroom could blow his nose with two million dollars—his half of Beale & McBroom was worth at least one hundred times Beale's laughable—but non-negotiable—offer.

That stupid smile on Beale's face was just killing Mc-Broom. Just killing him.

During the five-day grace period from Beale, McBroom had thought it all through, and, after facing the sad truth that two million dollars was the best he was ever going to get from this ugly situation, he realized that what he hated most was that he'd be leaving Beale a wealthy, wealthy man. McBroom would walk away (all the way out of the country if he knew what was good for him) with an insulting token of the vast resources he had earned for the firm while Beale sat there in his office, smirking and pretending he knew anything about finance.

Beale had inherited his half of the investment house from his ruthless but infallible father, and "Beale, the Sequel" (as McBroom thought of his partner) had spent the last ten years sitting on his father's leather chair, smoking cigars and paying various escort services. The only business sense he had ever shown was to catch McBroom red-handed in the most criminal moment of his life. And to save all the evidence on a floppy disk.

McBroom couldn't do anything about that disk. He didn't believe stories about spies and safe crackers and those caper artists who could get past all sorts of security technology. McBroom was afraid even to touch Chase Manhattan's ATM machines, for fear of setting off some alarm with his fingerprints.

He *knew* that was paranoia, but correctly diagnosing his condition did nothing to improve that condition.

And he couldn't do anything about Beale's two-million-dollar slap in the face. McBroom would have to take the money and leave the other man sitting on hundreds of millions.

It was that image of Beale sitting on a mountain of greenbacks, growing fatter and fatter like some obscene new mushroom, that had gotten into McBroom like a slow poison. He could *taste* his own creeping envy.

McBroom could never regain what he was losing. Beale had him nailed down and wrapped up and folded in a drawer—and any other metaphor McBroom could concoct for his feeling of entrapment. That the author of this misfortune was McBroom himself was merely an additional layer of torture over the much greater misery of Beale's happiness. Beale was so goddamned happy. He smiled all the time.

McBroom could stomach getting caught by his lazy partner, and he could take the ripoff buyout of two million dollars, and he could even stand the need to emigrate, but he couldn't tolerate Beale's bovine countenance with that bucolic smile of bliss.

So, on the fifth day, McBroom decided to kill Beale.

That wouldn't save McBroom's position, because his partner's death would inevitably result in the opening of that safe deposit box by Beale's estate. The only small triumph available to McBroom was the prevention of further enjoyment on the part of the mindless man who was ruining him.

The fifth day was Friday. An "official bank check" from Citibank (written by the bank on its own account and payable to the bearer) for two million dollars had been lying on Beale's desk, under one of his silly executive toys, since Beale had issued his ultimatum. McBroom would have to take the check immediately.

Facing the consequences of his own illegal operations was unthinkable. Massive. Opaque.

McBroom had his passport and a ticket to São Paulo, where no U.S. law or law officer could touch him. Brazil— and McBroom had researched better spots than Brazil without coming up with that unique and necessary nonreciprocal extradition policy, except in places where Americans were treated like slime—was a place where a man could set up a comfortable life on a foundation of two million dollars. Comfortable, yes. Exciting, no. Beale was sending McBroom away from the excitement of everything Manhattan's sparkling skyline symbolized. What the hell was McBroom supposed to do in Brazil?

Murdering Beale would not be a problem for McBroom. He knew he could pull the trigger. Especially if Beale had that cow smile on his fat face.

But, whatever else happened, McBroom needed that check, which was as good as cash at his own Citibank branch. Before he cashed it, though, McBroom planned to shoot Beale with Beale's own gun. Beale was only available to McBroom in his office. It wouldn't be like dropping his partner off a lonely cliff; the office was in the heart of New York City, and that would mean the cops.

McBroom had tried to persuade his partner to allow him to visit Beale in his Connecticut mansion, but Beale snorted and smiled and said he hadn't acquired *full* ownership of Beale & McBroom by being a fool.

To get away—to get a pass from the cops—it was absolutely necessary that the two-million-dollar check should never be found, on the premises or in McBroom's possession.

McBroom was perfectly resolved on his course, but he had yet to decide what to do about the check until he came to work Friday morning and caught a glimpse of that blind man and his dog. McBroom felt a flicker of annoyance that a blind man could apparently arrange a life without interference while he, McBroom, was having his life lifted from him like a piece of lint.

That blind man was always there, always looking up at the stupid sky, always holding that cup, always standing by his dog. Nobody bothered *him*. And everyone fawned over the dog. Except McBroom, who had better things to do with his time than play zoo with a blind man.

McBroom was about to enter his office building when a thought struck him. He looked back at the tin cup with its pencils. He looked at the peaceable dog. He looked at the man who wasn't looking at anything. *What a remarkable thing,* McBroom thought. *What a remarkable thing.*

Of course.

McBroom went up to his office on the twenty-fourth floor and looked down on Fifth Avenue. There was the man, looking up at him, or so it appeared.

McBroom checked his watch. It was quite early, but Beale would be in. *The earlier the better,* McBroom thought, now that he had a plan.

McBroom stood in the center of his office and did a slow turn, searching for something that he couldn't live without, something that would have to go in his briefcase and with him to Brazil. He looked and looked. There was nothing really. Those certificates and diplomas on his ego wall meant nothing to him. They were merely the objectifications of intellectual property. There was nothing. No little photo, no precious memento, nothing.

All he needed was the check.

He put his briefcase on the floor beside his desk, pulled a pair of surgical gloves out of his pocket, put them on, opened his door, and walked down the hall to Beale's office, hands in his pockets.

He entered without knocking.

Beale was sitting there, scratching his nose, smiling up at McBroom. They simultaneously glanced at the check on the desk.

Beale did not pick up the check to offer it to McBroom. McBroom did not bend to extract the check from under the toy.

Instead, McBroom returned Beale's smile and stepped to the other man's side.

He yanked open the bottom drawer of the desk and grabbed Beale's revolver, which he then pointed at Beale.

Beale kept smiling. *McBroom has the gun,* he thought, *but none of the big boy weapons.* Beale wasn't afraid. McBroom was the smartest man Beale had ever known, as well as the most self-centered, and there was no way McBroom would offer his neck for a noose. He was up to something. A bluff. An eleventh hour trick. Beale smiled—quite genuinely—out of curiosity to see what McBroom would do next.

McBroom stuck the gun on the smooth skin between Beale's eyes and pulled the trigger.

Beale's body crashed backward in his cushioned executive chair and then—almost like a ricochet—bounced forward onto the desk.

McBroom had no need to check Beale's pulse. Not in that mess.

He almost vomited as he took the dead man's plump hand and wrapped it around the gun, forefinger on the trigger.

McBroom hurried into Beale's bathroom and shoved up the window, which, since Beale had grabbed the southern exposure, faced Fifty-sixth Street. McBroom snapped off his surgical gloves, balled them together, and pulled the latex up to secure the ball. He gave the ball of gloves a frantic toss and saw it go sailing out and eastward toward Madison. It landed in the street, and traffic flowed over the ball the way Manhattan traffic flows over everything in its path. That ball would be nonexistent within the hour.

McBroom used his fingertips gently but quickly to pull the Citibank check off the desk without disturbing anything. And he left the room, a shocked look on his face in case anyone should be in the hall this early.

Nobody was.

McBroom ran to the elevator, pushed the button, and folded the pale blue (and, even now he told himself, "unfair") check in thirds, sliding it into the inside pocket of his jacket.

At street level, McBroom slowed down. He went out onto the sidewalk toward the blind man.

Lucy arose from her comfortable position on the rug and wagged her feathery tail at McBroom. She let out a low, sad whine and licked his hand.

McBroom had no time for the dog. He ignored the friendly, sniffing overtures of the animal and stuffed the incriminating check into the tin cup.

He quickly re-entered the building, took the elevator up twenty-four floors, and called the police. That was a hell of a lot smarter than sitting all afternoon at the airport with two million dollars on him.

By ten o'clock, McBroom had expressed his dismay so many times that he had come almost to believe that his partner had indeed shot himself. And McBroom drank too much coffee, because his throat was dry from so much talking. He was hyper, from nerves, caffeine, an inability to organize his chaotic thoughts. McBroom was so frightened that once—just once—he knew an impulse to jump out the twenty-fourth floor window and go snatch his check.

The police were sympathetic.

Did McBroom know of any reason for Beale to take his life?

Had Beale been despondent?

Did McBroom know of any reason why Beale had never married?

Could McBroom tell them exactly what time he had heard the shot?

Why did Beale keep a gun in his office?

How long had Beale kept it there? Who else knew about the gun?

Were the firm's finances in good order?

Did Beale always come to the office so early?

Whom should they notify about the death?

By eleven o'clock, McBroom was starved. He asked the officer in charge if he could leave to get a bite to eat. But the detective, who was busy consulting with a crime scene photographer, asked McBroom to wait until they could just straighten out a few things about Beale's morning commute, and go over McBroom's story once more of arriving at the office within minutes of the gunshot, which McBroom said he hadn't heard.

So McBroom waited in his own office with a uniformed police officer, occasionally drifting with jittery steps over to the window to look down on Fifth Avenue at the blind man looking up at him.

Even from twenty-four stories up, the man's face had a peculiar blankness, and McBroom didn't like looking at him.

At noon, Capote's customary island on the sidewalk was empty. McBroom knew where the man had gone—to St. Patrick's, to have his lunch with his dog.

What McBroom didn't know was that Lucy always led her master inside the big church, to the shrine of St. Francis of Assisi, where the man lit a candle. The blind man loved that shrine because he had always heard that this particular saint had taken care of animals. Here, when Capote looked up, what he couldn't see were the towering Gothic planes and arches, the rose window, the other stained glass that told the story of Christianity, window by window in the clerestory.

Capote lit the candle by picking up one of the long sticks and feeling around for the heat of a candle already burning. From that fire, he borrowed enough flame to light the wick of a candle he'd found by touch. He had burned himself more than a few times, but that didn't bother him. He loved that shrine.

Then, at a command from Capote, Lucy led him behind the main altar to the Lady Chapel, where he could look for a priest.

Half an hour later, Capote returned to his regular spot on Fifth Avenue. And within five minutes McBroom was by his side.

Lucy once again stood up at her master's side, keeping her eyes on McBroom, sniffing his trousers and wagging her tail. She licked McBroom's hand.

Grateful for Capote's clocklike predictability—oh, the timing was superb—McBroom reached his hand inside the tin cup, as if he were making a donation.

The cup was empty.

Empty. To McBroom it felt like a well, and no matter how far he pushed his hand, down and down and down, lower and lower, there was no bottom.

The goddamned cup was empty.

This was impossible. McBroom knew that this blind beggar was very successful among the regulars on this street. How could his cup be empty?

McBroom, shaking his head to clear it, realized in a flash that the blind man emptied the cup himself and put the money on his person.

McBroom had bought all the time he could afford. He had to have that check. None of his other personal assets were liquid, and he knew the police were having difficulty with the picture of suicide painted by McBroom in Beale's office. And there was nothing he could do to fix it. No little touch he could add, no little flourish. He wasn't sure what was bothering the cops, but he also didn't care. He couldn't think. All he wanted was the check, and a cab to the airport.

He glanced around. The sidewalk was too closely packed with people for anyone to see what anyone else was doing with his hands. McBroom reached into Capote's coat pockets and turned them inside out. Nothing.

And Capote did not object. He stood there like a statue, looking up at the invisible sky. After all these years, Capote barely noticed any touch from the crowd.

Desperate, McBroom put his hands in Capote's pants pockets. Nothing.

Lucy edged closer to Capote, leaning against the big man. The dog whined at McBroom and lowered her head, begging him to scratch her ears.

McBroom was ready to scream. He didn't dare touch the man again. Someone would notice, even in this impossible crowd. Damn it. Someone would see. And McBroom had a plane to catch. Where was that check?

McBroom cleared his throat.

"Your cup's empty," he said, only loud enough for Capote to hear him. "Where's your money?"

Capote said nothing.

"Come on, man. I've lost something. Where's your money? What did you do with it?"

Still Capote stared at the sky.

McBroom's nervousness was now so electric he was afraid he'd give himself away by dancing in place, that some spasm would set him into frenetic motion.

"What have you been doing with your money?" he shouted.

Lucy let out a low, sad whine and lay on the rug at Mc-Broom's feet.

The blind man still stared at the sky, but he answered, quite readily—now that he knew who was asking the question.

"You the man put that check in my cup. Lucy knows you. Mark him again, Lucy."

And the dog stood to lick McBroom's hand and sniff his trousers.

McBroom backed away the few inches the thick tide of people would allow him.

"That paper didn't feel right," Capote said, "so I took it to the priest and axed him what Capote had there. God bless you, sir. I tithe every Friday, but I never thought I'd be able to do any real good."

McBroom couldn't blink. His eyes felt dry, but he couldn't blink. He stared at Capote but saw blankness. There was nothing ahead of him, nothing at all.

The dog, sensing McBroom's discomfort, edged to his side and nudged his cold hand.

"Lucy know you plenty," Capote said, staring ever unblinking, at the invisible sky.

McBroom didn't notice them, but several police officers were coming out of his office building.

"Maybe God give you a nice day. Ain't that right, Lucy?"

Doggone

Jonnie Jacobs

JONNIE JACOBS is the author of two mystery series. Her first, noted for its wry take on murder,
malice, and motherhood, features amateur sleuth
Kate Austen; the second, attorney Kali O'Brien.
Kate's dog, Max, and Kali's dog, Loretta, play active roles in the stories. A former practicing attorney, Jonnie lives near San Francisco with her
husband and two sons. The antics of the dogs in
"Doggone" are based on those of the now deceased
family Airedale, Moska.

Danny Kellman learned in March that his mother was
dying. He hadn't seen her in nearly ten years, although he
talked to her on the phone from time to time. She called
regularly on his birthday, Christmas, and Easter. Occasionally she called other times, as well. For no reason at
all. And she wrote letters—often as many as two or three a
month.

Not that she ever had anything interesting to say. It
was always the same old stuff about her garden, her many
volunteer projects, or some neighbor he'd long forgotten.
And, of course, she wrote at length about her babies—
Samuel, Hank, Otis, and Tootsie. Christ, they weren't
babies, they were dogs. Smelly, flea-bitten, spoiled-rotten

four-legged things she'd rescued from the pound. Nonetheless, they probably ate better than he did, and they certainly led a more pampered life.

Danny sent his mother a box of candy each Christmas, but he tossed most of the letters she wrote him without opening them, which is no doubt why he didn't know that his mother was sick until the doctor called.

"A brain tumor, I'm afraid," the doctor said gravely. "She's partially paralyzed on her left side, and her eyesight is going. I give her a couple of months at the most."

"I see." Danny was sure there was more he ought to say, but he didn't know what it was. Besides, the call had come in the middle of a *Simpsons* rerun. Danny was trying to follow the show at the same time he was listening to the doctor.

"I'm afraid you're going to have to find a nursing home for her," the doctor said, "unless, of course, you elect to care for her yourself."

Fat chance of that, Danny thought. He was willing to bet that age and illness had done nothing to make his mother's company more tolerable.

"You find a nursing home," Danny told the doctor. "How do you expect me to pick one from two thousand miles away?"

"Maybe when you come to visit . . ."

"I'm not planning any visits."

The doctor seemed surprised. "Surely you'd like some say in the matter?"

Bart Simpson said something funny but Danny missed it. "Choose whatever nursing home you want. It's no skin off my nose."

Danny hung up the phone and gave the television his

full attention. He put the matter of the nursing home out of his mind. He wouldn't even have mentioned the call to Madge except that she'd been in the next room and wanted to know who had called and why.

Madge was always poking her nose into his business. She acted so much like a wife he hated to think what she'd be like if they were actually married, a state of being he'd tried over the years to avoid like the plague. He and Madge didn't see eye to eye about that, among other things. But she was a decent cook and better looking than a lot of women her age, so Danny hadn't ever come right out and told her he wasn't the marrying kind.

His conversation with the doctor would have been the end of it as far as Danny was concerned, if not for the call a week later from his mother's attorney, Harlan Rainsford.

"I'm calling about the nursing home," Rainsford said.

"Hey, what am I? An expert? I told the doc to choose one himself."

Rainsford cleared his throat. "They're very expensive."

So that was it. He should have known. "Sorry pal, I don't have a cent to spare." It was the truth, too. Payments on his Porsche took a big hunk of his paycheck, and Madge was forever hankering after some new bauble. Danny sometimes wondered if it wouldn't be easier to marry her, after all. Then he wouldn't always have to be showing her what a nice guy he was.

"I wasn't calling to ask you for money," Rainsford said. "Quite the contrary. You see, if your mother's savings go to pay for the nursing home and care, then there will be very little left for your inheritance. She's quite concerned about that."

Danny had the beer bottle half-way to his lips. "My inheritance?"

"Right. She explained it all in her letters so I won't bother you with the details. You might like to know, however, she's touched that you're too embarrassed by her largesse to respond. But she understands how talking money and death with someone you love can be uncomfortable. That's why she asked me to do it."

"My inheritance?" Danny asked again. As far as he knew his father had died penniless. Surely his mother couldn't have saved much during her years as a waitress at the Stop 'N' Go.

Rainsford chuckled. "That was one lucky lottery ticket, I tell you. And, of course, she invested it wisely. All told, I'd say there's about one and a half million."

The words sank in slowly. "And she wants to leave it to me?" Danny asked. He was afraid to sound too incredulous lest the lawyer realize there must be a mistake.

"You're her only child and she wants to provide for you. She's worried, though, that if she has to buy into a care center, and that's the way the best ones often operate—"

Danny interrupted. "No, that won't be necessary." He wasn't about to see his money frittered away on nursing care. *His money.* "Of course I'll care for her myself. I mean, she's close to the end, isn't she? She should be with family."

He'd barely hung up the phone when Madge popped into the room, barely able to contain her excitement. "We're moving to California?" She'd apparently been eavesdropping again.

We. Danny hadn't given any thought to Madge's role in this undertaking. He wasn't entirely sure he wanted her to tag along. This was his chance to start fresh, after all. A man of means. And California was full of all those young, athletic blondes in spandex. But there was no denying Madge would be a help with housework and cooking and all. He wasn't about to spend his days at his mother's beck and call, even for one and a half million.

In fact, the visions that came to Danny's mind didn't include much work at all. He'd have to quit his job in order to make the move, and it wouldn't make sense to tie himself down with something else while his mother needed his attention. That's why he was moving, after all, to care for her.

The more he thought about it, the more Danny warmed to the idea. No more getting up at six A.M. and heading off to the factory. No more time clocks and picky bosses. He'd sleep in till a reasonable hour, help Madge around the house a little, confer with his mother's attorney when necessary, brush up on his golf game and sip long, cool drinks in the evening. And his mother wouldn't be spending a cent of his inheritance on nursing care.

Danny turned to Madge. "I'm afraid there's no choice but to go. My mother needs me."

"Danny, honey." His mother gave him a wet kiss on the cheek. "It's so good to see you again."

She looked older than when he'd last seen her, and she used a walker to get around, but she seemed pretty lively for someone on her deathbed.

She turned to Madge. "You, too, honey." Their hug was interrupted by a flurry of canine enthusiasm. "And here are my babies," his mother said proudly, as four dogs leapt and yipped and wiggled with the excitement of company.

"They're adorable," said Madge, getting down on her knees to scratch their necks.

Danny looked at her with mild admiration. He hadn't known she was such a good actress.

"I always get the dogs who are close to being put to sleep," his mother was saying. "I do them a good turn by saving their life, and they do me a good turn by keeping me company. I used to keep more than four, but since I've gotten older, four is about all I can handle."

"I'm going to love playing with them," Madge said.

Danny swatted at the scruffy, brown-and-black terrier his mother called Samuel, then looked down when he felt something warm and wet on his leg.

"Oh, dear," his mother exclaimed with a laugh. "Samuel has a little bladder problem when he's excited."

Holding the fabric from his trousers away from his skin, Danny hobbled across the room and grabbed a roll of paper towels. Tootsie, who looked more like a dust mop than a dog, stood a few feet away and yapped shrilly.

While Danny was mopping up his leg, the third dog, who looked like a curly-haired Irish setter, grabbed the roll of paper towels from his hand and took off running.

"Otis is still a puppy," his mother explained. "He likes to tease."

Hank, a jowly creature with a skin condition, was the only one of the four who acted the way a dog was supposed to act. He sat quietly.

Madge had picked up Tootsie and was cuddling the thing in her arms. She seemed oblivious to the white dog hair that was clinging to her sweater.

His mother beamed. "I'm so happy my boy has

finally settled down. I've waited a long time for a daughter-in-law."

Before Danny had a chance to skirt the issue, Madge blurted out, "Oh, we're not married."

His mother frowned. "Oh?"

Danny knew he had to do something quickly. "But we're going to be, aren't we, sweetheart?"

Madge gave him a funny look.

"I'm glad to hear it," said his mother. "I won't allow any hanky-panky in my house."

Madge giggled. "You don't have to worry about that. Danny's a straight arrow when it comes to sex. Missionary position is about all he knows."

Danny choked. Luckily his mother seemed suddenly hard of hearing. "We put the wedding plans on hold to come out here," Danny hastened to add, nudging Madge's foot with his own to silence her. "We were just about to tie the knot."

"You can have the spare bedroom, dear," his mother said to Madge. "Danny can sleep on the sofa in the den. It won't be a problem at all."

It was a problem, but Danny decided he'd worry about it later.

After a few false starts, their days fell into a routine. Madge balked at doing all the cooking and dishes (she's your mother, Madge reminded him). She took care of the personal stuff like combing his mother's hair, sitting in front of the television with her, and, as the weather got warmer, rocking with her on the back-porch glider. But that still left a lot for Danny to do.

They'd been there less than a month when he began to

wonder if even a million and a half was worth the effort. Living with his mother was not easy. In fact, it was harder than any day he'd put in at the factory. And the house had few of the creature comforts he'd come to count on.

His mother had only one television, so old it didn't even have a remote. No VCR and no cable, either. She didn't own a microwave, a dishwasher, or even a clothes dryer. And her car was a real clunker. Some days Danny missed his Porsche so much it hurt.

His mother was a nonstop talker, too. When she wasn't talking to him or Madge, she talked to the dogs. Talked and then waited for an answer, if you could believe it. From the dogs, no less.

Dogs. They certainly didn't help matters. They needed to be walked and fed and cleaned up after. It seemed like every time Danny turned around, one or the other of them needed a trip to the vet or the dentist or the groomer. Hank passed a lot of gas and made the house smell. Samuel continued to have accidents, even when he wasn't excited. Tootsie shed constantly. And the puppy, Otis, had enough energy to send a rocket to the moon.

Otis liked to chew, too. He'd already gone through a pair of Danny's shoes and his forty dollar umbrella, and the stupid mutt thought it was great fun to tug at Danny's blanket just before sunrise each morning.

What with the house, his mother and the dogs, Danny didn't have much time for golf.

Or for tall drinks. His mother disapproved of alcohol as much as she did hanky-panky.

But Danny was willing to be patient. His day would come.

* * *

By June his patience had just about run out. He'd met with Rainsford, the attorney, to see about getting an advance on his inheritance, but that was not, apparently, the way things worked. He'd met with the doctor, too. Danny observed, being careful to keep the disappointment from his voice, that his mother's condition hadn't deteriorated as quickly as predicted. The doctor nodded encouragingly. Love, he said, was potent medicine.

Danny was tired of tending his mother's needs. He was tired of dog hair and muddy footprints and the barking that erupted at odd intervals day and night. And Danny wanted Madge.

He hadn't been to Madge's bed since they'd arrived. His mother might be old and frail, but she wasn't deaf. Whenever he tried to slip up the stairs to Madge's room, the floor would creak, one of the dogs would start yapping, and his mother would turn on a light and want to know what was happening. Madge suggested that they get married right away. Then there wouldn't be a problem, she pointed out. Not that particular problem, Danny thought to himself, but plenty of others. He'd avoided marriage this long; he could certainly weather his mother's unexpected good health without giving in now.

One warm afternoon Madge and his mother were sitting outside in the yard sipping iced tea. The dogs were sprawled at their feet—all except for Otis, that is. He was busy fetching the tennis ball Madge threw for him.

Danny had come outside to ask for dinner suggestions when his eyes fell upon an oleander bush at the back of the yard. He didn't remember much from his years as a boy scout, but he did remember that oleander was poisonous.

Maybe it was time to help things along, he thought. His mother was going to die anyway. What was a few more months? Besides, the slow withering away of life was unpleasant and often painful. He would be doing her a favor really.

"How about a cookout this evening?" he asked, infusing his voice with all the enthusiasm he could muster.

Both his mother and Madge were delighted.

"A picnic," Madge exclaimed, clapping her hands.

His mother nodded. "I haven't had one of those in years. It's simply lovely having you two here. I'm blessed to have family who care."

Madge squeezed his mother's hand. "It works both ways, you know."

Danny bit his tongue and looked longingly at the oleander bush.

Otis dropped the tennis ball and leapt for the shopping list in Danny's hand, smearing his muddy paws on Danny's pants in the process. With the list between his teeth, the dog took off racing around the yard, daring someone to chase after him.

Madge laughed. "Otis, you're a scamp."

Danny counted to ten silently. He decided they would eat early that night.

Later, while Madge was helping his mother with her bath, Danny cut a stalk of oleander and stripped the leaves. Then he skewered two hot dogs for his mother. He speared hot dogs for himself and Madge on willow branches, careful to keep theirs separate from his mother's.

Danny whistled as he built the fire that evening and held the hot dogs over the open flame. He'd picked up some potato salad and chips at the deli and set the table outside like it was the Fourth of July. Independence Day, he laughed to himself at the irony.

He could have used a beer, but he figured one last night going without was a small price to pay. When the meat was done, Danny set it on a platter and poured more iced tea.

"I guess summer's really here," his mother said, sounding almost like a kid.

Madge agreed. "Isn't it wonderful?"

While the women were waxing poetic about the joys of summer and Danny was refilling the glasses, Otis moseyed around behind the table and snatched the skewer closest to the edge, which happened to be the one Danny had prepared for his mother. Danny made a grab for it and missed, but Madge was able to catch Otis by the collar after a brief, playful tussle. By the time she retrieved the hot dogs, however, they were in no shape for eating.

"Let him have them," Danny muttered irritably. That way, at least, his efforts with the oleander wouldn't be for nothing.

But Madge and his mother objected. Rewarding bad behavior, they insisted, was no way to train a dog. Madge lectured Otis, then tossed the oleander-spiced links into the garbage. There was, as Madge pointed out, more than enough to eat without them.

Danny would have tried cooking out another night except that his mother and Madge were in agreement that while charred hot dogs had a certain nostalgic appeal, they weren't something a person wanted to eat more than once a year. So he tried instead to bide his time patiently.

Each morning he checked the kitchen calendar, counting the days they'd been there, making bets with himself about the number left to go. The doctor had said his mother's death was only a matter of time, and although she was hanging on longer than expected, the outcome wasn't going to change.

While Madge read to his mother and spent long hours listening to his mother's stories about her girlhood, Danny took care of the shopping and cooking and cleaning. And he filled his mind with visions of what his life would soon be like.

He'd come to see what an aggravation owning a house was. Give him a condo any day—with a view and a pool, maybe even a hot tub. That was one of first things he was going to do when the money was his. He wanted a modern place, one that didn't allow pets, with a big-screen TV and a sound system wired into every room.

Danny liked to shut his eyes and pretend that he was snuggled on the leather sofa with a svelte young blonde. They'd be sipping smooth martinis from crystal glasses while she nibbled on his ear. He'd be wearing a fancy silk shirt and maybe a diamond pinkie ring. He hadn't quite decided how he felt about the ring. But he knew that fine dining, expensive gin, and country club golf were right over the horizon.

By August his mother's health had deteriorated noticeably. While Danny found this change encouraging, he also found that it made for more work. His mother now needed help eating and moving about. And she couldn't be left alone, even for an hour. Finally, his patience ran out.

The oleander had been a stupid idea, he decided. Amateurish. What he really needed was something more reliable.

Danny called his mother's doctor and explained that she was having a difficulty sleeping at night. She wasn't, of course. The woman could fall asleep at the drop of a hat. But the doctor was sympathetic.

On the afternoon that Danny filled the prescription for sleeping pills, he felt a bounce in his step that had been missing for months. He'd fix a nice dinner that night—his mother deserved that much—and make sweet, rich chocolate pudding for dessert. He didn't think the taste of the pills would be discernable at all.

When all the ingredients for the pudding were assembled, Danny started to open the vial of pills. But then he heard Madge return from walking the dogs. Hastily, he slipped the pills under the newspaper on the kitchen table.

Madge kissed him on the cheek. "What are you making?" she asked, dropping the leashes and Otis's tennis ball on a nearby chair.

"Pudding. It's my mother's recipe. She loves it."

"You're so considerate, Danny. The way you've disrupted your own life to care for your mother. It's a very attractive quality, you know." Madge gave him a seductive smile and slipped her arms around his waist. "Speaking of which . . ."

Danny felt his pulse quicken. Despite his mother's dislike for hanky-panky, they'd managed a few trysts here and there. But only a few. He wasn't inclined to let opportunity pass him by.

Of course, by tomorrow he wouldn't have to worry what his mother thought. But Madge was here now. And she wanted him.

Danny pulled her closer. Tootsie heard a noise in the

yard and started yapping. Hank had another attack of gas, and Samuel, chin still dripping with water from his dish, flopped to the floor at their feet. Danny tried to ignore them all.

Otis, who was never in any mood to be ignored, started for his tennis ball. But the newspaper, hanging over the edge of the table, seemed a better choice. He tugged at it, sending the vial of pills rolling across the floor. Ever eager for a new game, Otis chased the vial, grabbed it in his mouth and raced into the yard.

Danny panicked. He let go of Madge and chased after the dog, but by the time he got to the yard, Otis had dropped the vial, or maybe buried it. In any case, it was no longer in his mouth. Danny hoped the stupid dog hadn't swallowed the pills.

Although he spent the rest of the afternoon searching the yard, Danny didn't find the vial. Yet Otis showed no signs of being sleepy, either, so Danny figured they had to be somewhere. Tomorrow, he reminded himself, was another day.

Dinner that night was lovely, and his mother so appreciative Danny felt a brief flutter of guilt.

"Such a sweet boy you are," she told him, giving his hand a gentle squeeze. "To tell you the truth, I suspected you might put me in a nursing home."

"This is something I wanted to do," Danny said simply.

His mother smiled. "As you know, I'm going to make it up to you eventually."

Danny returned the smile. He hoped that "eventually" wasn't too far off.

* * *

When Danny still hadn't found the vial of pills a week later, he decided to take matters into his own hands. Literally. It was what he should have done from the start. A pillow over his mother's face for a couple of minutes was all it would take. And her death would look to all the world as though she'd passed gently in her sleep.

Sneaking up on his mother wasn't going to be easy—her hearing was as keen as ever. But what the heck, Danny thought. She wasn't going to be around to identify him as a killer, was she? When he walked the dogs that afternoon, Danny was as excited as a kid on Christmas Eve.

"I hope you're enjoying yourselves," he told the dogs. Talking to them was a habit he'd picked up from his mother and Madge. "Tomorrow it's off to the pound with all of you."

Danny had decided to list the house with a realtor right away. He had one already selected, in fact. And he'd been collecting travel brochures all summer. He hadn't decided between Europe and the Caribbean, but now that the time was close he'd have to choose quickly.

He'd call the attorney in the morning. After the ambulance had taken away his mother's body, of course. Danny knew that legal dealings took time, but his mother had hinted that she'd set things up to avoid a lengthy probate. Danny was glad. He didn't think he had it in him to wait any longer.

After dinner that night, Danny was tense with anticipation. When his mother and Madge went up to bed, he tried watching TV but couldn't concentrate.

He waited until he heard Madge snoring, then crept up the dark stairs to his mother's bedroom in his stocking feet. He was prepared for the dogs this time, too. He had their favorite chew treats in hand. That would keep them occupied and quiet for the short period of time he needed.

Sure enough, by the time Danny reached the top of the stairs, the dogs were there, sniffing and wagging their tails like they hadn't seen him in a week. Danny gave them each a rawhide chip and grinned at the ease with which he'd outsmarted them. Stupid animals.

And then, two steps onto the landing, he stepped on Otis's tennis ball, lost his balance, and fell backward.

The doctor said he was lucky. Only one broken leg, a broken wrist, and a dislocated shoulder. Danny decided that he and the doc didn't exactly see eye to eye on the matter of luck.

Danny was now as helpless as his mother. Moving around the house was a major challenge. He couldn't even dress or bathe himself. He spent a lot of time sitting on the couch with the dogs, watching fuzzy, orange images on TV and listening to his mother talk.

"I feel so bad that you hurt yourself coming to check on me," she told him not long after the accident. "I had no idea you were that worried about me."

"Well, I . . ." Danny lowered his eyes, which he found was easier than an outright lie.

"I know I've been a burden on you. I can't tell you how grateful I am for all you've done. You gave up your job, put off your wedding. I want you to know I won't forget it." She took his hand in hers. "It's been wonderful having you here, Danny. And Madge, too. She's a fine woman."

He mumbled something meaningless.

"I've had a good life," his mother said after a minute. Her voice grew soft. "I've been a very lucky woman."

The past tense caught him by surprise. "You make it sound like you're dying."

A smile played at the corners of her mouth. "I am. That's why you're here, remember?"

"But I mean . . ."

She gave his hand a squeeze. "I know this embarrasses you, dear. But it shouldn't. Everything is all taken care of."

Within the month his mother was dead. She died peacefully in her sleep with Samuel, Hank, Tootsie, and Otis by her side.

Madge wept. Danny called the attorney.

They gathered in his office the next day for the reading of the will. Rainsford began by clearing his throat. "I want to tell you how sorry I am about your mother's passing."

Danny nodded impatiently. One and a half million, plus the house. His day had finally come.

"She was very grateful for all you did for her," Rainsford continued. "You should find solace in the fact that she died happy, knowing she had a son who cared."

At least she'd died, Danny thought, even if she took her own sweet time about it. "The will," Danny prompted.

Rainsford pulled a pair of glasses out of his pocket. "Yes, the will. First off, your mother felt very guilty about causing you to postpone your wedding. She wanted to make sure that once she was gone, you made that your first priority."

"Wedding?" Danny asked, pulling himself back from the white sand beach he'd been mentally lounging on.

"So she made that a condition," Rainsford continued.

"Once you're married, the house is yours—for as long as you want to live there."

"As long as—"

"In addition, you'll receive a monthly allowance, income from principal really—"

Danny pulled at his ear, sure that he'd misunderstood. "Income from principal?" he asked. "What about the principal itself?"

"As you know, that will be held in trust until you no longer need it. Then it goes to the humane society. It's all just as your mother explained in her letters. We didn't change a thing, except for the wedding stipulation."

All those letters he'd tossed. Danny couldn't believe he'd been so stupid.

"You'll get your allowance regularly," Rainsford continued. "Just as long as you continue to live in the house and raise a minimum of four dogs rescued from the pound. Of course, you'll start with Samuel, Hank, Tootsie, and Otis."

Danny's fantasies came crashing down around him. No elegant condo. No pool and hot tub. No babes in spandex. Instead, he was stuck with Madge and four dogs. It was either that or move back to Pittsburgh and put in his forty hours a weeks at the factory.

By the time Danny got back to the house he was so low he felt like crying.

But Madge met him at the door with a kiss. They had a nice dinner, preceded by a shaker of dry martinis. He figured with a little redecorating, there'd be room in the den for a large-screen TV. And the dogs—well, at least his mother hadn't been into rescuing snakes.

Sleeping Dogs Lie

Laurien Berenson

LAURIEN BERENSON is the author of the Melanie
Travis mysteries, a cozy series that uses the dog
show world as a backdrop. The current titles are
Watchdog, *Hair of the Dog*, *Dog Eat Dog*, and *A Pedigree to Die For*. She is a three-time winner of the
Maxwell Award for Fiction from the Dog Writers
Association of America and is a long-time breeder/
exhibitor of miniature poodles. She lives in Atlanta
with her husband, her son, and six dogs.

"It's not much to ask, really. He's such a dear little dog.
I know he won't be any bother."

Peg Turnbull looked askance at the tricolor Jack Russell
terrier clutched in her neighbor's arms. She'd been a dog
lover for all six decades of her life, but Peg was no
pushover. She knew trouble when she saw it; and Digger,
a hyperactive mischief maker with no obedience training
to speak of, was big trouble.

Sensing imminent rejection, Mabel Watkins hurried on.
"It will only be for a week. Harold and I just can't leave
him in some big, impersonal boarding kennel with nobody
to look out for him. Surely you, of all people, understand
that."

Of course she understood, thought Peg. She had nine

dogs herself, didn't she? Hers were standard poodles; big, beautiful dogs with jet-black coats and intelligent eyes. The Cedar Crest line was renowned in the elite circles of the dog show world for its good temperament. Digger, now snuggled in his mistress's arms and chewing one of the gold buttons on the front of Mabel's blazer, looked as though his forebears might have been famous for their impudence.

Feeling her gaze, Digger glanced up at Peg and curled a lip. Peg answered with a sneer of her own. Mabel mistook the gesture for a smile.

"I knew I could count on you!" she said quickly, thrusting Digger forward.

"But—"

Before she could finish, the little terrier had jumped nimbly onto her ample bosom, his paws winding around her shoulder as he clung like a monkey. Reluctantly, she lifted her arms to give him support.

Mabel dusted off her hands, whether in satisfaction or in an attempt to rid herself of Digger's hair, Peg couldn't tell. The woman's top button hung by a thread, but she didn't seem to notice. With the Jack Russell in residence, destruction of property was probably a habitual occurrence.

"You're such a dear to do this for me. You know I'd never ask for such a large favor except . . ." Mabel's expression clouded.

Peg knew what was coming. She'd heard it before, many times. Unfortunately, her neighbors had a tragedy in their past from which they'd never recovered. Their son, Will, nineteen years old and a vehement opponent of the Vietnam War, had been drafted and sent to Southeast Asia in the last year of the fighting. Doing his duty, Mabel pointed out, in spite of his beliefs. Serving his country to the best of his abilities because that's the kind of a boy he was.

Five months later, the letters home had abruptly stopped. Will Watkins had disappeared. Missing in action, Mabel said. That was the official designation. It didn't mean dead, only missing. She called her son "our neighborhood hero" and refused to give up hope.

As the years passed, Mabel had eventually stopped speaking about her son. Peg wasn't sure if that made things better or worse. She had never had any children of her own; still, she could feel the magnitude of Mabel's loss.

So when her neighbor stopped by every so often and asked for a favor, the scope of which often left Peg gasping, she still had a hard time saying no.

"But my garden club luncheon would be so lovely on *your* terrace," Mabel had said one summer. "And you know how Harold can't stand to be around crowds. Too many questions he says. And never any answers." So Peg had found herself playing hostess to thirty-eight silly, chattering women who spent the afternoon discussing shrubs Peg had never heard of and gossiping about their friends.

"I have to sell my old car," Mabel had announced on another occasion. "I've placed an ad in the paper and you know how Harold gets when the phone rings. He thinks every call will be the one." She paused to wipe a tear from her eye. "I've put your phone number in the ad. You're such a dear, you wouldn't mind taking a few messages, would you?"

The calls arrived at all hours of the day and night and

were spoken in a surprising number of languages. By the time a buyer was finally found, Peg had been tempted to purchase the car herself just to put an end to her misery.

Now Mabel was back again. This time the favor she wanted was squirming impatiently in Peg's arms. Peg was heartily tempted to hand him right back. Then Mabel played her trump card.

"I know you'll take wonderful care of him. We have to leave Digger with someone we can trust. You know how attached Harold and I have become to him. He's almost like a member of the family. You understand. We'd never be able to bear it if we lost him, too."

Peg sighed. She seemed to do that a lot when Mabel was around. It looked as though the Jack Russell was hers for the duration. She felt a tug and saw that her sleeve was in the dog's mouth. Digger's teeth had already began to fray the cuff. She suspected it was going to be a very long week.

By the end of the first day, Peg wanted to strangle Digger; by the end of the second, she nearly had. It was an accident, of course. Peg adored dogs, at least she always had. Now that she had more than a nodding acquaintance with her neighbor's Jack Russell, however, Peg realized that perhaps she shouldn't have been so quick to include the entire canine population in her affections.

She started by taking the little dog into the house and introducing him to the various members of her canine family. Five of her poodles were house dogs; the remaining four, a stud dog and several rambunctious puppies, were quartered in the kennel building out back. The house dogs, all show champions, all but one retired from the ring, formed a curious circle around the little interloper and gave him a good sniff.

Digger responded by growling in their faces.

"None of that," said Peg. "For the next week, you're going to get along."

The poodles got the message. They backed off and wagged their tails. Ignoring them, Digger trotted purposefully over to the sofa and lifted his leg. Before Peg could snatch him up, he'd succeeded in marking his territory and Beau, the only male poodle in residence, looked like he was thinking of following suit.

"No!" cried Peg.

Beau sat down looking chastened. Digger sat down as well. Obviously he was used to being yelled at. He hadn't even flattened his ears. The expression on his face was smug.

Peg went to get some seltzer water and a rag to clean up. As usual, her five big black dogs trailed along behind. "I'll need you to set a good example," she told them firmly. "And for heaven's sake, keep him out of trouble."

Maybe the poodles weren't listening. While Peg cleaned up in the living room, Digger trotted up to her bedroom and found her favorite pair of slippers. Old slippers, to be sure, but well broken in and worn in such a way that they molded to Peg's feet, keeping her warm on even the coldest nights.

Digger destroyed the heels first, then went to work on the toes. By the time Peg found him, the slippers were in shreds.

Stifling her outrage, Peg tried to look at things from Digger's point of view. This was obviously her own fault. She never should have let him out of her sight.

With that in mind, Peg spent the remainder of the day keeping a close watch on the Jack Russell terrier. While she ate lunch, he explored the kitchen, poking his nose into cabinets and kibble bins alike. When she puttered in her garden that afternoon, he raced in the fenced yard with the poodles. That evening when she sat down to work in her office, Digger finally went to sleep, surrounded by the poodles who'd begun to accept him as a friend.

Peg's current show dog, Lillith, stretched out on the floor beside him, and her long, luxurious coat fell across Digger's body, covering him like a blanket. All Peg could see was his little white feet, which twitched and trembled as he chased imaginary rabbits in his dreams.

Now that he was finally still, he really was a rather cute little dog. Of course there was bound to be an adjustment period, thought Peg. But now that Digger knew what was expected of him, things would go much more smoothly.

She managed to hold that thought until bedtime when Lillith gave a sharp yip as she rose to go out. The reason for her pain became immediately apparent. Lying beneath her, Digger clutched a mouthful of long black hair between his teeth. Not only that, but the floor around him was littered with similar debris.

"You little devil, you've been chewing on her show coat!" Peg's face grew white at the enormity of this new transgression. "Do you know how long it took me to grow that hair?"

Her fingers searched hurriedly through Lillith's side, evaluating the damage. The standard poodle would be out of the show ring for months. Sensing her fury, Digger got up and ran. The poodles quickly followed suit.

The Jack Russell terrier spent the night in a crate, howling at the unaccustomed loss of freedom. By morning, Peg thought he ought to be more concerned about possible loss of life. After breakfast, she'd calmed down enough to let him have a run in the fenced backyard. She watched as he treed a pair of birds, then sat down at the foot of the trunk to wait for them to come back down.

"It's not your fault you're not the brightest boy," she said grumpily. "Nor that you haven't had any training. And you certainly can't spend your entire visit in a crate. Let's see what we can figure out."

Moments later, Peg was dragging a portable exercise pen through the back door of the house. The round wire mesh enclosure had walls four feet high and opened out to provide a space six feet in diameter. Once she pushed the table to one side, it fit rather nicely in the middle of her kitchen.

Peg added a bowl of water, a rawhide chew toy, and a piece of old blanket that Digger's busy paws could mold into a bed. Then she popped the little dog over the side and stepped back to have a look.

The Jack Russell jumped up against the wall of the pen, his stubby tail wagging back and forth energetically. He could see everything that was happening around him, he just couldn't reach it. Digger didn't seem to mind. He touched noses with Lillith who was standing outside the pen, then dropped back down to all fours and went to investigate his new toy.

"Finally," Peg said as the dog lay down his rawhide bone between his front legs. "Now I'll get some peace."

She was in her office late that afternoon when the sound

of furious barking made her sit up straight and glance out the window. Visitors? Her standard poodles were excellent watchdogs, but the driveway and front walk were empty. A neighboring dog in the yard perhaps? Peg stood up to have a look. She didn't see a thing.

"What?" she asked as Beau came racing down the hall. "What's the matter?"

Peg had always talked to her dogs; she didn't consider that unusual in the least. She did, however, find that their answers were sometimes less than satisfactory. Beau jumped up and down in place, whining under his breath. Then he turned and ran back down the hall, stopping halfway to see if she was following.

"All right." Peg set her book aside. "I'm coming."

The closer she got to the kitchen, the louder the commotion became. All five poodles were circling and spinning in the small room, their frenzied attention centered on the ex pen in the center. As Peg turned the corner, she quickly saw why.

Digger had managed to climb the side of the pen in an obvious bid for escape. Going over the top, however, the little terrier must have slipped and as he'd fallen, his leather collar had snagged on one of the supports. Now he was hanging by his neck from the top of the pen, his little feet paddling ineffectually in empty space, his mouth open and gasping for air.

"Oh, dear Lord!" Peg cried. She leapt forward and snatched Digger up, pulling him free. "Oh, my goodness!"

Her fingers quickly unfastened the collar as she cradled Digger in her arms. He coughed several times, his whole body racking with the effort. Peg massaged his neck and let him catch his breath.

Legs suddenly rubbery, she sank into a kitchen chair, still holding Digger tight. "You very nearly killed yourself, you silly animal. How would I ever have been able to break the news to Mabel?"

That poor, sad woman, thought Peg. Something like this could have been the last straw. Mabel had been through so much. Not just the loss of her only child, but the uncertainty, the lack of a resolution had to make it all that much worse.

Mabel rarely talked about Will anymore, but Peg knew she had to be thinking of him. Lying awake at night, perhaps, and wondering where he was. After all these years, Peg wondered, had Mabel finally given up, or did she still hold out the tiniest shred of hope that someday her boy might come home?

"Your troubles are nothing compared with that," Peg told herself sensibly. "Now let's get on with it."

She decided to put Digger in the kennel. At that point it seemed likely that was the only way they'd both survive their association. Of the dozen pens in the kennel building, more than half were empty. The Ceder Crest line of standard poodles had been a force in the dog show world for three decades, but since the death of her husband, Max, several years earlier, Peg had been scaling down. It wasn't hard to find a place to put the Jack Russell terrier.

The pen inside the building was made of solid wood. If Digger attempted to climb out, he wouldn't find any purchase on the smooth sides; and even if he somehow managed to succeed, he'd still be trapped within the building. A dog door led outside to a gravel-floored run surrounded by six-foot chain-link fencing.

"Gotcha," she said with satisfaction as she watched

Digger explore his new home. "It may not be as plush as you're used to, but at least I'll know where you are."

For the first time in three days, Peg got a good night's sleep. As someone who prided herself on her expertise in dealing with dogs, the problems with Digger had proven unsettling, and she was pleased to finally have the situation resolved. That feeling of complacency lasted until after breakfast the next morning when she went down to the kennel to feed.

Joker, the stud dog, immediately jumped up in his pen to greet her. The puppies yipped and yammered and rolled around on the floor. The only pen that was quiet was the one that should have housed Digger. Peg peered over the side. No little dog was waiting to see what new mischief the day might bring.

She stepped over to the back door and poked her head out. Digger's run was empty, too. "Lordy, lordy," Peg moaned, hurrying around to the end of the pen. As she unlatched the door and stepped inside, the means of the terrier's escape immediately became apparent. A dog-size hole had been dug beneath the fence; Digger had tunneled his way to freedom.

"Digger," she said, frowning and feeling inutterably stupid. "I should have known."

It only took a few minutes to ascertain that Digger wasn't within the fenced boundary of the yard. "Probably climbed out," Peg muttered. "The little Houdini."

She paused in the house only long enough to call around and ask if any of the neighbors had seen a small tricolor dog running loose in the area. No one had. Then she grabbed up a leash and a box of dog biscuits and set out.

Summer in Connecticut was a glorious season. If Peg

hadn't been so worried, she would have enjoyed the walk. Houses in back country Greenwich were spaced wide apart with spacious lawns and patches of woods filling the area in between. Unfortunately there were plenty of places where a little dog could disappear.

Peg visited the neighbors who had pets first, guessing that's where Digger's curiosity and inquisitive nose would lead him. She saw a Keeshond running free, a Great Dane on a chain, and an orange tabby cat asleep in a patch of sun. But no little Jack Russell terrier.

She called Digger's name. She shook the box of biscuits. She assured him all was forgiven. If Digger was close enough to hear, he didn't deign to make his presence known.

By ten o'clock, Peg had gone back for her car. Digger's legs might be short, but they were sturdy. She needed to cover a wider area in her search.

Peg rolled the windows down, drove slowly, and listened for any scrap of sound that might lead her in the right direction. Who knew where Digger might decide to run now that he was free? If it took all day, if it took all week, she had to find him.

Mabel's parting words played a steady refrain in her head: *"He's almost like a member of the family. Harold and I would never be able to bear it if we lost him, too."* No matter what she thought of her neighbor's pet, Peg was not about to be the one responsible for causing Mabel Watkins any more pain.

She circled the neighborhood twice, pausing at the end of each long driveway to gaze at the quiet houses and empty lawns. Once a flash of white, half seen out of the corner of her eye, had her shifting into reverse and speeding up a Belgian block–lined drive. It was only an oversized flowerpot, painted ivory, planted with impatiens and used to mark the boundary of a terrace.

Damn it, Digger! Aunt Peg thought. Now she was growing angry. If the dog had decided to run, he could be halfway to town by now. When she got home, she'd call the police and the dog warden. But even that effort would be compromised. Peg remembered all too well the jangle of Digger's identification tags as she'd taken off his collar the night before and left it on the kitchen counter.

Maybe he'd come home when he got hungry, she thought hopefully. Resourceful a little dog as he'd turned out to be, Peg couldn't imagine him hunting for his dinner. On the other hand, he probably wasn't above raiding a garbage can or two.

Home, Peg thought abruptly, her foot easing off the gas pedal. If Digger was looking for the comfort of familiar surroundings, he wouldn't come back to her. He'd return to his own house.

She whipped into the nearest driveway and turned her station wagon around. What had she been thinking? Rather than passing the Watkins' house by because it was empty, that was the first place she should have looked. She might be growing older, but Peg hated to think she was losing her touch.

On approach, Mabel and Harold's home looked peaceful and still. What had she expected? Peg asked herself irritably. Just because she'd had one bright idea, did she really think that Digger was going to come running down the driveway and throw himself gratefully into her arms?

She parked in the turnaround near the front door and got

out, taking her leash and her biscuits with her. Peg paused to listen. After a moment, she shook her head, scratched her ear and listened again. There was still no sign of Digger, but Peg could swear she heard music.

Unconsciously she began to hum along, realizing after a moment that she was humming the theme from the game show *Jeopardy*. How very odd—

The thought was cut short by the sound of an excited yip that came from the direction of the backyard. Digger! Peg hadn't sprinted in forty years, but that didn't stop her from racing around the house. But by the time she reached the back, the Jack Russell seemed to have disappeared.

Then she saw him. Digger was up on the back porch, his nose pressed against the locked door, his front paws scratching busily on the wood in an attempt to get in. Peg hurried up behind him and grasped the wiggly little body in both hands.

"What do you think you're doing?" she asked in exasperation as she slipped the looped end of the leash over his head. "There's nobody here."

Digger barked in reply, then braced his hind legs and tried to jump out of her arms. Knowing the leash would hold, Peg lowered him to the ground. Immediately the terrier began to throw himself against the door again.

Peg twisted her end of the leash around her hand and hauled him back. "Get a grip on yourself. Your family isn't in there. They're not home."

Digger refused to be appeased. He whined, he spun in a small circle, and when he could reach, he attacked the door again. "Oh, for Pete's sake," said Peg. "Come up then and have a look for yourself."

She lifted Digger up and held his nose to the window.

They both looked into the kitchen. As Peg expected, the room was empty. She was surprised to see, however, that the sink was filled with dirty dishes. Mabel was a meticulous housekeeper. Peg couldn't imagine why she'd left a mess like that behind.

"See?" she said thoughtfully. "I told you no one was home."

She put the dog down and walked him back to the driveway. His latest rebellion a rousing success, Digger was happy to trot along in her wake. As they came to the car, Peg stopped and stared at the house. If she listened very carefully, she could still hear the faint strains of . . . something . . .

Peg put Digger in the car, shut the door firmly behind him, then marched up the front steps. She knew the house had a security system but still, with Mabel and Harold out of town, it wouldn't hurt to have a look. Two tall, narrow windows flanked either side of the door but offered only a limited view of the front hall.

Never one to stifle her curiosity, Peg inched sideways behind a holly bush to the next window. A light was on in the living room, and a television sat against a side wall. A commercial for laundry detergent filled the large screen. Peg gazed around the room, but saw nothing amiss.

Easing away from the window, she told herself that everything was fine. Harold had obviously hooked some of their appliances up to a timer. Lots of people did that. It helped make a house looked lived in when its occupants were out of town. Now that she had Digger back, everything was just as it should be.

Peg drove Digger home and put him back in the kennel. It took two hours to refill the hole he'd dug and make sure the accommodations were once again secure. While she worked, the terrier watched the proceedings from the next run. He didn't even have the grace to look guilty.

That night, she left him inside his pen in the kennel building, with the door to his outside run fastened shut. "I dare you," she said, as she checked on the dogs one last time before going to bed. Digger merely looked at her and grinned.

Confident that she'd finally succeeded in outwitting the little dog, Peg still found she had a hard time dropping off to sleep. Something was bothering her, but it wasn't until the early hours of the morning that she realized what it was. On occasion Peg had enjoyed matching wits with the *Jeopardy* contestants herself. And she knew for a fact that the show only came on in the evenings.

Peg had read enough history to know the pitfalls of overconfidence. Still, she wasn't prepared for the following morning to be a repeat of the one before.

"He can't be gone," she said incredulously to Joker, who cocked an ear and listened obligingly. "How did he get out this time?"

A quick scan of the outside runs provided the answer. In the bright morning light, the upturned dirt of a freshly dug hole was clearly visible. Somehow he'd scaled the inside wall into the adjoining pen, then used that dog door to escape. Gazing at the evidence, Peg felt a tug of unwilling admiration for Digger's ingenuity. It didn't stop her from cursing his perseverance.

"Hog-tied," she muttered under her breath as she marched around the house to the garage. "Hobbled. Crated.

Sedated. I don't care anymore. There has got to be a way to keep that dog out of trouble for the next four days."

At least this time, she knew where to go first. Peg drove straight to the Watkins' house and parked, once again, in the turnaround. As she got out of the car, Peg paused to listen. A swallow chirped, a lawn mower sounded from afar. No barking dog. No game show theme.

Feeling vaguely disappointed, she called out Digger's name then began to search the area. Following the lawn around the house, Peg felt the oddest sensation. Her shoulder blades twitched; the back of her neck prickled. She could have sworn she was being watched.

Peg stopped and wheeled around. Nobody was there. "Digger? Is that you?"

Still no answer.

She skirted the big rhododendron bushes flanking the side of the house and emerged in the backyard as a sudden breeze rattled the back door. Frowning, Peg stepped closer. The door was closed but not latched, and the wind had pushed it slightly open.

It hadn't been like that yesterday, Peg thought, remembering Digger's frantic attempts to get inside the house. Then it had been securely locked. And speaking of Digger, where was the little monster anyway?

As if in answer to her question, the Jack Russell began to bark nonstop, loudly, and shrilly. The cacophony came from inside the house. It was followed by a crash and the sound of someone—male—swearing at the top of his lungs.

Without thinking, Peg ran up the steps and pushed the back door open. Caution arrived too late, but it did keep her from rushing headlong into the house. It didn't matter. Looking through the kitchen and into the dining room beyond, she could see the source of the problem.

A man was standing next to the table, brandishing a newspaper and yelling at Digger who was nipping at his feet. The remains of a broken mug littered the floor around them and a dark stain was spreading across the rug.

"Damn it, dog! Leave me alone!"

Peg backed away in alarm. Her first thought was to get to her car phone and report a break-in. Digger, the little dog who couldn't seem to do anything right, had cornered himself a burglar. Then she stopped, took in the whole scene, and reconsidered.

Even the most casual of burglars was unlikely to rob a house wearing a bathrobe and slippers.

The man aimed an angry kick at Digger's head. The Jack Russell dodged nimbly to one side, easily evading the blow. He jumped up, grabbed the terry cloth belt that dangled within his reach and gave it a sharp tug.

The robe fell open. He was wearing nothing underneath. Caught between blushing and laughing, Peg decided to was time to make her presence known. She cleared her throat softly. Man and dog were making so much noise that neither paid any attention.

"Hello?" she said, rapping her knuckles on the back door.

Digger spun around and began to wag his tail. The man glanced up in surprise. He gathered his robe quickly around him, aimed a last, futile kick in Digger's direction, then raked his fingers back through his hair.

In his forties, Peg estimated. Not bad looking, but with a shiftiness around the eyes that didn't speak well of his character. A family friend, perhaps? But then why would he be visiting when the Watkins were out of town?

Digger trotted over and sat down at Peg's feet, looking very pleased with himself.

"Who are you?" Peg asked. She remained in the doorway, careful to keep her avenue of escape open. "What are you doing here?"

For a moment, the man said nothing. He looked up, down, anywhere but at her. Clearly he was very uncomfortable, this stranger making himself very much at home at Mabel and Harold's.

Feeling more secure, Peg glared at him, reinforcing her right to demand some answers. She studied his features, committing them to memory, just in case she should ever be called upon to pick him out of a line-up. Then unexpectedly, as she continued to stare, she realized who he was. He wasn't a stranger at all.

"William?"

He still didn't answer, but Peg refused to be deterred.

"You're Will Watkins, aren't you?"

Slowly he nodded.

"Oh, my Lord!" Peg's heart did a little leap as she imagined Mabel's response. "Where did you come from? How did you get here?"

"In a car." Will looked baffled by the question. "I came by to visit my parents. I guess I should have called ahead."

"Called ahead? What are you talking about? You've been missing."

"Missing?" Her questions didn't seem to be helping his confusion any. "No, I haven't."

"Yes, you have," Peg insisted. Was he crazy, or was

she? "Nobody knew where you were. It's been years! Mabel told me all about your stint in Vietnam, how you went missing in action—"

"AWOL," he interrupted her. "I wasn't missing, I was AWOL."

"But . . ." Peg's voice trailed away as the import of his words sank in.

"Mother told you I was MIA?" Will shook his head. "That's just like her to clean things up. Everything always has to be presentable. Including me. There was no way she could own up to what I'd done."

Peg sagged back against the door frame. "Not missing? Never missing?" She knew she was babbling. It didn't seem to matter. "But it's been years. Where have you been all this time?"

"After I worked my way back, I went to Canada. There was plenty of support for people who felt like me up there. I was able to get in touch with my family. Then amnesty was declared and most of the guys I knew went home. The only problem was, there wasn't any amnesty for deserters. I can't ever come back, not permanently. There's still a warrant out for my arrest. Every so often, I sneak down for a visit. It's a bitch of a way to live."

Peg tried to muster up some sympathy and found she couldn't even come close. "Mabel's known all along that you were all right," she said softly.

"Yeah, I guess." Will bent down and began to pick up the pieces of broken mug. "Now what happens? Are you going to turn me in?"

Peg sighed, visions of garden club ladies and used car buyers flitting through her head. There was only one thing to do. She leaned down, picked up Digger, walked across the kitchen and thrust the little dog into Will's unwelcoming arms.

"Here," she said. "He's all yours for the rest of the week. That will be punishment enough."

Manor Beast

Lillian M. Roberts

LILLIAN M. ROBERTS writes the Andi Pauling, DVM, series of veterinary mysteries. (The series debut—*Riding for a Fall*—was shortlisted for an Agatha Award.) As a practicing veterinarian herself, Roberts can't recall a time when dogs weren't a part of her life. She lives in Palm Springs, California, with three cats, two parrots, and a very tolerant mastiff named Moby.

Rachel Burdick sounded like a panicked child instead of the almost-thirty I knew she was. It was six o'clock on a Saturday morning, and my brain had barely stretched. I didn't recognize Rachel's voice, and was on the brink of hanging up when she got the words out.

"Ham—Ham—the dogs! They killed him! Hammond's dead and the dogs—"

Hammond Roone. One of the few clients who had my home phone number. One of my few celebrity clients, in a town full of celebrities. "Hammond's dead?" I blurted stupidly. "No, he can't be. His dogs would never do that." His dogs wouldn't kill him, and therefore he couldn't be dead. Logical, huh?

One of the lessons any veterinarian learns early, and repeatedly, is never to predict what a dog won't do. It isn't the snarling rottweiler that will bite you, but the friendly Lhasa with the sore ear, wagging her tail while she snaps in self-defense. But kill? Hammond's Doberman pinschers were among the mellowest I knew.

"Please come, Andi! They're in there with him, there's blood everywhere! Oh, God, they must have thought . . . we had this awful fight last night . . . and then I left! How could I? I can't look at them, I can't. Please come, Andi. Please?"

I was fully awake now, and reaching for a pair of jeans and a scrub top. "Are the dogs hurt?"

"Nuh-nuh-no. I don't think . . . I can't . . . I can't look! Please, you didn't . . . see him. When can you get here?"

It was the first time I could remember her actually *asking* me for anything. Usually she orders people around with equal dismissiveness, be it the gardener, the maid . . . or the vet. Everyone but Hammond, who was, after all, her meal ticket. He, in turn, had both indulged her and ignored her. Much as her father always did. Come to think of it, most people tended to adopt the same attitude with her, myself included. It was simply efficient.

So I went. It occurred to me as I drove that, by moving in with Hammond and embracing his world, she may have lost her peers. Her father had not approved the relationship. Her mother, I seemed to recall, lived in Australia. Although I was a few years older than Rachel, she may have called me because I was the only female of her generation she didn't feel competitive toward.

Rachel, you see, was beautiful. That was her identity. I am not, nor have I any interest in trying to be.

The Hammond Roone estate is five acres in Rancho Mirage, an attractive block wall shielding the house from the curious eyes of tourists. Roone had owned it since the Six-ties, since the time he was Hollywood's seventh-most-popular leading man. You might remember him—the usual tall, muscled frame with an aloof bearing and tousled dark hair and a wide, thoughtful brow. Blue eyes to give Mel Gibson a run for his money. Beyond that, he had moderate talent. I'd seen his movies and the man could make me laugh or cry or scream at the injustice of life. Perhaps if he'd been two notches more popular the city would have named a street after him. That's the way they do things here in Palm Springs.

But now he was dead. Hard to grasp.

Maybe he'd get that street after all.

My theory as to why Rachel had called me was blown out of the water by the presence of Rachel's father. He was getting out of his car when I pulled through the gate, which he had left open.

Geoffrey Burdick was technically my colleague. He and my first partner, Philip Harris, were among the first vets to set up shop in the Coachella Valley. Harris opened Dr. Doolittle's in the Forties, and Burdick erected Vista Veterinary Hospital in the mid-Fifties. That building was still a landmark. However, Rachel's dad seemed to regard me as a threat. He had lived through enormous changes in the profession; to him, I represented the surplus of recent graduates carving out chunks of what he saw as his pie.

I saw him as a dinosaur. I admit it. The ornate facade of his showplace hospital disguised antiquated. "It-was-good-enough-forty-years-ago" equipment, and several of his patients that I'd seen for second opinions had never been worked up even marginally. On the plus side, I knew the practice was up for sale and he was nearing retirement.

At any rate, this was not in the bargain when I'd agreed to come to Rachel's aid. Surely she didn't need two vets? I could just check on Rachel and go, stop by Starbuck's on the way home, then head to the clinic. I still had to work all day.

He stood by his car and watched me get out. He wore khaki pants and a long-sleeved button-down shirt despite the June heat. His silver hair was brushed back, revealing a face that had aged gracefully.

I spoke first. "Good morning, Geoff." It was hard for me to call him by his first name, but necessary. It reminded him that I was a doctor as well, however much he may dislike that fact.

Rachel came running out to meet us. She had dressed in tight white shorts and a clingy tank top and pulled her hair back with a scrunchy, but it was the first time I'd ever seen her without makeup.

"Andi! Thank God!" She flew into my arms. This was a definite first, but I gave her a hug. Her thin, muscular frame felt fragile and insubstantial. Her hair smelled of marijuana, her breath of toothpaste mingled with stale tequila from the night before.

"How are you doing?" I asked gently, wondering why she had come to me instead of her father.

She pulled back, her lower lip quivering violently. Her wide green eyes were swollen, the perfect cheekbones pale and blotchy. This was not a face that handled grief well. Somehow that made me like her better. At any rate, I couldn't just leave her.

Geoff approached and she submitted to an embrace.

"Thanks for coming, Daddy." She didn't look at him, and I wondered if her relationship with Hammond had hurt this one. Rachel had been working for her father as a veterinary technician when I came to the desert. Hammond had been his client then, and somehow that fact had led to this one. I'm not sure what it says about a young woman's relationship with her male parent when she takes up with a man older than he is, but it definitely says *something*.

"Where are the police?" I asked.

"I just called them. I wanted you here first."

I couldn't imagine why. "Where are they?"

"The police? I told you . . ."

"The dogs. Where are the dogs?"

"Oh. God. They're . . . still in there. With . . . with Ham. I can't look at them."

"What is it you want me to do?"

"Just take them away." Shades of the old Rachel.

I glanced at the Miata, then back at her, my irritation showing. "Animal Control will do that, but I'll get them out of the room and sedate them if necessary. Show me the way." It seemed like a good idea to keep her moving, but what did I know?

She led me through a wide hall tiled with Mexican pavers that resembled fine leather in the subtle light. The whole house was built on the theme of a Spanish manor house, with intriguing small rooms in unexpected corners, atria and patios and broad stairwells along the outside walls beneath a wide tile roof. I had always loved this house, but had never been up the stairway I now climbed behind Rachel. Her father lagged but followed.

The bedroom doors were heavy oak with iron hardware, made to look rough-hewn. Rachel stood to one side and gestured at them. Apparently she expected me to go in alone. A tall window and two skylights provided the only illumination here, but I could see she was ashen beneath her tan. Understandably, as it turned out. She'd already been inside.

Only Bart rushed to greet me as I slipped through the door. He darted from me to the bed and back. The bed was an *abattoir*.

My mind at first refused to recognize the form in its center, instead taking in Abe and Clancey—black and tan, inseparable and nearly indistinguishable from each other, lying side by side as if guarding the bed's grizzly contents. I did not at first spot Delilah, the bitch.

Steeling myself, I crept closer. Hammond Roone was dead, all right. His throat had been hacked, chewed, destroyed. With the brief glance I could not have determined what had created the wound.

I stroked the head of Bart, the big male, who leaned against my left thigh waiting for me to put things right. At that moment we needed each other equally, and I knelt down to hug him. An odd reaction, maybe, given where we were, but I had been taking comfort from canine companionship for years and to me it was only natural.

But as I leaned over I saw the blood on his muzzle. It flecked his lips and jowls in a pattern I knew had not come from placing his head on the bed. I backed away from him in horror.

He whined in confusion.

What had happened here last night?

I found Delilah sprawled on the floor on the far side of the bed, near a glass door that led to a balcony and a sweeping staircase to a patio with a Jacuzzi. As I pulled the heavy drapes open a faint sound of trickling water reached me from the artificial waterfall that fed the pool.

Delilah raised her head with obvious effort. Her face drooped, and her third eyelids covered much of her gentle brown eyes. I bent to examine her—no blood. But the posture, the laborious movement, was familiar and recognizable.

"She's been sedated," I said out loud, then looked up to make sure Rachel and Geoff were still in the doorway. They were not. The door was closed.

I patted Delilah's head. Judging from her attitude and the fact that the drug had not yet worn off, I guessed someone had given her acepromazine in food. In fact, I now realized that Abe and Clancey were logy as well. And I remembered needing a larger-than-expected dose once to sedate big Bart. If someone had tossed tranquilizer-laced food to these guys, it was entirely consistent that Delilah, bless her gluttonous little heart, would have snatched more than her share, and Bart would have been less affected—thus back to normal sooner.

Conscious now that I was disturbing a crime scene, I took Bart's collar and led him from the room. We left through the glass door, which was not locked, and down the weathered wooden stairs to the patio.

I did not see the blood until Bart growled. There, by the Jacuzzi—drops of dried brown, where they should not be if the dogs had torn their master's throat out and remained in the room with him.

I led Bart around the house, trying doors as I found them. Most were locked; a few appeared nailed shut, for security. Bart occasionally pulled against his collar, but he was well mannered by habit. Still, I wished for a leash.

Two police cars arrived as I approached the open patio door through which I'd followed Rachel the first time. One uniform emerged from each—a tall, sandy-haired man whose name tag said Jansen, and a shorter, paunchier man named Sanchez. They were clearly intimidated by their surroundings. I didn't blame them—this could be a high-profile case, the kind that made careers—or ruined them.

I waited and introduced myself. Bart raised his hackles and growled but I had no trouble restraining him. Still, his presence made the officers more uncomfortable.

Sanchez said, "Is this one of the dogs that . . . attacked Mr. Roone?"

I said, "I don't think that's what happened." I explained why I was there, and what I'd seen. The men asked a few questions and we all went inside. We found Rachel and her father on either side of a small wrought-iron table in a breakfast nook off the main dining room. A pot of coffee and two mugs sat on the table but neither appeared to be drinking.

Bart went nuts. He nearly jerked me off my feet as he lunged. The table went over, the insulated coffeepot spilled on the tile, and a mug exploded like a shot.

Rachel shouted, "He hates men! Get him away!"

Geoff screamed, "Get that damned monster out of here!"

It was all I could do to comply. Bart struggled against me and it took both hands and all my strength to drag him into the dining room and close the door. He growled and scratched at the door but could not damage it.

Both officers had drawn their guns, and now put them away looking embarrassed.

We all trooped back up the stairs. The officers glanced inside the room and called for detectives. We went back outside and sat on patio chairs to wait. Inside I could still hear Bart's distressed efforts to escape. My heart went out to him.

I asked, "What happened last night?"

The cops looked ready to stop us talking, but did not interrupt.

Rachel said, "I feel so horrible! I told him I was leaving! I want to go back to school. Daddy said I could move back home if I need to. I've got a little money set aside, and I'm turning thirty next month. I want to do something for myself."

Geoff said, "She's been saying that for a year." He turned to his daughter. "Why should he suddenly believe you now?"

"He believed me all along. That's why he changed his will."

"For God's sake, Rachel, shut up about that!" Geoff's face was crimson.

Rachel blinked. "Why? Everyone knows about it."

I didn't, but kept quiet.

She turned to me as if two police officers were not there. "He always said he loved me but I never really believed him. I mean, I know he liked to look at me, and I, you know, took pretty good care of him. But a few months ago he changed his will to leave me practically everything. To prove he was sincere, he said. It almost made me stay. For a while, it did. But last night we fought. He was drinking. Okay, we both were."

"And you told him you were finally leaving?" Inside, my stomach clenched and my heart screamed, *"Mur-*

derer!" I had liked Hammond and no one deserved to die that way.

"I . . . I did leave. That's why I feel so . . . responsible. The dogs always loved me. I'm afraid they . . . well, you have to know this, I guess. At one point he shoved me. I almost went down the stairs, but I caught myself on the wall. That's when I ran out the door."

"Where did you go?" Could she have an alibi? Was I completely off-base? Maybe, as a former veterinary technician, she had given the dogs a tranquilizer afterward. Like this morning, when she discovered Hammond's body. Acepromazine was cheap and stable for years, and one of the few sedative drugs not tightly controlled. Her father might have supplied her with some just to have on hand in case the dogs needed it, for any reason.

"I went to Barnaby's. On one-eleven. You know, Daddy. I called you from my cell phone." Geoff nodded absently, his face miserable. I felt a twinge of compassion. I don't have kids, but it's not a stretch to imagine the horror of thinking your child is a killer.

Rachel went on. "I stayed till closing. Everyone saw me, at least twenty people asked me what was wrong." Her lip trembled. "Oh, Ham!" she said in a tiny voice. It took her several tries to get her control back. "Then I went to Denny's for coffee. It's next door and I wasn't ready to come home."

"Receipts?" I asked.

She shrugged and shook her head. Who keeps receipts from Denny's?

The weird thing was, I found myself wanting to believe her. On the one hand, I had not looked closely at Hammond's wounds. And there was the blood on Bart's face.

Perhaps Rachel's interpretation of events was accurate after all.

On the other hand, dogs are not vindictive. They do not wait to exact revenge. If the Dobies attacked Hammond in response to his shoving Rachel, they would have done so immediately. They would not wait until he passed out in his bed and was no longer a threat.

"Did you give the dogs anything this morning? Drugs?" I asked, just to be sure.

She shook her head, confusion and revulsion on her face. None of her performance seemed like an act, but how could I know?

The officer named Sanchez cleared his throat. "Detective'll be here in a few minutes," he said. "They'll have plenty of questions."

So we sat. I fidgeted. After less than a minute I got up and made some more coffee, rescuing the pot that Bart had knocked over. When he went ballistic. After he saw . . .

"Geoff? Aren't you warm in long sleeves?"

After a long moment he looked at me. He knew that I knew. The malevolence on his face went far beyond professional rivalry.

I held his gaze, standing across the table. "I saw blood outside near the Jacuzzi. It only makes sense if the killer left that way. Bart has blood on his muzzle, but I'm willing to bet tests will show it isn't Hammond's blood."

He was trembling. "I don't know what you're talking about."

"No? Then how about rolling up your sleeves? Bart bit someone, but it wasn't his master. He didn't kill Ham. He was trying to protect him. But you doped him first. I could have told you he'd need a larger dose."

As the cops watched expectantly, Hammond unbuttoned his cuffs. "I'm a vet. A bite wound on my arm doesn't prove anything. Dog bites are part of the job."

It was a fresh wound, the punctures dry and barely scabbed. They were spread over his right biceps. Bart was a big dog with a long, Doberman snout. I was sure his dental impression would match the wounds. DNA would prove the blood on Bart's fur to be Geoff's. The blood on the patio would also match. But none of it would explain why.

Rachel's eyes went huge with betrayal. "You? You, Daddy? Why would you kill my Ham?"

He glared at her furiously. He didn't answer, so I speculated.

"You were finally leaving Ham for real," I said. "He was sure to change the will back, disowning you. Your father's practice has suffered in recent years, and it's been on the market quite a while—I'm betting he isn't having any luck selling it. He needs money, even if it's yours. He knew you'd let him manage your money."

"Oh, no, Daddy. Is it true?"

"For God's sake, shut up!" he growled between clenched teeth.

On the other side of the door, Bart fell silent. It was almost as if he knew. He'd told his story and could rest now.

Foolproof

Taylor McCafferty

Writing as TAYLOR MCCAFFERTY, Barbara Taylor
McCafferty authors the Haskell Blevins mystery
series. Writing as Tierney McClellan, she authors
the Schuyler Ridgway series. And writing with her
twin sister Beverly Taylor Herald, she coauthors
the Tatum Twin mystery series. It's a good thing
she has dogs for company, as she doesn't get out
much. Sharing her home are Ogilvy, a half-German
shepherd/half Old English Sheepdog, and Taylor,
a small, auxiliary dog who is prepared to kick in
and do the Big Dog Job if Ogilvy should ever fail.
Coincidentally, Taylor was the name the Humane
Society had already given him before McCafferty
adopted him.

The plan worked perfectly—without a single hitch,
without one misstep, without so much as a ripple in the
smooth flow of events. Of course, there was never any
doubt that the plan would work. It was, after all, foolproof.

Funny, I remember using that very word on that Saturday morning when I first told Marisa what I was planning
to do. I'd gone over it again and again, as I drove over to
the grocery out on Highway 61 to meet her. She'd phoned
me shortly after eight that morning, crying again and

wanting to see me. This had gotten to be a strange sort of routine for Marisa and me, our meeting like this, my standing and listening while she poured her heart out. If there was no one around, I'd hold her in my arms while she cried against my chest. It was pretty much how we spent a routine Saturday morning following one of Ben's routine Friday nights drinking up his paycheck.

Pop's Grocery on Highway 61 was the first place I'd thought of when Marisa asked me to meet her. Ever since the Hebron SuperMarket had opened up a couple miles on down the road, not many folks came by Pop's Grocery anymore. So I was pretty sure we wouldn't be seen together. And even if we were seen, it didn't really matter.

Hebron, Kentucky, is one of those rural small towns that folks traveling Interstate 65 zoom by in a blink of an eye. With only 3,500 people, most everybody here knows everybody else. Still, if anybody who knew us happened to be driving by we would be just a guy and the wife of his best friend standing out in a grocery parking lot, passing the time of day. Hell, even if Ben himself had driven by, there was nothing to give us away.

Except for Marisa's eyes.

Her big blue eyes had looked even bigger than usual as she'd stared at me. "Foolproof?" she'd repeated. "You think your plan is foolproof? Eddie, are you crazy?" Her voice shook, and the two bright spots of color appeared on each of her pale cheeks. "You'd be betting our lives on Bruiser! *Bruiser,* for God's sake!"

At the sound of his name, the dog's ears perked up. Marisa had brought Ben's dog with her, just like she always did. The mutt had bounded out of the car and come running over to lick my hand the second Marisa had opened her car door.

Marisa told me once that the reason she always brought the dog along was because she didn't feel safe driving down lonely country roads all by herself. She said she needed Bruiser for protection. The idea of Bruiser protecting anybody, though, was pretty laughable. The mutt only weighed twenty pounds, if that. It was a funny-looking little thing, too. It had the brown and black markings of a German shepherd, the body of a beagle, and the short, stubby legs of a dachshund.

All it took was one look at that mutt, and you knew it wasn't Bruiser protecting Marisa. It was Marisa protecting Bruiser. Bruiser had probably needed protecting that morning, too. When Ben got to drinking, the slightest thing would set him off. Like, for instance, Bruiser licking his hand. Or Bruiser barking at a car going by outside. Ben didn't need any more reason than that to give old Bruiser a kick that would make the little dog limp for a week.

Of course, sometimes Ben kicked Bruiser for no reason at all. Ben had pretty much hated the dog from the moment he'd finally figured out that the puppy he'd brought home from the pound wasn't going to be the huge watchdog he'd been sure he was adopting. Hell, that's why Ben had named the dog Bruiser in the first place. More than once, when Bruiser was a puppy, Ben had pointed out how big the dog's paws were and told me, "Man, just look at the mitts on that damn dog. That's how you can tell how big a dog's gonna be, you know. Old Bruiser here is gonna be a monster one day, you wait and see!"

Well, Bruiser-the-Monster was two years old with the largest paws you ever saw, and I was still waiting. I had no doubt that the way Ben saw it, Bruiser had made a fool of him. What's more, every time he called the dog by name, Ben was reminded just how big a fool that happened to be. I think Ben might've gotten rid of Bruiser— he might've left the dog by the side of a remote road somewhere, or maybe even worse—except that everybody in Hebron would've known what had happened and who had done it. Not to mention, if Ben got rid of Bruiser, it would've been like admitting in public that his big paw theory had been so far wrong, he'd ended up adopting a dog he couldn't stand.

Hey, I hated to break it to Ben, but it was pretty obvious—whether he got rid of Bruiser or not—Bruiser's big paws had turned out to mean nothing more than that. Big paws. In fact, on that last Saturday, Bruiser had actually tripped over his big paws twice as he came running over to lick my hand. The dog's tongue had felt wet and slobbery, and its licking was more than a little annoying. I moved my hand out of reach as I said, as calmly as I could, "Marisa, Bruiser is just a small part of my plan. A very small—"

With my hand no longer available for licking, Bruiser had started licking the top of my shoe. I moved my shoe out of the way as Marisa interrupted me again. "Well, Eddie, you'll just have to think of something else. You can't possibly gamble our entire future on a dog!"

Obviously, she hadn't been listening, because that was not exactly what I'd said. Marisa's attitude might've made me mad, and her using that tone with me—like maybe she thought she was my mother or something—could've been even more irritating than Bruiser's constant licking. Except that I realized that Marisa wasn't herself. Lord knows, she had to be rattled. We were, after all, quietly discussing how to go about murdering her husband—and my best friend.

Marisa was probably in some real pain, too. The whole time we were talking, she was holding her left wrist as gingerly as if it were made of crystal. Even though her right hand covered most of the bruising right around her left wrist, I could still see the ugly purple marks discoloring the upper part of her forearm.

Looking at what Ben had done to her, I could hardly breathe. If he'd been standing there in front of me, I think I could've killed him right then and there with my bare hands. Even as Marisa watched.

But then again, I guess Ben's temper was not exactly a surprise. Ben always had been a hothead, even as far back as the seventh grade when I'd first gotten to know him. That year I'd had to pull Ben off some kid who'd stepped ahead of him in line at the lunchroom. That's all the kid had done, and Ben had bloodied the kid's nose before I could get him to stop.

After that little incident, Ben had himself a reputation. The word around school was that Ben Crenshaw was somebody you didn't want to mess with. I think Ben kinda liked knowing folks were afraid of him, too. Because every once in a while, just in case anybody had forgotten who was the meanest, toughest guy in school, he reminded everybody by picking a fight with some poor fool who just happened to be in the wrong place at the wrong time.

Ben had himself another reputation back then, too. Even at thirteen, he was already sneaking bottles out of his parents' liquor cabinet and stealing cigarettes out of his mother's purse. He'd stash all of it in his locker until after school, and then, hiding whatever bottles Ben had brought in that day under our shirts, he and I would sneak off somewhere. Lots of times we'd end up sitting under the bleachers in the back of the gym. I reckon, at the ripe old age of thirteen, we thought that we were all grown up, sitting under there, drinking and smoking.

All of this was no doubt the reason Ben and I had gotten to be such good friends in the first place. Ben seemed to have an unlimited supply of alcohol and cigarettes—which, I've got to tell you, is a major attraction for a kid in the seventh grade. Hanging out with Ben meant thumbing your nose at your teachers, at your parents, at just about everybody. Because Ben Crenshaw was as wild as they come. And when you were with Ben, you felt wild, too.

As far as I could tell, Ben didn't follow any rules ever. He drove as fast as he wanted to, regardless of the speed limit. He drank every single day in high school, and he kept right on even after we graduated and he was hired as a production worker at Pell Conveyor. I was hired the same day as Ben, and working the line next to him, I couldn't help but notice how many times a day he took a quick swig out of the small flask he carried around with him. The times he noticed my looking at him, he always gave me a real big grin. "There ain't no such things as rules," Ben told me more than once. "They're just suggestions."

The last time he'd said this to me, I'd just looked at him. We were in our mid-twenties by then, and Ben's shenanigans were beginning to get real old. A couple times he and I had ended up in fist fights ourselves, he'd get so damn mean when he was drinking. "So, Bon, you think then that should've been what they called them stone tablets that

Moses brought down from the mountain?" I said. "The Ten Suggestions?"

I was being sarcastic, but Ben threw his head back and laughed like that was the funniest thing he'd ever heard. "Yeah," he said. "That's right, Eddie! The Ten *Suggestions*."

Yep, Ben was outrageous, all right. His being so outrageous might've been his appeal for Marisa, too. Her family moved to Hebron when Ben and I were just starting high school. I think she walked into our homeroom, took one look at Ben, and never saw anybody else. She sure never saw me, even though a whole lot of the time, I was standing right next to Ben.

Staring at her.

God, she was something. With long brown hair, pale ivory skin, and lips so red she looked as if she were always wearing lipstick, Marisa was easily the prettiest girl I'd ever seen in my entire life.

I think I fell in love with her the first second I saw her. I can still remember what she was wearing that first day she walked into Ben's and my homeroom. A pale blue blouse that made her eyes look even bluer, and a little flip of a skirt that showed off her long, slender legs.

Of course, I realized fairly quickly that I had to put her right out of my mind. Because it got to be obvious pretty damn soon that Marisa belonged to Ben. I wasn't really surprised. With shaggy blonde hair and blue eyes, Ben looked enough like Brad Pitt that girls were always falling for him. It seemed like the most natural thing in the world that the best-looking guy at school would end up with the best-looking girl. Marisa and Ben were going steady three days after they met, and they were married five days after they graduated from high school.

As Ben's best friend, I was best man at the wedding. Standing there, watching Marisa come down that aisle, looking like an angel in white, ready to say out loud that she wanted to spend the rest of her life with Ben—well, it was one of the roughest things I ever had to do in my life.

And yet, no matter how I felt about Marisa, I knew that fooling around with your best friend's woman was just about as low as you could get.

The only thing a man could do that was any lower, in my opinion, was to beat your wife.

I reckon that's why Marisa didn't tell anybody what was going on for the longest time. She was trying to keep folks from finding out what kind of man she'd married. Hell, I was Ben's best friend, and I didn't find out myself until they'd been married six years.

After they were married, Marisa and Ben had rented a house in the Knob Acres subdivision on the outskirts of Hebron, so I didn't see her all that much. Ben and I mostly got together by ourselves—we'd go shoot a little pool, do a little bowling, that kind of thing. I reckon Ben must've thought that all the rules governing marriage were just suggestions, too, because not even a year after he and Marisa had tied the knot, he was running around on her. He'd pick up women right in front of me, winking at me over some bimbo's head, just as if Marisa wasn't waiting at home for him.

Watching old Ben operate, I couldn't help but wonder how long it would take before Marisa found out. Evidently not long, because it was only a couple months later that Ben started complaining about how "his old lady" was always on his back. "I tell ya, Eddie," Ben said, "I should never have gotten hitched. And you know why?

Because women just wanna own you, they just wanna put you on a damn leash."

We were sitting at the bar at Jake's Pool Hall, and Ben was about half sloshed, as usual. I tried to nod and look sympathetic, but all I could think was, *Man, I'd sure love to be on that damn leash.*

I'd just broken up with Cindy, the third relationship I'd had go sour in as many years. It seemed as if it always came down to the woman I was dating wanting me to make some kind of commitment, and I just never could bring myself to do it. I reckon I always knew my heart was already committed.

I found out just how committed it was when I ran into Marisa at the Big Lots in Hebron one Friday night. Big Lots is a store filled with just about everything, from hardware to underwear—it's mainly odd lots and discontinued stuff being sold at discount. I went around a corner, and there Marisa was, standing on tiptoe, reaching for a roll of paper towels. She was wearing a long-sleeved shirt, even though it was July and plenty hot outside, but her sleeve had fallen back as she reached up. You didn't even have to try to see the bruises on her arm.

I have to hand it to her. Marisa tried her best to convince me that she'd fallen, but when she saw I wasn't buying it, she told me the truth. After that, we went out to the parking lot, got into my car, and she cried for a half hour.

It's funny, but now as I look back on everything, it seems as if once I knew, everything picked up speed. First, there was Marisa and me, just meeting and talking. And then, it seems right after that, there was Marisa and me, meeting and making love. I hadn't really meant it to happen, but somehow I just couldn't help myself. We drove all the way to Elizabethtown, a good forty-five minutes away so nobody would see us together. In fact, it was on the way to E-town one time that Marisa gave me the diamond earring. Well, actually, it wasn't a real diamond, it was one of those cubic zirconia things, but it sure looked like a diamond.

"I want you to get your ear pierced and wear this every day, Eddie. So that you always know, no matter where you are, that a part of me is always with you." I was driving, trying to keep my eyes on the road, and she put her arms around my neck and kissed my ear. "If you ever doubt that I care about you, if you ever think I'm not thinking about you, just reach up and touch this diamond, okay?"

I thought I might actually burst, I loved her so much.

Things kept picking up speed, and it seemed as if it was practically the next day, and there was Marisa and me, meeting and talking about what she was going to do about Ben.

At first, she thought she could just divorce him. But she found out real quick that just mentioning the word enraged Ben so much, he'd go wild. He'd beat her so bad, he wouldn't let her go until the bruises went away on her face. "You will *never* leave me, you understand?" he'd yell at her. "*Never!* If you think about leaving, I'll kill you!"

This from the man who'd told me that he wished he'd never gotten hitched.

"And you better keep your damn mouth shut, too," he told her over and over. "You tell anybody anything, I'll make you wish you were dead."

I'd been intending to try to talk to Ben myself, but when I heard that, I knew it was hopeless. Ben wasn't about to listen to me. He would just be furious at Marisa for telling on him.

Looking back, I know that everything actually took months—long, horrible months during which I could hardly think, hardly work, hardly do anything, what with worrying so much about Marisa and what Ben might be doing to her—and yet it seemed as if it were no time at all until it got to be Marisa and me, standing out in front of a grocery, on a Saturday morning, talking about murder. "Marisa, my plan is foolproof. It really is. Listen to me, I—"

She interrupted me, just as if I weren't still talking. "Eddie, if we got caught, it'd be all over for us. I mean, we're talking the electric chair—"

Okay, she didn't have to remind me that murder is punishable by death here in Kentucky, and that the way that particular sentence is carried out in this state involves several thousand volts.

"It'll work," I said, trying to stay calm.

She was still shaking her head. "No, Eddie, we need a plan that has absolutely no chance for a slipup. No chance at all."

Obviously, she hadn't been listening to a word I was saying.

So I laid it all out for her again. "It's got to happen tonight, understand? We can't wait. This kinda thing never gets better." I'd been doing some reading on spouse abuse, and everything I read said it always got worse. "Marisa, one of these days Ben's gonna put you in the hospital. Or—or—" I couldn't bring myself to say the words.

Marisa actually shivered, looking at me.

"It's gotta be tonight," I said.

Marisa's eyes were showing the whites all around. "Tonight," she repeated.

"During the Blanchards' party," I said. Shirley and Al Blanchard were a middle-aged couple who lived across the street from Ben and Marisa. The Blanchards must've loved having a house full of people because they were always throwing Saturday night parties and inviting everybody within a twenty-five mile radius to drop by. They had this real small ranch house, too, but they always invited so many people that they spilled out onto the patio into the backyard.

The Blanchards had even invited me, and I barely knew Al Blanchard. He was just another one of the guys on the line at Pell Conveyor, like Ben and me.

Ben had never been any too crazy about the Blanchard parties, so there was some doubt he would even go to the party. But it didn't matter. If he went, he wouldn't stay long. He never did. "With the thing being right across the street, Ben won't question it if you tell him that you ought to put in an appearance. Just to be neighborly and all."

Marisa nodded, her eyes on my face.

"I'll be watching for you, and when you get to the party, I'll go over to your house and do it. Okay? Or if Ben has come to the party, I'll wait and follow him home. There will be enough people in that house and milling around the yard that nobody will notice if I'm gone for a few minutes."

Marisa didn't nod this time, she just kept looking at me.

"After it's done, I'll come back, and when Bruiser starts barking, it'll be just like the O. J. Simpson case. You know, when everybody assumed that the time of . . ." I took a deep breath at this point, not wanting to say the word out loud, "well, it'll be like when Nicole Simpson's dog started barking. Everybody assumed that she and that guy were killed when the neighbors heard the dog. That's exactly what they'll think this time." I paused.

Marisa glanced down at Bruiser. That dumb dog was licking the top of Marisa's left shoe now. She actually smiled a little, watching that stupid mutt. Hell, you might've thought she wasn't even listening to what I was saying.

"That's why you have to make sure that Bruiser is asleep before you leave to come to the party. So that he doesn't wake up and start barking until after I'm back. That way everybody at the party can testify that I was right there in full view of a lot of witnesses when they first heard Bruiser."

I gave her the pills then, and explained how she was to open the capsules and mix the powder inside with some canned dog food. So that Bruiser would be sure to eat all of it. "It should start working within minutes," I said.

Marisa was now staring at the small capsules I handed her. "What is this stuff?"

I shrugged. The bottle had said "acepromazine," but I didn't even know how to pronounce that. "It's stuff they give dogs to tranquilize them. I knew somebody who had a dog they wanted to take on a long airplane flight, and so the vet gave them this."

Actually, it had been Cindy, my ex-girlfriend. I'd remembered the pills she'd given her golden retriever the time she'd taken it with her to visit her parents in California, and so I'd called her up a couple days ago, asking to talk. She'd agreed so quickly, I'd actually felt a little bad, knowing that the only reason I'd wanted to see her was to go into her bathroom and steal a few of the pills out of the bottle I knew she kept in her medicine chest.

"You open the capsules, and sprinkle the powder inside on Bruiser's canned dog food."

Marisa was still looking at the capsules. "How many do I give him?"

Cindy had given her dog three. "Oh, three, I guess."

Marisa's eyes widened as she slowly turned to look at me. "You guess?" she said.

"Okay, just give him two then. Whatever makes him sleep."

Marisa continued to stare at me. "Eddie, if we give him too much of this stuff, it could hurt him."

I couldn't believe she was standing there, talking about killing Ben, and then worrying about hurting the damn dog. "Marisa, it'll be fine."

She was still just looking at me, her eyes very large. "I don't know, Eddie. This seems really risky."

I couldn't believe it. "Risky?" I was the one taking the risk. All she had to do was give the damn dog a little powder. "Marisa, it's risky for you to live another minute with Ben."

She didn't say anything for a moment. She just stood there, looking at me, with the oddest expression on her face. It was as if for a second there she didn't know who I was. God, did she really think that I wanted to do this? Did she really think that I was the sort of man who would kill his best friend just to get his woman? Was that what she thought?

That's when I grabbed her by the shoulders, and gave her a little shake. "Sweetheart, listen to me," I said. Her blue eyes were so big now, they seemed to fill her entire face. God, she was beautiful. "We don't have a choice. Ben will never let you go. And he for sure will never let us be together."

Marisa blinked. Just once. And then her mouth tightened, and her eyes seemed to go a shade darker as she looked at me. "You're right, Eddie, of course. There *is* no choice. We'll do it tonight."

As it turned out, Ben didn't come to the Blanchards' party. I got to the thing a little early, but it seemed as if half the population of Hebron was already there. I was calming my nerves with a Scotch and soda when Marisa walked in the front door. She gave me one quick glance that told me that she'd done what I'd told her to do, and then she walked right past me, disappearing into the Blanchards' backyard.

My legs trembled as I snuck out the Blanchards' side door and made my way across the street, hiding behind shrubs and the like, until I found myself at Marisa and Ben's back door. Once inside, I didn't give myself time to think about it. I went to the living room, saw Ben asleep on the couch, and I picked up the poker from the fireplace. It was amazing how little time it took. There wasn't even that much blood, not at all like I'd been imagining. I had to wash up a little in the bathroom, but for the most part, it was as if I'd never been there. I thought about checking on Bruiser before I left, but I didn't really know where the dog was. And, let's face it, I was pretty anxious to leave before Bruiser woke up.

I was back at the party in less than fifteen minutes. I'd gotten myself another Scotch and soda when Marisa seemed to appear from nowhere. Pulling me into the hallway, she whispered in my ear. "Is it done?"

I took a sip before I could trust my voice to answer her. "It's done."

She kissed my ear then, her lips so soft, so sweet. And then she was gone.

It didn't occur to me until hours later, when Bruiser had not yet barked and Marisa had spent the entire night at the Blanchards' party without once looking my way, to reach up and feel for the diamond earring she's given me.

It was, of course, gone.

Gone like Marisa had been for a few minutes shortly after I'd returned from across the street.

Gone, like all the foolish plans I'd made for her and me.

The police, of course, found the earring right where Marisa had planted it. Next to Ben's body. They didn't find Bruiser at all, because Marisa had taken the dog to her mother's. As always, Marisa was making sure that damn dog didn't get hurt.

Like I said at the beginning, Marisa's plan was foolproof. And, sitting here in this cell, staring at these cold gray bars, I reckon I'm the fool who proved it.

Nosing Around for a Clue

Valerie Wolzien

VALERIE WOLZIEN is the author of the Susan
Henshaw suburban mysteries and the Josie Pigeon
seashore mysteries. Susan Henshaw made her first
appearance in *Murder at the PTA Luncheon*, which
became the television movie *A Perfect Little Murder*.
And now Susan reappears—with her trusty golden
retriever, Clue—in "Nosing Around for a Clue."

"No one pays any attention. I sometimes feel like I'm a
cipher in my own house. Oh, they expect me to do the
shopping for them. And they'd all starve if I didn't cook.
And entertaining . . . well, if I made just half of what a professional caterer would make on all the parties I've given,
I'd be a rich woman, Clue. A rich woman."

Susan Henshaw, middle-aged suburban housewife, mother
of two almost-grown-up children and wife of an adver-
tising executive now busy at work in New York City, was
spending the morning as she usually did on these warm
June days. She was walking her dog in one of Hancock,
Connecticut's, well-groomed parks.

"They don't even listen. No one. Not Jed, although I
suppose that may just be the result of twenty-six years of
marriage. Not Chad or Chrissy, of course, but what do you
expect from a couple of kids in their twenties? Even Kath-

leen, my very best friend, seems to think I'm nuts this time. She says not to worry, that the answer will come to me. What sort of advice is that? Clue, you're the only one who gives me her complete attention."

The golden retriever looked up at Susan with love in her eyes. She was a great dog, Susan thought. A bit overweight, perhaps. Getting just slightly gray around her muzzle. As usual, she could use a good professional grooming. But she cared. And she listened. Oh, how she listened. And just now Susan needed a good listener. Just now she had to decide what to do with her life now that the kids were out of the house.

"It's called empty nest syndrome, Clue. And I had no idea what it meant. For years I've been laughing at the entire concept, telling everyone that I was dying to get the kids out of the house, that I would be happy to spend my days puttering around, reading, sleeping late, going to the Club and . . . . and what, Clue? That's the problem. What did I think I was going to do with my time? With my life?"

They were circling a large pond. Clue, whose entire name was Susan Hasn't Got a Clue—a backhanded tribute to Susan's involvement in murder investigations—was walking sedately by Susan's side. The migrating geese were gone for the summer. The squirrels were apparently content to remain out of reach in the tops of the trees. And the only other dog walker in sight was a fabulously chic woman strolling beside her equally chic afghan hound.

"I hate to say it, Clue, but we look pretty dowdy compared to those two."

Clue didn't give a damn. A long line of young children, on a field trip with a local day care center, had appeared snaking across the horizon. Potential ball throwers, Clue seemed to think, pulling on her leash.

"No, Clue. They're busy. And their teacher wouldn't appreciate a hundred pounds of enthusiastic animal joining her group." She noticed that the afghan wasn't pulling away from her owner. "Be good, Clue!"

Oh, fine, now she was worrying about her dog's behavior the way she'd worried about that of her children when they were young. Clue, ever aware of the changing environment, was now focusing on a large branch lying on the ground. Susan accepted the inevitable and allowed her dog to "retrieve" the branch.

Clue had never learned that picking up anything by one end would cause the other end to dangle—or, depending on its length, drag on the ground. Or, as in this particular case, smack into Susan's legs as they continued their walk around the pond.

The afghan hound and its owner were still trotting toward them. Susan was wondering just what would happen when the two dogs met when Clue dropped the stick, jerked the leash from Susan's hand, and ran into the pond.

Damn. She should have been prepared. Clue had been trying to get into the water every day for the last week or so. Now what the hell should she do? Beside, of course, jumping up and down on the edge of the water yelling for Clue to return.

"Your dog doesn't seem to be paying attention to you."

Naturally, this was the moment the afghan and its owner would reach her side.

"She . . . there must be something out there that she wants to retrieve," Susan was inspired to explain. "She is a retriever, you know."

"A very wet retriever."

Who would have thought it was possible? Even the afghan looked supercilious.

"My dog wouldn't have done that without a reason," Susan insisted stubbornly.

"Maybe." It was obvious the woman doubted it. "A friend of mine runs obedience classes. Perhaps you would like her phone number."

"I . . . I suppose so." Susan didn't want to admit that she and Clue had gone to dog training classes together one night a week for almost two years. Susan had learned that most other dogs were more obedient than her own. Clue had learned to sit, lie down, and stay—when she felt like it.

"We'll be here at this time tomorrow. Perhaps I can give you the information then."

"Yes. Yes. Thank you."

Clue was starting to swim back toward shore and Susan found herself alone. And then minutes later, she was soaking wet as Clue shook herself dry.

She picked up the dripping leash. "Let's go home, Clue."

The next day, Susan was late getting to the park. Her phone had been ringing all morning with news of the disappearance of a long-time resident of Hancock. Harriet MacHugh had moved to town as a young bride. After raising five children, she had become very active in volunteer work. Her executive abilities soon became apparent, however, and for over two decades she had run almost everything that needed running in town. Susan and Harriet had known each other for years and, when Harriet announced her retirement from volunteer work a few years ago, Susan had organized a huge benefit dinner dance in Harriet's honor.

Two weeks ago, Harriet MacHugh had left her home in Florida saying goodbye to friends down there, telling them it was time she went home to Hancock. She had gotten off the plane in New York City that afternoon, flagged down a taxi, told the driver to take her to Connecticut, and disappeared.

Actually, Susan thought, absently scratching Clue's head, that was the story she had managed to piece together from six different phone calls. She was hoping to learn more when her friend Kathleen Gordon arrived. They were meeting to walk their dogs. Recently, Kathleen had succumbed to her children's desire for a puppy, so a small black Scottish terrier had become part of her household. Today was to be the puppy's first public appearance.

"And you're going to be good, aren't you, Clue?" Susan asked.

"Do you ever think maybe you spend too much time talking to that dog?" Kathleen had arrived.

"Wait until you've spent a little more time with Licorice, you'll end up talking to him, too."

"Maybe." Kathleen sounded as though she doubted it. "So what do you think about Harriet MacHugh? The rumor I heard at the grocery store this morning was that she was murdered."

"By who? Everyone in this town loved her."

"So I've heard. But, as an ex-police officer, I have to tell you, I find that a suspicious statement. No one is loved by everyone."

"Okay, and maybe love isn't the right word. But I do think most people in town respected her. Even my kids remember her as that kindly lady who always had a few Tootsie Rolls tucked in her purse to give away to children. If someone killed her, it was the cabdriver who claims to have driven her here from Kennedy Airport."

"Nope. Three separate people saw her here. Two even spoke to her. At least that's what I heard. Hey, there's Brett." Kathleen pointed to the good-looking man who had just stepped out of a car, bearing the logo HANCOCK POLICE DEPARTMENT on its doors. "We can ask him all about it."

But Brett Fortesque, chief of the local police department, was the one asking questions.

"So, I don't suppose either of you saw Mrs. MacHugh here in the past few days?" he asked immediately after greeting them.

"Here? You mean in the park?"

"Not just here in the park, but right here beside this pond. We've found two other dog walkers who report seeing her early last week."

"Was she murdered?" Kathleen asked.

"There's no reason to think so. There's not much reason to think anything right now. The story, as I have it, is that she told her friends in Florida goodbye and that she was going to return to Hancock. Apparently everyone assumed she was going to fly back to Florida after a few days away and, when she didn't, people down there started to worry, called mutual friends up here, and apparently they hadn't seen her. That, coupled with the fact that she was certainly here, has got a lot of people worried."

"And?" Susan asked, as Clue drooled on her foot.

"And she was last seen standing fairly close to where we are now. Just looking out at the pond. Alone. Early in the evening exactly ten days ago."

"And no one has seen her since then?" Kathleen asked.

"Not that we can discover."

"Maybe she just saw what she wanted to see, got back in a cab, went to the airport, and flew to . . . to wherever she wanted to go next," Susan suggested. "Why are the police involved in this?"

"Her children are convinced that she came to Hancock for a purpose—something important."

"Any idea what?"

"Nope, but they're worried. They all say she wasn't a woman to do things casually and that she had been recently talking about a change in her life. All five of them have been ringing the phone off the hook down at the police station for the past few days."

"But you know how family can be—overly concerned," Kathleen suggested.

"Maybe, but—"

"But Harriet's children include a congresswoman, a Pulitzer prize–winning journalist, a television talk show host, a Tony Award–winning actor, and a drummer for one of the most famous rock-and-roll bands in the country," Susan interrupted. She had lived in Hancock longer than her friend and had kept better track of its past citizens.

"Oh. I didn't know."

"So you can understand why we're particularly interested in finding out what happened to Harriet as quickly as possible."

Kathleen nodded, a serious expression on her face. "Nothing's worse than political pressure."

"Usually." Brett frowned. "But it's more than that. The truth is I really liked Harriet. She was . . . she is a very special woman. You all know what a fabulously affluent town Hancock is, but there are always citizens who are hurting—either financially or emotionally. What you probably don't know is that Harriet MacHugh endowed a discretionary fund that can be used to help these people. It's called the Mayor's Fund and there are a group of trustees who administer it. A lot of people have been helped with that money. And, as far as I know, none of them have had any idea where it came from."

"Really? I didn't know the MacHughs were particularly well off."

"They weren't. But she sold that big old Victorian she raised her family in for a large profit and moved into a very small apartment down in Florida. I understand she wanted her money to help people, rather than using it to keep her in a luxurious lifestyle."

"Good for Harriet." Susan was impressed. Here she was worrying about how to spend the last third of her life when this woman had simply decided to help others as much as possible with the resources she had. She would have said something about it if Clue hadn't suddenly taken it into her fuzzy little head to do a repeat of yesterday's impromptu swim.

"Clue! Come back! Now! Come, Clue!"

"Licorice! Licorice! Stop! Come back! Susan, he'll drown!" Kathleen joined her friend yelling for the two dogs to return to shore.

"You don't have to worry. It is natural for a dog to swim." The afghan's owner had joined them. Her dog, of course, sat sedately at her side, looking at the pond with disdain on her face.

"You see, the terrier is turning around."

Kathleen knelt down and flung her arms out. "Licorice. Come here, honey."

In a flurry of muddy water and fur, the Scottie ran out of the pond and into Kathleen's arms. Clue, as she had been the day before, was back in the middle of the pond, doing a fine example of the doggy paddle.

The afghan's owner was not impressed. "You might want to keep your puppy away from older, untrained dogs," she said to Kathleen. "Terriers are very impressionable, you know. And a bad influence early in life can create habits that are very, very difficult to break."

"Clue is not a bad influence! Clue is . . . she's a loving, sweet, kind . . . tell her, Kathleen, tell her what a wonderful dog Clue is!"

Kathleen was ineffectually trying to clean her puppy's head with a Kleenex. The task seemed to need her full attention.

Susan looked up at Brett. "Brett, tell her. Clue is a wonderful dog. All retrievers are like that. They . . . they retrieve things."

"What precisely is your dog retrieving now?"

"I don't know, but—"

"But it might be something important," Brett interrupted, grabbing the two-way radio that hung from his belt.

The three women exchanged looks. Kathleen and Susan had serious expressions on their faces. The afghan's owner seemed mystified. "If we're not needed here, Shalimar and I will just continue our walk," she announced. "We have a four-fifteen appointment with the hairdresser, don't we, sweetie?" Since no one objected to the plan, the elegant twosome continued their stately trek around the park.

"Do you think the same man does both dog hair and people hair?" Susan wondered aloud.

"Look, Susan, she's on her way back!" Kathleen cried, pointing to Clue.

"She always comes back. I have a pocket full of dog biscuits," Susan explained, standing up. "You all might want to be prepared to back up when she starts to shake off. . . . Brett? Did you hear me?"

Instead of moving away, Brett was walking toward the approaching dog. "Yeah, I heard you. Does Clue always swim around the same spot?"

"Sort of. I hadn't really thought about it. But, yes, I guess so."

"And she's been doing this every day since . . . since when?"

"She been trying to go in for days. Usually I manage to keep her with me."

"But how many days has she been trying to go in?"

"For the last seven . . . no, eight days."

"Are you sure about that?"

"Yeah. I brought her here after church a week ago Sunday, and that was eight days ago. She ran in then. I remember because I was wearing a new white linen skirt and it's at the cleaners now. She shook all over me then, too." Susan finished her statement as Clue repeated that particular gesture.

"Susan, could I borrow Clue this afternoon?"

"You want to borrow Clue? What for?"

Brett had finished mumbling into his two-way radio, and he flicked it shut and reached over for the dog. "I think

Clue may know something we need to know," was all he would say, petting Clue's soaking wet head.

"You can have her for the afternoon, but, you know, you're getting wet." Susan pointed to where her dog was leaning against the police chief's leg.

"It doesn't matter. And if things turn out the way I think they will, I'll probably be getting a whole lot wetter."

A line of trees circled the pond, around which bright yellow scene-of-the-crime tape was wound. A good number of citizens of Hancock, pausing in the middle of afternoon runs, jogs, walks, and strolls, were crowding about the tape. Susan and Kathleen sat on the hill where the day-care children had been tramping the day before. Kathleen's daughter, Emily, rolled around on the ground nearby with Licorice.

"So Brett asked you to stay away?" Kathleen was asking her friend.

"He thought I might be a distraction. You know, that Clue would pay more attention to me than to whatever is—might be—in the water."

"I've heard of this type of thing," Kathleen began, making sure her daughter was out of hearing before she continued. "As I understand it, the body has to be in a state of decay before it can be detected by the dog. And that's a dog which has been trained to find bodies. And I sure didn't know that anything could be detected under water."

"Brett called an expert from some sort of rescue group—this man trains goldens and German shepherds to find bodies, and he said that dogs can detect bodies under as much as thirty-five feet of still water. The pond is probably much shallower than that."

"But the body would have to have been down there long enough to decompose, right?"

"True. But if Harriet disappeared two weeks ago, her body might be . . . um . . ." She realized she was beginning to feel slightly ill. The thought of a body decomposing under water had been on the edge of her mind since Brett explained what he was going to do. Giving the body a name and a face was just a bit too much.

"I know what you're saying." Kathleen made it unnecessary for her to continue.

"Brett said there was something else, but he didn't get a chance to tell me," Susan added, glaring at three trucks from local television stations parked so close to the crime-scene tape that the yellow ribbon bowed in toward the water. "Those vultures showed up and started shoving microphones in people's faces."

"If Harriet was murdered, it's news. Big news."

"Yes, but don't you think she would have hated this? I mean, if Harriet's down there, she certainly wouldn't have wanted all these cameras around when she . . . when she was pulled out," Susan said, starting to stand. "Do the divers have something? Do you see a . . . a . . ."

She didn't have to finish the question. What came out of the center of the pond, supported by three frogmen on loan from the Connecticut State Police department, was very obviously a body. A body dressed in a bright red flowered dress.

"So it was Harriet?"

"Yes. But she wasn't murdered. Brett says it was suicide."

That evening, Susan and Jed Henshaw were sitting

together in a booth at the Hancock Inn, too upset to do more than pick at the wonderful meal on the table between them.

"How does he know that?"

"Apparently she sent a letter explaining her intentions to the lawyer who handled her financial affairs—unfortunately he was on vacation the week it arrived at his office. Since the letter was marked personal, it wasn't opened until he came back to the office this morning. His call came in to Brett's office while he was with the frogmen at the pond this afternoon."

"Did she say she was going to drown herself?" Jed asked.

"No, but it makes sense. The pond was named after her husband ages ago. Most people in town don't even know that."

"Or have forgotten it if they ever knew," Jed said. "Now that you mention it, I remember going to the dedication ceremony."

"Yes. That was years ago."

They picked at their food a bit longer and then gave up and ordered coffee and brandy.

"You know what I've been wondering?" Susan asked. "I've been wondering if I should still walk Clue in that part of the park."

"I don't think Harriet MacHugh would be happy if she thought she was keeping people away from one of the most charming spots in Hancock," her husband answered, reaching across the table to take his wife's hand in his.

It was three days later that Susan took her husband's good advice and returned to the path around the pond. The grass still bore evidence of being crushed by the crowd that had continued to mill around for over twenty-four hours after Harriet had been found. The tire tracks created by the television news vans had already been raked up and seeded by the efficient crews of the Hancock Parks Department. There were a few more walkers than usual, but other than these things, life had pretty much resumed its normal pace.

Until Clue dashed back into the water.

Susan and Jed were back at the inn, the evening of the same day, this time drinking glasses of white wine and laughing together.

"So Brett did the entire thing again. Hung the scene-of-the-crime tape? Called out the frogmen? Talked with reporters?"

"Yes. And there were even more people in the park this time. I think everyone in town had heard about it this time and then . . . and then . . ." Susan was laughing so hard she had to take a deep breath and a sip of wine before she could continue. "And then the frogmen came up to the surface with a red patent leather purse and Clue went nuts. I tried holding her. And one of the frogmen tried, too. Brett finally opened the purse and found a glob of chocolatey paper that had once been Tootsie Rolls and gave them to her. She swallowed them in one gulp and just sat down with this contented expression on her face. That's when all the cameras began to click. Clue's photograph may be on the front page of tomorrow's paper."

"Fabulous. Here's to Clue. A natural search-and-retrieve retriever if there ever was one."

"And, you know, I've been thinking. Maybe Clue found more than she was looking for in that pond," Susan said, suddenly serious. "Maybe she found a new career for both of us. The man who trains goldens said he would call in the next week or so. What do you think? Would that snotty woman with the well-groomed afghan be impressed if Clue and I became a professional search-and-rescue team?"

"Maybe." Jed's expression became more serious. "But I do know one thing. I know Harriet MacHugh would be glad to know that the Tootsie Rolls she always carried in her purse were appreciated even after her death. Who would have thought our dog would go back into the water for some water-soaked candy?"

"Anyone who knows her," Susan said, laughing. "Anyone who knows her."

Cooking the Hounds

S. J. Rozan

S. J. ROZAN is the author of the Lydia Chin/Bill Smith series (*China Trade*, the Shamus Award-winning *Concourse*, *Mandarin Plaid*, and *No Colder Place*). An Edgar Award-winning short story writer, she shared fourteen years with a large yellow mutt named Simon (named for Simon Templar, the Robin Hood of modern crime), and Peggotty, a beagle with whom she shared only a few years, but who defined the word *loyalty*. Rozan dedicates this story to Simon and Peggotty.

Turner rapped the glass on the damn bar for what, the third time? Not like McGill, the fat slug, hadn't heard him. Turner knew he had. McGill didn't like him, Turner knew that too, didn't like any of them, McGill too high-and-mighty in this falling-down place, sour smell, bad wiring, cheap booze, but McGill with a real attitude, mostly about the fights. Like the dogs were good for anything else, Turner curled his lip, like any of them would have places to sleep and people to feed them, if they didn't fight. Like the damn dogs didn't *like* to fight, didn't yank their leashes when they saw where they were headed, Turner's place, like they didn't jump and yelp and snap while they waited, you could see their hearts pounding and they drooled, they wanted it so bad; but you couldn't tell McGill that, McGill just copped this attitude, like Turner and the guys were some bad element kind of thing, lousing up his bar for the pushers and pimps who liked to drink there, do their business in the corners.

Well, screw McGill. If there was some other joint to drink in in this godforsaken neighborhood, sure as hell they'd do it, but there was no place to go, so they came here, and damn if they weren't what you call your steady customers, paid cash, didn't they? So what the hell was McGill's beef, anyway?

Not that they'd been so steady lately, Turner had to admit, felt a little morose, staring around the place, peeling paint, grimy floors, bar your shirt stuck to. Somebody'd shot Roland, a month ago it was, shot the damn dog too, pit bull named Duke, both of them, right through the heart. That was bad, Roland trying to muscle in on his cousin's territory, get into the dope business, didn't seem to be going about it in a smart way to Turner, and it looked like the cousin didn't think so either, though he swore up and down he didn't do it, didn't order it, was gonna kill the guy who did when he found him. Yeah, right, Turner thought; and it was too bad about the dog, but there were other pit bulls, popular dog, so Turner's action hadn't taken too bad a hit, not from that.

Few days after that, though, that Dominican kid, Miguelito, he called himself, they found him in the river, kind of chewed up, like maybe his dog had gotten him or something, but Turner didn't believe it. Dog was a Doberman, strong, tough, usually a winner, could've maybe gone crazy, torn the kid apart, but it didn't push him in the river, did it? Dog was gone, though, nobody'd seen him, not at the kid's apartment, not around, everybody making bad jokes, hey, saw Miguelito's dog the other day, yeah, Satan, he was asking me where you lived. Turner never liked Miguelito, kid was psycho, liked to hurt people, liked to pretend to trip, brush your arm with his cigarette, smiling, hey, I'm sorry, an accident, man, but it never was a damn accident. Other people's dogs, too, if he could get away with it, just for fun, but boy, you even looked cross-eyed at Satan and Miguelito was ready to call you out. Probably someone else—probably lots of people, you think about it—felt the same way about him Turner did, so someone offed him and Turner didn't care, but Satan, that was a problem. Not a lot of Dobermans around, not these days, and if Turner set up a mismatch he had to give heavy odds and he always lost money, so not having Satan, that cost him.

And then, since last week, Joey, nobody'd seen him, nobody'd seen the dog either, German shepherd named Groucho, funny name for a fighter, but Joey, he was always funny, always bought a round when Groucho won, right here in McGill's, and where the hell was McGill anyway with his goddamn refill? Turner banged with the glass again, hollered for McGill, who was down the end, leaning his lard on the bar, talking to some girl. McGill looked over slowly, like he couldn't be bothered, but he lifted himself, waddled over, dribbled some Scotch into Turner's glass, stingy goddamn shot, you asked Turner, especially he was drinking the crap McGill kept in the well, probably watered anyway, but that was McGill.

Who was the girl? Turner asked him. Hadn't seen her in here before, not like he cared, but a new chick, you know,

and McGill told him her name, Joan, new in the neighborhood, that was all he knew about her. That wasn't a lot,
you looked at the way McGill had been hanging over
the bar, and Turner didn't know about that new business,
had the feeling he'd seen her before, small, short blonde
hair, better tits than a skinny girl usually has, he could see
that under her sweatshirt. Strong-looking, though, maybe
something about her hands, but anyway, if he had seen her,
he didn't know where, and she was seeing him look at her
and she smiled, so he picked up his glass and went down
that end.

Hi, they both said, and haven't seen you around here before, told each other their names, she said, yeah, she just
moved to town a month or two ago, drove a cab, would
you believe it, at night, that's why she could sit here, have
a drink in the middle of the afternoon, what about him?
And he said a cab, a little thing like you, dangerous job,
you're not scared? And she smiled, said, no, I take care of
myself, truth is, I kind of like the danger, makes it fun.
Turner smiled, because he sort of felt that way himself,
that's what the fights were about, really, besides the
money, it was the sweat and fear in the air, the blood, the
pounding hearts, like he was one of the dogs, he got so hot
when they fought. He smiled, but wasn't going to tell her,
because who the hell was she, really, and the fights were illegal anyway, but she tilted her neat little head and said,
wait, she knew him, wasn't he the one who ran the dog
fights around here, the ones in the basement, matched
dogs, he took the action, and Turner was so surprised he
said yeah, that was him, and how did she know?

Oh, she said, this guy Miguelito, picked him up in her
cab once, he told her about the fights, about this bar. That's

why she started coming here, Miguelito said it was an okay place. The guys got together here, this Miguelito said, he told her about Turner, the arranger, and now, the lightbulb just went on, she was putting it together. Yeah, he said again, that was him, and what a bummer about Miguelito, did she know? And she knew, nodded, sipping her beer, and he sort of whispered, not really to scare her, but maybe sort of, that they said the dog Satan chewed him up. She nodded again, yeah, yeah, she was pretty sure that was true, but she was smiling, and Turner thought, damn, he liked this girl.

It wasn't half an hour, they were walking, Turner and the girl, across the park, the girl—Joan was her name, McGill had it right—kicking leaves with her foot, yellow and brown. She had her hands stuffed in her pockets, and Turner was glad, for two reasons. It sort of accented her hips, this one, that one, as she walked; and it meant Turner didn't have to hold hands with her, girls liked that when they felt romantic, and Turner, he didn't know anything about romantic, he just felt his heart going, knew he was going to score.

I used to walk in this park, she was telling him, with my little dog, all summer, you know there are flowers here, daisies, even in a neighborhood like this? And Turner, not really listening, more wondering if her hair was blonde all over, still he knew it was his turn, so he said, summer, I thought you just moved to town, a month or two, and she said, yeah, well, not really—here, we go this way. So this little dog, she said, as they turned a corner, went down a different path, I only had her about six months. I'm not really a little dog type, I like big ones—she smiled at

Turner, his blood racing—but where I lived, the guy upstairs, his wife ran out on him and left the dog behind, little
Maltese. He took it out on the dog, beat her up, she'd howl
and cry, so one day I went up there with a baseball bat,
broke his arm the minute he opened the door, took the dog
with me. Kind of dumb, but sweet, followed me everywhere, that dog worshiped me. Skittish, in the beginning,
from being beat up on, but dogs, mostly they can be retrained, if you know what you're doing.

Then, one day, over there—pointing to one of the
benches—I'm walking her, out of nowhere there's this pit
bull, throws her in the air, blood everywhere, I grab him so
he drops her, bites me, look here, and she shows him a scar
on her arm, yeah, teeth, Turner thought, and said, bet that
hurt. Damn right, she said, and then from across the park
some bastard whistles and the pit bull's gone. When he
gets back to the guy he gets a bone, a reward, the guy
waves at me, he fucking waves, and they walk away! She
was looking at Turner, her eyes blue and hot, and Turner
said, jeez, because he didn't know what else to say. Here,
she said, here's my building, and unlocked a basement
door, took Turner down a hall, let him into her place.

Boy, Turner, said, you travel light, looking around the
room, couch, chair, TV, coffeemaker in the kitchen, door
over there to the bathroom, that was all: no rugs, no pic-
tures on the wall, no books, magazines. Yeah, well, she
said, sit down, you want a drink? Sure Turner did, and she
took out a bottle, better Scotch than Turner usually drank,
better Scotch than McGill ever saw, he was sure of that.
So, as she poured him a glass, took out a beer for herself—
what she'd been drinking at McGill's—so, Turner said,
what happened to the little dog, because he figured she

hadn't told the end of that story, and girls, they liked to talk beforehand, it put them in the mood better.

Died, she said. Sit down, and she pointed at the chair. I had eight stitches, she said, I wanted to go after that bastard, not go to the hospital, but the paramedics, they made me, dog was dead already, bastard and his pit bull were gone. Took me, she said, bringing Turner his Scotch, six weeks after to find out who the guy was. She sat near Turner, on the arm of the couch. No one wanted to talk to me, she said, people who'd seen what happened; guy was well known, everyone afraid of him. So it took a while. Name was Roland. Dog was Duke, he was keeping him in training for fights. Used to set him on squirrels, dog could even catch pigeons, he was that good, and sometimes, he thought he could get away with it, he'd set him on dogs, little ones like mine.

Jeez, Turner said again, well, Roland, he got his, Duke, too, I guess you heard, and she clinked her beer bottle against his glass and said, yeah, I heard, cheers.

Turner drank his Scotch, thinking, this was one weird chick, a hot babe not afraid of much, breaks a guy's arm with a baseball bat, lives in an apartment with nothing in it, keeps around bottles of expensive Scotch. Wanted to go after Roland and Duke! Lucky for the dumb bitch someone took them out, that was for sure.

She pulled the sweatshirt over her head, threw it on the couch while he drank some more. She had on a T-shirt under it, he could see the little hard ends of her tits, Turner suddenly confused, didn't know what to do so he lifted his glass, drained it. She smiled, tipped the bottle over his glass again, more than McGill would have done, and he drank some more.

I was sorry about the dog, she said, the pit bull, he was only doing what he'd been taught, but I couldn't have retrained him, he was too far gone, he liked the blood too much, you could see that. Huh, said Turner, taking another sip. She said, but he didn't feel it, the bullet went right through his heart, he never knew. Roland, too, even though that was too good for him, but it's when you get fancy that you lose.

She was looking at Turner, those hot blue eyes, and he thought, speaking of losing, I'm lost, and it was a funny joke, so he laughed. What do you mean, he said, Roland, the dog? Bullet went right through his heart? Well, it did, she said. Miguelito, that was different.

She stood up, went to the fridge to get herself another beer, and Turner looked at his glass, the beautiful brown stuff, and thought jeez, this is some Scotch, because when he watched her walk back from the fridge the room swung itself, back and forth, round and round, and when he closed his eyes it didn't stop. He'd had two at McGill's, this was only his third, but maybe the good stuff acted on you harder than the crap McGill had, Turner wouldn't really know, he didn't drink stuff this good all that often.

He opened his eyes, because what good was keeping them shut doing, and besides, he liked to look at her, her tight little butt and her tits. She was standing over him, leaning forward a little, smiling, and he remembered the last thing she'd said was weird, so he asked her about it: Miguelito?

Well, she said, I mean, it was the same with him, bullet right through his heart, but not the dog. Not a bad dog, Satan, you could retrain that dog. No, Miguelito had to be dead, otherwise Satan wouldn't have done it, but after three days, he didn't see him as Miguelito anymore, just a piece of meat. Miguelito, Turner thought, maybe it's Spanish for meat, and he wanted to tell the girl, because maybe it was funny and she'd laugh, but he couldn't get his mouth to work right. The Scotch glass had gotten really heavy, too, he tried to lift it to drink some more, because it was so good, but his arms felt like lead, he just looked at the thing, what was this? And he felt her fingers brush his hand as she took it away from him. Some Scotch, he said, but she said, no, Turner, it's not the Scotch, it's what I put in the Scotch. He looked at her, leaning over him, and she said, good, okay, now listen because there isn't much time left, and I want you to know. Turner asked, want me to know, what? Though it sounded funny to him, his own voice, but funny weird, not funny something you'd laugh at, and she wasn't laughing.

The shepherd, she said, he could've been retrained, too, but he wasn't healthy, he had that hip thing shepherds get, he never should have been fighting, dog was in pain, or sometimes all drugged up. None of them should be fighting, Turner. Turner thought, jeez, you been talking to McGill? And must have said it out loud, though he didn't hear it, because she said, yeah, McGill, he told me where to find you, told me where to find each of you.

She stood up again, so Turner had to look up to see her, the room spinning, and she said, I don't really live here, I just rented this place to do some business in. Turner asked, what business? his words echoing like in a cave or something, and she said, business like you, Turner. Business, Turner was lost, like drifting on the ocean, listening to her saying, so the shepherd and Duke, the pit bull, I had to shoot those dogs, but Miguelito's dog, Satan that was different. And the guys, it was this way: Roland, that was because of my little dog. Miguelito, guy was a creep. Jesus, you know, second time in my cab he tried to hit on me? This guy, Joey, I didn't know him from a hole in the ground, but the way he had that sick dog fighting, you could just tell about him. And now you, Turner, because you're the worst, you're in it for the money.

The room swaying, darkness fuzzing the corners of his sight, Turner watched her blue eyes hot and shining, her tits hard, and Turner wanted to tell her no, not just the money, tell her about the sweat and fear and pounding hearts, but he didn't know how. So instead of telling her, he asked her, asked her something, from something she'd said, he didn't get any of it, really, but this he wanted to know: Miguelito, he said, Satan, you kept the dog?

She moved backward, walking to the bathroom door, put her hand on the knob as the room spun around. Turner heard, even over the growling, the snarling—and it was the last thing he heard, like the last thing he saw was the sudden blast of short glistening black-and-brown fur, of muscles straining and gleaming white teeth—Turner heard when she said: yeah, I kept the dog.

Daisy and the
Archaeologists

Anne Perry

ANNE PERRY is the author of two highly successful mystery series set in Victorian England. The
launch of her long-running series about Police
Superintendent Thomas Pitt and his wife Charlotte
came with *The Cater Street Hangman*. A newer cycle
of novels, featuring private investigator William
Monk, began with *The Face of a Stranger*. Perry
lives on the east coast of Scotland with a mixed
breed named Daisy (who appears in the following
story).

Isadora shot in through the cat-flap absolutely bristling
with anger. Her tail was straight up like a flue brush.

"It's the best field, and they're going to build on it!" she
said instantly, before anyone could even ask her. Bertie
was sitting on the kitchen table washing himself. He ignored her, because he hasn't much patience with kittens.

The Boss was out, so I was in charge, being the most
senior dog. Actually I have lived with Boss since I was
two weeks old. She has all sorts of embarrassing pic-
tures of me being fed with a bottle, and being fed por-
ridge on a spoon. But that has nothing to do with what

155

happened next. I merely explain so you will understand my responsibilities.

Willow, my half-sister, rather more of a spaniel than I am, was asleep by the stove. She usually is there, or on the landing upstairs. Anyway, she ignored Isadora, who was obviously very upset.

"What field?" I asked, so she wouldn't feel ignored. Besides, it might matter. I don't like changes, no sensible dog does. Things are very well as they are.

"The one in front of Friend's house," she replied, still bristling. "It's the very best field for mice!"

"How do you know they are going to build?" I pressed. After all, she is only a kitten. She doesn't always get things right.

She looked at me furiously. "Do you think I haven't seen enough building to know? They are digging great big holes, long ones and square ones, just like those that Friend had them dig before all those new rooms were added on to her house. And like Boss is doing now!"

This caught Bertie's attention. He stopped washing his foot and listened. Even Casper listened. He is a very large puppy with legs like stilts. He says his mother was a collie, and I suppose he must know, although I don't remember mine. And his father was a pointer or something. Casper does stand around pointing with his nose sometimes, so he could be right. He looks like a dalmation to me, except he hasn't enough spots.

"It's enormous!" Isadora went on desperately. "It's going to take up half the field, and there'll be a hundred people there!"

"Rubbish!" Lewis responded. I didn't know he'd even been listening. Lewis is about fourteen or fifteen, older than any of the rest of us. He's white, when he feels like being clean. He's a very eccentric cat. He climbs up trees and can't climb down again, so he just lets go and falls. He also went through the combine harvester one year and broke all his bones. He got better again, but he isn't very fond of fields, and he gets terribly stiff sometimes. "You don't even know what a hundred is," he added dismissively. He hasn't a lot of patience with kittens either.

"They're digging it out with spoons and paint brushes," Isadora went on. "I've seen them!

"What?" That really made me pay attention.

"They're digging it out with spoons and paint brushes," she repeated, glad that at last someone was taking her seriously.

Casper was the only one who believed her, but he believes anything.

"People dig with shovels and tractors," Bertie said, washing his tail.

Willow went back to sleep again.

I admit I dismissed it, too, until the Boss came back in the late afternoon and we all got into the Woofer Wagon— that's the special car that is for us—and went to the beach for our walk. Boss's Friend from next door came, too, as she often does, which meant Tara came as well. She goes for walks down to the village sometimes. Labradors get fat if they don't walk a lot.

We were down on the sand, scuffling around at the water's edge, smelling things and swimming a little. I've just realized I really like swimming—I used to think I didn't—so I mentioned this business of building.

"Oh, yes," Tara agreed. "There are lots more people than there used to be in that field. Passed by today, and got tied on a lead." She was digging up a stone as she said it, but the expression on her face eloquently revealed her disgust. She doesn't usually get put on the lead.

"Really?" I enquired. Finding a rather good stone myself, I began to dig to loosen it so I could carry it around for a while. "Are they building anything?"

"They're digging holes," Tara answered, digging a beautiful hole herself. "Lots of them in lines and squares. There are people all over the place. Had to wait for ages at the shop. All sorts of people I've never seen before."

This was not good news. Ours is a very small village. We notice newcomers, even in the summer. They're all right, as long as they go away again. It sounded as if these ones intended to stay, and it worried me. Tara seemed not to mind, but Labradors are like that, always insufferably cheerful.

I wandered off back to where Boss and Friend were talking. I saw Mother Perry coming along the beach. She is Friend's mother and is very old indeed, but Bertie says she is also very wise. She walks stiffly sometimes. I have wondered if she might have gone through the combine harvester, too. Nobody mentions it, perhaps it is embarrassing. Lewis never talks about it either, and he can't have forgotten.

"Of course they were going to go at the end of the month," Mother Perry was saying. "At least Professor MacAllister was. Apparently they hadn't found anything really new."

"But there are more of them coming!" Friend protested. "There are half a dozen new tents up."

"What did they find?" Boss asked, looking at Mother Perry.

"As far as I know, it's not so much what it was, as where," Mother Perry answered very seriously. "It means the whole site is a lot bigger than they had supposed. It would mean it was one of the largest Pictish habitations anywhere in Scotland. Now they are thinking it might stretch halfway up the hill." She looked very unhappy. "I'm so sorry."

Boss and Friend were both very grim.

I presumed she meant our hill, and that was bad—in fact, it was terrible.

"The farmer won't be very pleased," Friend remarked glumly. "They'll be digging up all the crop. And Isobel will have people past her front door coming and going all the time."

"The corner's tight enough as it is," Boss added. "We don't need any more traffic on it. It's only a one-way track, with a passing place."

"The shop was full of people when I went today," Friend went on. "Carlo was too busy for me to ask him what it was all about."

"Young Catriona'll be pleased, anyway," Mother Perry said, with a shaky little smile.

"Who's Catriona?" Boss and Friend asked at the same time.

"One of the students on the dig," Mother Perry explained. "She's rather in love with Professor MacAllister, and she was very upset when he got fed up and said he was going."

"Maybe she put it there?" Friend suggested in a sort of throwaway manner as if it were half meant to be funny.

"No, she didn't!" Mother Perry contradicted her quickly. "She was astonished when it was found." She gave a little smile. "I thought Mr. Caldicott was going to be furious, because you know how he hates Professor MacAllister, but he seemed to be quite interested. Apparently it was sufficiently important a find for them to forget their rivalry long enough to investigate it."

"What a pity," Boss retorted. "Still, there's nothing we can do about it." She looked down at me. "Come on, Daisy. We'd better collect everybody and go home. Casper! Willow!" she shouted. "Goodbye, Mother Perry."

Friend said goodbye to her mother, collected Tara, and we all piled into the Woofer Wagon and went back up the hill.

I thought about it a good deal the next day, but nothing unusual happened, except there seemed to be a lot of cars going past and around the road to Rockfield. I suppose they were lost. Of course they all came back again because there are only a dozen houses there, and the road goes no further.

"You can always hunt in our own field," Boswell said, trying to be comforting to Isadora. He is also a black kitten, about the same age, but bigger.

Isadora sat in a huff. "I don't want to! That's your field. I like the one with the corn. It has mice in it."

"Our field has hares in it," Boswell replied.

Humphrey sauntered in and heard the end of the conversation. He is ginger and white and very big. Sometimes he lives here, sometimes at Friend's. He has two of every meal.

"Pansy caught a hare once," he remarked.

Pansy is one of Friend's cats. She is as old as Lewis, but she never went through the harvester . . . at least not that I

know of. She was a great hunter in her day, so that could
be true. I've heard Friend say she caught rabbits, moles,
and a pheasant once.

"If all those people come, they'll scare everything
away," Isadora replied, and curled up with her nose in her
tail, ending the conversation.

It was a whole week later when the next thing happened, and it was Willow who told me about it. Anyone
else and I wouldn't have believed her, but Willow has the
best nose of all of us. She finds things other people have
given up on months ago. But she can't count.

She must have thought it was a Saturday, when Boss
goes out all day and Friend comes over and takes us for a
walk. Willow won't come with us up the field, but sneaks
out and runs across the drive to sit on Friend's front
doorstep until she gets back, then shoots inside, first of all
to see if the cats have left anything in their dishes, then to
spend the rest of the afternoon with Friend.

It wasn't Saturday, but Boss went out anyway. Somehow Willow got misled. Friend was working. There was
no one else there. I think it was what they call a "Bank
Holiday." Anyway, Willow got fed up with sitting alone
on the doorstep, so she wandered off down the road, which
is most unlike her. Maybe she was talking to Roddy, who
does gardening for Friend and throws sticks for Willow
and makes a fuss of her. She likes him.

Anyway, she came back home later with the most ex-
traordinary story. She was wagging her tail so wildly she
was in danger of dislocating her back. But then she does
that for no particular reason, so I took no notice.

"It's dishes!" she announced.

"Boss'll get them back," I said, presuming she meant that Casper had taken the cat dishes again, hoping there was something left in them.

"You aren't listening!" she accused. "It's dishes down in the field. That's what they've found, very old dishes. Hundreds of years old, thousands of years old!"

Casper sat up. "Is there any food in them?'' he asked hopefully.

We ignored him. I was beginning to understand what it was all about. Humans are very odd. Some things they like new and when they get old they throw them away; other things, the older they are the better they like them. But with dishes there don't seem to be any rules at all.

"They got terribly excited about the one they found this afternoon," Willow went on. "Which was all very silly."

"Why was it silly?" I asked, assuming there was more to this than she had explained.

She took a long drink of water before she answered, dripping it over the kitchen floor. "Because it was where they found it that mattered," she replied at last. "They kept saying how important it was, and how much bigger it made the settlement, and that nobody had touched it in about four hundred years."

"What is silly about that?" I asked her. "I think it's very bad, because it means there'll be even more of them coming here."

Bertie got up off the table and stretched. He looked miserable as well. Boswell took his place. Humphrey came in through the cat-flap and saw that we were having a very important conversation, so he sat down to listen.

"Because somebody had touched it," Willow replied. "If they'd been dogs they'd have known that. I was right there when they uncovered it, just as if it had been there all that time, but it smelled of the young girl they call Catriona."

This was really interesting. It might mean something.

"Are you sure?" I pressed, although I did not really doubt her. Willow doesn't say a lot, and some of what she does say is nonsense, but her nose is never wrong.

"Yes, I am sure!" she said a little sniffily. She doesn't like to be disbelieved.

"Does that mean she put it there?" Boswell asked.

"It must," I replied.

"Why?" Casper looked at us one at a time. "Why would anybody bury dishes? Humans don't do things like that!"

That was a very sweeping statement for someone his age—he's only a puppy. But nonetheless he was right—they don't. Then I remembered what Mother Perry had said about this Catriona liking the Professor, and being afraid he would go away. She must have put it there to make him stay. I said so, explaining it carefully so the younger ones would understand.

Everybody looked very serious.

"It doesn't solve the problem," Willow said. "She didn't put the first one there. Mother Perry said she didn't."

"It wouldn't solve the problem even if she had," Bertie pointed out. "Because they don't know that, and we can't tell them."

All this was true. It was very upsetting.

"We must do something," Humphrey said after several minutes.

We all looked at him.

"I have an idea," he announced.

"Well, what is it?" I asked.

He stood up. "I shall go over and see what Pansy and Thea think."

Thea is Friend's Siamese. She is a very odd creature, long and thin with a voice that hurts my ears. She has a pedigree back to the Ark, but she is quite clever in her own way and not really so difficult once you get to know her. Pansy is odd, too. She used to live with Friend since she was a kitten, then when Boss took over Friend's house and we all moved here, Pansy wouldn't go with Friend, she stayed with us . . . for four whole years. Then suddenly, without a word, she took off and went back to Friend. She told me afterward that it was something Mother Perry said to her, but she didn't say what. As I told you, she is peculiar.

None of us thought much of Humphrey's idea, and he took off in a huff.

He came back the following morning, looking for a second breakfast.

"It all depends on the first *find*," he said with great importance. "The second one doesn't matter. It wasn't real, because this Catriona girl put it there."

It was good sense, even if it didn't help.

"She didn't put the first one there," Bertie recalled my having said so.

"Then we should find out if someone else did," Humphrey said.

"Why?" Boswell asked, looking at me.

I didn't know, but at least it was something to do.

"The more we know the better," I replied to him.

"Now?" he said eagerly.

It was time to start thinking hard. "Bertie," I said very

seriously. "You must get in the car next time Boss goes to see Mother Perry. You haven't been to visit her for a while, and she always likes to see you. Listen to everything you can, and come back and tell us. Humphrey, you had better go right back next door and tell Tara to listen to everything she can, and if she's off the lead at all to go into that field and hear everything there is to discover, sights, smells, everything. And if Friend is angry with her, just make the best of it. It won't be too bad. She'll make a lot of noise, but she won't do anything. She might deprive you of a few biscuits, but it's all for a very good cause."

Humphrey looked pleased with himself, and went off with his tail in the air.

It was two long, impatient days before we even had an opportunity to follow our plan, let alone have any success. Tara came over for her evening run up the field, bouncing with news. She's always bouncing with something. You'd think at six years old, she would have settled down a bit. She thinks she is six, but she has done so for ages; she might be seven by now. But Labradors don't grow up. They aren't responsible, like collies. I'm mostly a smooth-haired collie . . . more or less . . . more than I am anything else, anyway.

"Well, what is it?" I asked, running to keep up with her. We were heading over to the pond for a swim. I could hear Boss shouting after us, "No, Daisy! No swimming!" But we ignored her. I had to hear what Tara said. And I like swimming.

"Mr. Caldicott hates Professor MacAllister," Tara replied. "Just as much as I hate that dog next door at the back. It's the same sort of thing."

"How do you mean?" I asked. I could still hear Boss calling out, "No swimming." We jumped into the water. It was lovely and cool and wet and muddy and smelled wonderful, even better than the sea.

"You know how that dog always comes right up to the fence and then barks all the time, and the little one dances across the top of the wall, shouting?" she asked, splashing beside me. "Well, he's just like that. Always putting his foot over the line onto your piece of ground, leaving marks on your patch, taking stones and sticks that don't belong to him. He'd take your toys and bones if he dared."

"I see." I did. It was perfectly plain. We all know dogs like that.

"The sort of dog who'll dig a hole in your garden and wait for you to get into trouble for it," she went on. "And sit there looking as if he knows nothing about it."

"Perfectly clear," I agreed. "He dug the hole for the first piece of dish, and put it there, to get Professor MacAllister into trouble."

"That's right." Tara found a ready good stone, a lovely big one, and turned her attention to trying to dig it up. I went to find one of my own.

On the way back I was rather in disgrace for getting wet. I saw Bertie coming toward us over the grass and so I hurried to meet him. He had that sort of swagger he does when he has something important to say, or thinks he knows something the rest of us don't.

"What?" I asked.

"Mother Perry is very upset," Bertie replied, watching the swallows swoop overhead, and half hoping one of them would come low enough to catch. "Professor MacAllister told everyone it's the biggest settlement in Scotland, and it could go halfway up the hill. They are going to stay here all through the autumn. We've got to do something!"

"Of course we have," I agreed. "But what? We know the truth, but there's no way we can make them understand it."

I went on thinking about it while Boss put the chickens to bed. We all walked over to Friend's garden to look at the roses and go around the pergola and the white garden and up the herbaceous border as we always do. Thea and Pansy came as well, and Archie, who used to live with us but seems to have moved in with Friend now. We all thought about it hard.

"There's got to be a way," Bertie said seriously.

"We'll have to think more," Willow urged.

"We'll all think." Lewis appeared out of the snow-in-summer. Being white, he can do that. "A lot more," he added.

Thea rolled in the dust, flipping over several times, showing off. "They are completely deaf in their noses, but their eyes are all right," she remarked.

"What is that supposed to mean?" I asked her.

"They can find things, but they never know who put them there," she replied, rolling over again and standing up.

I began to have an idea.

Pansy was sitting in the catnip in the rockery, looking a little glazed. I'm not sure if she was entirely sober.

"Lots of dishes," she said giddily. "Absolute nonsense."

I ignored her. She'd be embarrassed in the morning.

"Good idea," Bertie agreed, wandering a trifle unsteadily over to the catnip himself. "Total confusion."

Then I understood. Those diggers and dish finders

believed they knew exactly what they had found and where it had come from. That was why they were going to stay and tear up our field. If we could make them realize their mistake . . . that was the answer. "But there is a problem," I said aloud. "Where can we find more of those dishes they like so much? We haven't got any."

"It doesn't matter," Pansy said airily. "Any dishes."

"You can have mine," Humphrey offered. That was not as generous as it sounded. He ate out of any dish he could reach.

"And mine!" Isadora added. This field business had really upset her.

Casper said nothing. He wasn't parting with his bowl for anything at all.

"We'll take cat dishes," I decided. "They are far lighter. We can carry those."

The decision was made. I looked at Boss and saw her eye on me. It was not going to be possible to do anything without more careful planning. Twilight was always a good time for the odd adventure. I've noticed that before.

I wandered over casually to Tara, pretending I was investigating a smell.

"We need a diversion," I told her. "I shall suggest to Casper that he gets lost—visibly, of course. You might do the same. Then while they are looking for you, Willow and I shall go and take the dishes."

"Willow should get lost," she answered. "I can reach the cat dishes off the bench, I do it all the time. She can't reach. Besides, I'm a better digger than she is."

All this was true. She has feet like shovels. I was bound to agree. I made my way back to Casper again. This presented an immediately problem. He had just begun running around the lawn as fast as he could in circles. He does that from time to time. I used to think he was showing off, now I realize he just loves to run so much he can hardly help it.

I ran out in front of him the next time round, but he simply leapt clean over me and kept on going. It was embarrassing and it made me rather cross. But although I run pretty well, I hadn't a hope of catching him. So I went and told Willow our idea. She agreed reluctantly. She wanted to come with us, and she doesn't like getting into trouble for being lost, or for anything else. She is one of those dogs who mind. But she is also a good team player, and my half-sister, so she agreed. She knew it really mattered.

She started to wander off, and I sat in the shadows next to some white flowers. Then Casper began to realize he was all on his own, and might be missing something, so he stopped racing around and came to look for us.

"Run away and get lost!" I said to him urgently.

He looked very hurt. His ears went down and his tail went down. He really is only a puppy, in spite of his legs.

"Just long enough to make Boss and Friend go looking for you!" I explained. "So Tara and I can take the dishes to the field!"

"I can carry dishes!" he said eagerly. "I have done so, often! And I can reach all the cat plates, even the very back ones at the top of the shelf! And I can open the ring-pull tins and get what's inside!"

I wanted to skirt over that, because *I* can't, but I had to be fair. It was a considerable accomplishment. "I know. But what we need now is a diversion. And you can run faster than any of the rest of us."

He was mollified. He agreed, and loped off, skipping every now and then because it was an adventure, and he was part of it.

All was going according to plan, but I was a little nervous, because sometimes when one of us goes off, Boss thinks to shut the rest of us away before they go looking, so I kept a good distance. She can be very persuasive, but she can't carry me.

We did it perfectly . . . to begin with.

"Casper!" Boss called out. "Casper! Where is that dog?"

"Willow's not here either," Friend added.

That was our cue. Tara and I slunk off and ran over the drive to get the cat dishes from the utility room. We managed three very nicely, and decided to take two of them, a very good mouthful. We could always chew them up into bits when we got there. We ran down the road at a brisk trot. It wasn't very far, only to the bottom of the hill and then a right into the field. Everything was fairly quiet. There were dozens of tents up, all with lights in them, but nobody was around outside.

I looked at Tara, and she looked at me. We hadn't yet worked out quite where we were going to bury the dishes. If we put them too close they wouldn't mean anything, they would think they were their own things just lost. But if we put ours too far away, they might never find them at all.

We ended up choosing an excellent site, just at the edge of where they had been working that day. It had the extra benefit of being freshly turned ground and very easy to dig again. Isadora was right, it really does look like the trenches they make when they are going to build something. We all knew about this from what Boss and Friend had done at home.

We had just gotten started and were thoroughly pleased with ourselves when it happened. I was thinking how well it was going and that it was rather fun. I was covered with earth that smelled excellent and had reached a good depth, when I heard the yell. You can tell what people mean by the tone of their voices, even if you don't understand the words. This person was very angry indeed. There was a thud of feet and something heavy landed rather too close to my head for comfort.

Tara was so busy digging she took no notice. There was earth flying everywhere.

"Damn dogs!" the man bellowed furiously, hurling something else at us. "Get them out of here! They'll ruin everything!" And there was a pounding of feet and more people shouting.

"Run!" I barked at Tara, and as another stone actually struck her this time, she yelped and jumped out of the hole, and together we ran for all we were worth, ducking and dodging between people, trying to avoid being hit with long sticks they were waving about. Lights went on everywhere, torches swinging beams onto us, a lot more noise and yells and howls. Anyone listening would have thought we were a pack of wolves at the very least, not two very intelligent and good-natured, civilized dogs who had lived here in perfect accord since long before this lot of destroyers arrived.

It was all very undignified, and I hate being made to look silly. Running away is horrid, and even worse, we had left the cat dishes in the corn at the edge of the field.

We had to run all the way back up the hill again with an

army of enraged people shouting and banging behind us. It was all most unpleasant. It was also no use at all in getting rid of those digging up Isadora's best hunting patch and in restoring the general peace and tranquility of the village.

"What were you doing down there?" Boss demanded angrily when she saw us. "You stupid dog! You should know they'd chase you! Are you hurt?"

It was only my feelings, but I couldn't explain that to her. However she did seem to understand, because in spite of a thorough scolding, I still got my biscuit, and so did Tara.

However, that night in the kitchen I felt very glum. We had most definitely failed.

"We'll just have to try again," Casper said cheerfully. I gave him a filthy look. He hadn't been shouted at or hit with stones and chased out.

"They'll be watching for you," Willow warned. "Anyway, we can't get out now. The back door's shut."

"They couldn't see me," Bertie pointed out. Since he is entirely black, like a patch of ink, that is true. "And I can get in and out any time I like."

"So can I," Boswell said bravely. "And I'm as black as you are. I'll go with you."

Isadora was very much smaller, but it was her hunting patch, and her battle. She wasn't going to be left out. "And me," she added, but not very loudly.

I considered that for a moment. She was still only a kitten. Like everybody else, she was my responsibility.

"And me," she said again.

She's very black. Perhaps she wouldn't be seen. I agreed.

We went ahead with the plan. Casper retrieved one more cat dish from the back of the bench, and he and Willow and I took turns at chewing it until it was in several pieces, small enough for cats to carry. They have lots of claws, but their mouths aren't very big.

In the middle of the night, when it was as dark as it gets, which lasts for only an hour or so in summer up here, they set out off down the hill, each carrying a nice piece of red plastic dish.

They came back almost two hours later, dirty, satisfied and quite safe.

We learned the results of our escapade late in the evening, two days later. We had come down to the beach in the Woofer Wagon and, by chance, Mother Perry was there. She looked very pleased about something.

"What a wonderful day," she said to Boss and Friend. "Look at that sunset across the water. It's almost as if it knew."

"Knew what?" Boss asked.

"Oh, I thought I'd told you. I must have meant to," Mother Perry replied airily. "The archaeologists are all packing up and leaving for the winter. The village will be back to normal again in a few weeks. Apparently they realized that the special things they found that made it seem to be much bigger were only put there quite recently. They weren't real finds at all."

"Oh?" Friend looked surprised. "What made them realize that?"

"They found other things in the same areas that couldn't possibly be real. Bits of red plastic that were obviously thoroughly modern, but well buried and covered up."

"How on earth did they get there?" Boss was puzzled.

I looked at her to see if she had realized what they were, and there was a flicker of suspicion, but she didn't say anything.

"Heaven knows," Mother Perry replied, but there was great satisfaction in her voice. She leaned on her stick and gazed out over the sunset across the sea. "I think personally that Catriona buried something there to make Professor MacAllister stay longer, because she was a little in love with him. And Caldicott put something there so MacAllister would claim he had made a great discovery, and then look like a fool when it proved not to be. And they were both believed because each knew their own was false, but neither knew about the other."

"But what about the red plastic?" Friend pressed. "Nobody in their right mind could imagine the red plastic was Pictish from two thousand B.C.!"

"That's a mystery," Mother Perry agreed. "But it is what made them start thinking, and see how easy it was to attach meaning that isn't true."

"I suppose they'll now cover it all over again with earth," Boss said thoughtfully. "And then next year they'll come back and dig it all up again."

"Probably. But it'll be much smaller," Mother Perry answered. "Only the size it's always been."

I had heard enough. It was beginning to get darker and they might decide to go home soon. I stood up and went off down the sand toward the water, which beckoned irresistibly.

"No, Daisy!" Boss called after me. "It's too late! You'll go to bed wet! I'm not drying you off! Come back here! No swimming!"

I trotted into the foam at the edge of the sea. It was gorgeous! I went in and felt its delicious coolness all over me.

"No, Daisy!" Boss yelled at me. "No swimming!"

I took no notice at all. Neither did anybody else.

The Long Arm of the Paw

Jeffrey Marks

JEFFREY MARKS is an interviewer, freelance journalist, and short story writer. His work has won multiple awards including the Barnes and Noble Prize, and he received Honorable Mention from *DreamWeaver* magazine, and a grant from Malice Domestic. In addition, his author profiles and scholarly works on mystery authors have appeared in numerous national magazines. Marks also wrote a biography of mystery writer Craig Rice *(Who Was That Lady?)*, which has only appeared in French translation to date. Having been reared in the company of beagles and terriers (Bugular, Malady, Almanzo, and Busters 1–4), Marks lives in Cincinnati with a Scottie named Ellery.

As Norman trundled toward me, he slobbered over his latest treasure. Although technically a hunter, my beagle had only shown signs of tracking cookies and ferreting treats. Jewelry was a new avocation.

I didn't need to investigate the bauble to know what he'd found. We'd spent most of yesterday scouring my antique store for this particular necklace. Margaret Nuxhall, one of the thirty vendors who rented space at Oldies But Goodies, had caused much ado about the incident. Someone had pilfered a lovely piece of overpriced costume jewelry. The settings of the piece in question were eighteen-karat gold, but the genuine stones had been replaced with paste years ago.

Searching the store was an easy task. My grandmother had left me her homestead in Ross when she died and I knew every inch of the house. Her legacy had become my income. While she might have approved of my ingenuity, my grandmother would have hated my trusty mutt strolling through her former living areas.

By six o'clock last night, the only antique I wanted to see was twelve-year-old Scotch. Margaret had practically danced at her opportunity to collect insurance and warn the others regarding the perils of shoplifting. I dissuaded her from filing a police report, but I'd fully expected a performance of smelling salts on the divan. Subtlety was not her maiden name.

As Norman parted a gaggle of customers like a four-legged Moses, I questioned last night's assumptions. The dog had come from the rear of my store where three dealers shared my grandmother's erstwhile dining room. The room had a single entrance, the threshold Norman had just traversed. True, the piece might have been misplaced, but we'd ransacked the common areas and secured the house before leaving.

His stomach dusted the floor, which marked his first attempt at earning his keep in my store. I tickled Norman under his chin to release his death grip, but he was having none of it. He clamped down on the necklace and yelped. Dropping the sloppy jewelry into my palm, Norman whimpered off to the corner. Normally, he opted to lounge upstairs in the bathroom, but he seemed content to rest under a mahogany bookcase. His penchant for hogging the shower and attacking other occupants had led to comparisons with his namesake, Mr. Bates.

As a consolation prize, I tossed him a soft treat and walked to the cash counter. The necklace clanked on the glass top. The hardness of the paste jewels made me ponder the situation. I attempted to mark the glass one jewel at a time. On the fifth try, I struck gold. Perhaps *diamond* would be a better word. The bauble scratched the glass. Maureen's necklace had a real sparkler. Suddenly the meaningless shoplifting had nasty implications. If the necklace was hidden in the house, a dealer who rented space here had stashed it, recognizing another vendor's trash as treasure.

As if on cue, Maureen scurried through the front door and sat down next to me at the counter. "Dear, you found my necklace. Where was it?" She was an older woman with hair in that red shade peculiar to women of a particular age. Her ears, like satellite dishes, were barely hidden by tufts of hair and garish hoop earrings hung on her lobes. She wore a flowing white blouse and an ankle-length patchwork skirt that gave her the air of a Tarot card reader. I doubted that the cards held a solution to this problem.

I pointed to my four-legged friend. "Norman did, but he didn't give me any hints as to where that might have been."

Maureen slipped to the floor in her flowing skirt. She scratched Norman under the ear and talked baby-chatter. Norman ate it up, poking his nose skyward to show he didn't need me. At least until lunch.

I dangled the necklace by its clasp. "When was the last time you saw this?"

She shrugged and stood up, brushing her hands on her skirt. "Yesterday morning. I added some more jewelry to my display. I tried to wipe the doughnuts off my hands, but some stuck to the jewels. I noticed it gone after lunch."

Yesterday was slow. More dealers than customers. Another bad sign. And the doughnuts explained Norman's interest in the necklace. "Did you notice anyone lurking around your booth?"

"Not a soul, more's the pity." Maureen's voice made me feel bad. She had inked a deal with the store six months ago and her sales weren't up to her expectations. No accounting for retail tastes. Jewelry lingered while happy face mugs sold like gold coins for a dollar. "That's why I came up just now. What did you want to talk to me about?"

"Your necklace has a real diamond in it. That might explain why it was taken."

Her eyes widened and she carefully pulled the necklace across the counter. "I wonder then. Could the rings be real? They're gone, too, you know."

"Rings? When did this happen?" Nothing would run dealers out of the store faster than a gladhander with good taste and an eye for bargains. Just the thing to run up my insurance rates and run off the people who put food in Norman's bowl.

"Sometime today. I just noticed it a few minutes ago."

"Where did you get the rings?" My mind boggled at the number of places a band of gold could be cached. I checked Maureen's hand first, but she didn't wear any jewelry. From choice or from need?

Maureen smiled. "Maybe I have an eye for the genuine article. I bought these at an estate sale in Indian Hill. The heirs marked them costume, but now I wonder. One was a pearl and the other a red stone. I'd assumed colored glass. Rubies are red, aren't they?"

Maureen had signed on with the notion of getting rich quick. She watched the *Antiques Roadshow* like a game show, shouting out appraisals and sitting back to match wits with the experts. Her pricing reflected those hours of watching, either ten times the worth of a piece or next to nothing.

Eric St. James rushed through the front room of the store. The slight, elderly man in his linen jacket and bow tie looked more fragile than his wares. He carried a piece of pottery cradled in his palms. "I just found the most amazing thing. A Rookwood wall pocket for twenty-five dollars at a sale. What a steal." He gazed at it with a lust most men reserve for Pamela Anderson. The tiny vase with a flat back would hardly inspire most people with desire.

The words made me cringe. Eric would kill anyone who stole from his collection. I had a suspicion that he treated some of the Rookwood in his home more like guests than decorations. The only reason he sold pieces was to buy more.

I made a head motion to Maureen and we followed him back to his display in the dining room. Norman yawned and then decided his best chance of another snack rested with the crowd. He followed us, sticking his nose under Maureen's skirt a couple of times. I caught a glimpse of her ankle-high hosiery and unshaven legs.

Eric's displays were meticulous, glass spotless and shelves dusted. The better to admire his treasures. He had four cases of antique glass and pottery, along with a bookcase packed with odds and ends. Norman rested his considerable backside on the lowest shelf and watched as Eric gently stowed his treasure. He turned to look at us as he shut the case. "Did you want something, Brett?"

I shrugged and pulled a bud vase from the bookcase. "Nothing much. Just wanted to make sure that everything's okay with you."

"Never been better. I sold two signed pieces of Rookwood yesterday." He flashed a wad of cash at me. Had that bankroll come from misplaced jewelry? I tried to guess the amount of currency, but I knew I'd be as bad as Maureen and her pricing.

"Great." I continued to survey the room as I gently replaced the vase. The few pottery displays in my store sold well, amazingly so. Still there were too many places to hide a tiny necklace or two rings. Every Rookwood vase and Roseville candleholder had an opening, an orifice designed to hide things in.

Since the entourage showed no signs of dispersing, I decided to check out the other two dealers in the dining room. The next display was a little simpler to inspect. Laura Ashmore hadn't stopped by today, but yesterday she'd been here. More than enough opportunity to swipe a necklace and hide it in one of the huge furniture items she had in her space.

Eric tried not to stare as I inspected a few drawers of a breakfront. Nothing inside, but the goods could easily be taped to the back or bottom of a piece of wood. My search felt futile.

Margaret wasn't quite so circumspect in her search. She had gathered her long skirts around one arm and peered around the back of a nineteenth-century armoire. With a flourish, she ripped something from the back of the piece and held it over her head. "I found this."

Norman sat up and took notice. Hoping for a treat, he sidled up to Margaret, inspecting the strip in her hand.

She'd found a piece of tape on the back of the furniture. I doubted it was what we wanted. The adhesive had browned with age and two screws hung from the strip.

"I think you found the screws for hardware for the armoire." Eric moved closer, trying to make himself a part of whatever excitement we'd generated.

Margaret inspected the tape closely before pressing the tape back on the armoire. "Oh, well. Nice try. I wouldn't mind blaming this mess on Laura. She's always stopping by to point out that I've mispriced something."

I nodded. Despite her recently joining the shop, Laura had appointed herself resident expert in every area of antiques. She'd lectured Eric about an overpriced piece of Roseville yesterday. The worst part of her pedantry was that she was usually correct.

Having been denied a snack, Norman went back to resting on the floor.

Betty Parker's space proved the point that if you wait long enough, everything becomes an antique. She'd loaded her corner of the dining room with every possible kitchen device imaginable. The canisters and wares took me back to my own youth, while the clutter reminded me of my kitchen this morning.

Betty's deeply creased face turned to watch us approach. She wore a simple white shirt and plain jeans that belied her personal wealth. A husband's amassed fortune allowed her to play entrepreneur. With her impeccable Indian Hill heritage and genteel demeanor, I'd expected silver tea sets and bronze chafing dishes or Ben Franklin glasses to look down her patrician nose when she approached me about renting space. Instead, rusted Nabisco tins and dented Hershey canisters lined the back wall of her space. The Parkers must have used this space to unload leftovers from their deceased relatives' estates.

I was sure Betty's clutter annoyed Laura, who took great pains to dust weekly and polish monthly. Laura's schedule was fixed in stone. I could set the clocks by her methodical ways. I couldn't determine the year from Betty's habits. For example, she was supposed to come in yesterday at ten, but didn't bother to show by noon. So instead of paying the quarterly taxes due, I was forced to man the register for the first hours of the day. Not the best way to please the owner.

"Brett, how nice of you to stop back. Did you get your taxes done?"

I nodded in Betty's direction as I despaired of ever finding a clue in her kitchen utensils. Margaret found a box of spatulas under the Hoosier cabinet and rummaged through them like a woman possessed. The ring incident had pushed her into a frenzy that foretold police visits and accusations. I couldn't blame her anxiety at losing some good pieces, but the publicity would hurt my business for months.

I suggested to Margaret that we retire upstairs to talk.

As I closed the door to my office, Margaret sat down in

my chair behind the desk. "Well, I was going to have a problem in paying this month's rent, but given the circumstances, I don't think I'll have a problem." If she hadn't worn a skirt, I swear she would have put her feet on the rolltop.

"What exactly are you telling me?" I swallowed hard, waiting to hear the damage. I knew enough dealers and operators to hear one in action.

"I'll keep this to ourselves in exchange for some latitude on future rent. You wouldn't want the police involved." She bent over so our faces were inches apart. "Bad for business," she added with a wink. "Other people might be tempted to back out of their deals, but I'm willing to be more forgiving."

"I know, so what's the tally?"

"For a pearl ring, I'd say six months rent-free and six more reduced. Seems fair to me."

Norman looked dismayed to think of the number of dog biscuits that kind of cash could buy while I bit my lip to keep the zingers in check. I didn't want to see her mad if this was keeping her cool. We walked downstairs to draw up the papers. When I pulled out a sheet of writing paper, I couldn't believe my eyes. The necklace had disappeared again. Only the scratches on the glass top remained.

Before I could speak, Laura Ashmore tore into the store like a tornado in a business suit. "You went through my display today. Who authorized you to do that?" Her arms crossed her chest while she waited for a response. I'd suspected Eric called his neighbor for a less than kindly update on what was going on at the store.

I cleared my throat. "Well, technically it's in your contract with Oldies. The right to inspect your merchandise for illegalities."

"And what am I supposed to have done wrong? Did you search Margaret's display for her criminal pricing mistakes?" She pointed an accusing finger at the theft victim.

Margaret sputtered out a protest, but I mollified her with a pat on the arm. I explained the situation in as few words as possible—the precise number I was allowed to insert into the conversation. When I'd finished, Laura stared at Norman as if he'd deliberately instigated this mess.

"What did you hope to find in my booth? I wouldn't leave that kind of merchandise just tucked away in one of my drawers."

A smart-ass comment came to mind, but as father figure to these squabbling children, I thought it best to refrain. "So you knew those items were real and not costume jewelry. How did you know that?"

Laura managed to roll her eyes as she spoke with that air of bored *über*-intelligence. "Any idiot could see by the cut of the gems in the necklace that one or two of them stood out from the rest. It was simplicity itself."

Norman sniffed around Laura's leg and moved back toward me. Usually my beagle took to everyone, but Laura was beyond even his people skills. I reached for the box to give him a snack as consolation, but Laura brushed the box out of her way as she rested her arms on the counter. Norman whimpered and retired to his bed to pout. Nothing short of canned liver would console him.

I suddenly had an inspiration about the thefts. I slapped my leg and Norman galloped behind me as we went back to the displays. I pretended to hide a treat in part of one of the booths and stood back to watch.

Norman used his snout to flip the lids off a few canisters until I found what we had missed before. A Nabisco cracker tin held the two rings, not a prize I would have expected to find in any canister.

Margaret swooped down and slipped the baubles on her fingers. Laura took a long look at the pearl ring and shook her head. "That's an incredibly rare jewel you have there. I'm sure you didn't know that though since it's marked at ten dollars."

Margaret had the good graces to blush. "Not until Brett suggested that it might be the real thing. I certainly had it underpriced."

Laura tsked with her tongue. "I could have told you. Until you get the hang of this, you really should come to me with questions about pricing. But I can't figure out how you knew that Betty had taken the jewels. Why didn't she just buy them from Margaret?"

This time I could matriculate to Laura and I seized the opportunity with both hands. "If Betty continued to buy all the items from Margaret, she'd get suspicious about their worth. When was the last time you got something from here that wasn't marked at book price? So large purchases of jewelry would be a dead giveaway. Besides, she was greedy enough to want them without paying anything."

"But how did you know this is where Norman went?"

"When you moved the snack box, I realized that the only antiques that would interest this dog had to be food related. Pottery and furniture he sees all the time. But tins and kitchenware would definitely set his mouth watering. He sniffed through the tins low enough for him to break into."

I tickled Norman under the chin as I tried to figure out how I'd tell Betty that her space would have to be cleared by the end of tomorrow.

Best Served Cold

Dean James

DEAN JAMES is the coauthor, along with Jean Swanson, of the Agatha and Macavity Award–winning reference book *By a Woman's Hand: A Guide to Mystery Fiction by Women*. With Jan Grape and Ellen Nehr, he edited *Deadly Women: The Woman Mystery Reader's Indispensable Companion*, nominated for an Edgar Award for Best Critical/Biographical Work. His latest work of nonfiction, written with Jean Swanson, is *Killer Books: A Guide to the Popular World of Mystery and Suspense*. His short story "The Village Vampire and the Oboe of Death" was published in *Malice Domestic 7*. In addition to two cats, Dean has a poodle named Candy who anxiously awaits her appearance in a future story.

After eight hours on the road, I had had enough. Home was still a good two hours away, and at the age of sixty, I can't drive all day and all night like I could when I was younger. I had left Houston at six o'clock in the morning, and I was more than ready for a stop by the time I hit Jackson. Besides, I'd been owing Iva Jean Delancey a visit for quite some time. The fact that I hadn't called to warn her I was coming wouldn't matter. We had been good friends for too long.

I pointed my Jeep up into the driveway of Iva Jean's house a few minutes after two on a sunny but chilly October day. The house stood in the bell of a cul-de-sac on one of Jackson's oldest and quietest streets. Tree-shaded lawns, big rambling houses, and extensive yards made this area prime real estate. Iva Jean's family were all gone now, but she held on to the house and all the memories it contained.

Iva Jean's car was in the garage, and I parked my Jeep behind it, then got out and stretched. I could feel my bones pop, and my shoulders felt like they could use a long hot shower. Relief was blessedly only moments away. I followed the flagstones from the garage, across part of the yard to the back door. I rang the bell, expecting Iva Jean to swing the door open with a beaming smile on her face.

I waited for over five minutes, then started frowning. I rang the bell again, and somewhere inside the house, I could hear frantic barking. Iva Jean's dog, Gemma, otherwise known as the "Hell Hound," was disturbed about something. Maybe Iva Jean was ill.

I started hurriedly hunting for the spare key Iva Jean kept near the back door. Now which flowerpot is it? I wondered, as I hefted them around in turn. "Gotcha!" I said, after lifting a large pot of dying geraniums.

Gemma met me at the back door, nails scrabbling on the tiles. "What is it, girl?" I asked her as she bounced around. She always remembered me, no matter how much time passed between my visits. "Where's Iva Jean?" Gemma bounded away toward the front of the house, and my stomach slowly clenching in apprehension, I followed.

Iva Jean was stretched out on the sofa in the living room. There was an odd smell in the air that took me a moment to identify. A trace of vomit streaked Iva Jean's mouth, but her face looked almost serene in death. Iva Jean had vomited on the hardwood floor by the sofa, then had slumped down to die in comfort. Gemma took up a position beside the sofa near Iva Jean's head.

Stunned, my breathing labored, I reached over to assure myself that Iva Jean was really dead. No pulse, no sign of breathing. Dear God, I thought, she's only sixty, like me. What on earth happened?

Leaving Gemma anxiously guarding her mistress, I ran back to the kitchen and grabbed the phone. Punching in the numbers took all my efforts at concentration, the way the receiver shook in my hands. When an operator came on the line, I stammered something into her ear and waited for assurance that someone would be with me soon. Then I hung up the phone and rushed over to the sink, where I promptly threw up.

Some minutes later, my face still damp from repeated splashings with cold water, I went back to the living room to sit with Iva Jean until the police or the ambulance or whoever-the-hell got there.

"Who in blazes are you?" I asked the man I suddenly found standing over Iva Jean's body. He was awfully well dressed to be a burglar or a paramedic. Gemma barked excitedly, and I shushed her.

More startled even than I, he whirled around and almost slipped in the mess by the sofa. "Jesus!" he swore, adding a few other choice words as he danced to keep from falling. "I might ask the same of you, lady. Who the hell are you?" he asked as he got himself stable and upright a few feet away from Iva Jean. He matched my own six feet, but he was a good twenty years younger. Handsome, and knew it, I suspected, but his color was high right now, taking the edge off his looks.

"I'm Ernestine Carpenter, an old friend of Iva Jean's. I just got here, and I found her like this. Now, who the bloody hell are you, and how did you get into the house?"

He flushed again, unbecomingly. "I'm Mrs. Delancey's lawyer, Harlan Carr. I was by to see her at lunchtime, and I came back to check on her. I was a bit worried. And the front door was unlocked." He turned to look back down at her. "I knew she was in a bad way, but I never thought she'd do this." He sighed heavily.

"What do you mean?" My voice rose at least an octave. "That you think Iva Jean committed suicide?"

Harlan Carr nodded. The man was stark raving nuts. I'd known Iva Jean for over fifty years, and I'd swear on a stack of Bibles that she'd never kill herself.

"She asked me to come by today, since I live close by. Said she wanted to talk about something. I thought she wanted to draft a new will." He sighed again, his features composing themselves in an attitude of deep sorrow. "Her granddaughter's death really hit her hard. That's all she could talk about."

I nodded cautiously. Martha Lee Delancey, daughter of Iva Jean's only daughter Jeanette, had been killed in a car accident nine months ago, almost two years to the day that Jeanette had died from breast cancer. Iva Jean had taken it hard, but we'd talked on the phone a lot. She would have given me some hint if she'd been despondent enough to kill herself. She had borne too much tragedy in her life, but she was a survivor.

Gemma whimpered. That convinced me more than anything. Iva Jean would never have killed herself without making some provision for the dratted animal. Iva Jean adored her, but she was too rambunctious for anyone else, myself included. You never knew what she'd do next.

The doorbell rang, and then a voice called out, "Hello!" I marched out in the hallway and escorted the emergency personnel into the living room. Thank the Lord, they could take over now.

A police officer took statements from Harlan Carr and me, then the officer took a quick look around the house, particularly in the kitchen. After that I left Carr talking with the officer while I put on a pot of coffee. I badly needed something hot and strong.

The house fell silent about the time my coffee was ready, and as I sipped at the brew, feeling warmth seeping back into my body, I could hear stealthy sounds from the front of house. Frowning, I took my coffee down the hall toward the living room.

"Can I help you find something?" I asked Harlan Carr, who jerked upright, nearly banging his head on the edge of a table. He had been peering at the floor under the table.

"Er, no, just looking for something I thought I must have dropped earlier. But it's gone now," he said.

"Well, if you don't mind, Mr. Carr," I said politely, "I'll be in touch with you later. I know that I'm the executor of Iva Jean's estate, and I'll discuss arrangements with you tomorrow. Do you have a card?"

Normally I'm not so abrupt with people, but there was something about this lawyer that set my teeth a bit on edge. Maybe I was simply still in shock over Iva Jean's death, but I just had to shove him out of the house as soon as possible.

"Certainly, Miss Carpenter. It is 'Miss,' isn't it?" He seemed to smirk a bit at that. I nodded shortly as he handed me a business card. "I'm sorry that you've had to go through this, I know it's quite a shock. You can rely on me to help you with whatever you need." I nodded again, and his eyebrows arched briefly. Gemma escorted him to the door, nipping at his heels. The Hell Hound is a marvelous judge of character.

I locked the door behind Harlan Carr and stood there for a long moment, staring down at Gemma. If only she could talk to me, I sighed. Gemma, a Patterdale terrier, was a few inches over a foot long and weighed about fifteen pounds. She could do many things, but talking wasn't one of them. If I was lucky, she hadn't found my car keys and hid them, like she had the last time I was here. Iva Jean would laugh over the many items that Gemma made off with the TV remote. She always brought things back, but on her own schedule. And usually soggy.

Wiping away a few stray tears, I set about cleaning up the floor beside the sofa. Someone had taken away samples of the vomit, and I didn't want to think much about why. I cleaned up the residue, while Gemma watched patiently. Then I took Gemma out.

I let Gemma run around in the backyard and do her business while I unloaded some of my things from the Jeep. It might be a while before I made it home, and I might as well stay there. Staying in Iva Jean's house without her would be unsettling, but it was the most sensible thing to do for the time being.

Gemma and I had barely gotten back inside before the

front doorbell rang. I considered ignoring it, but thought it might be important.

I peered out the peephole and vaguely remembered the two women who stood talking to each other. They were neighbors of Iva Jean's I'd met at some point, though I couldn't remember their names.

"Hello," I welcomed my visitors. "Won't y'all come on in?" I was tempted to stall them on the front steps and not let them in, but I bowed to the inevitable.

"Hello," said the taller of the two women. A rail-thin redhead, she stuck out an expensively manicured hand with ridiculously long, red nails. "What on earth has happened to Iva Jean? Did she have a heart attack? We saw the ambulance and all the flashing lights. I'm Claudia Hood. You're Iva Jean's friend Ernie, aren't you? She's always talking about you. I'm afraid the last time we saw you was at poor Martha Lee's funeral." She nodded at the shorter, brunette version of herself who stood, in more ways than one, in her shadow. "This is Mayrene Lanier."

Mayrene Lanier chirped a greeting, and I followed as the two women marched right into Iva Jean's living room. The fact that both women, who were around my age, were far too old and far too thin to carry off such tight-fitting clothes aroused my sense of the ridiculous, mixed with a bit of pity. Who on earth were they trying to please? With no hips and no busts to speak of, and birdlike legs, the women looked like pipe-cleaner dolls draped in expensive and inappropriate clothes. If I wasn't careful, I'd start laughing and wouldn't be able to stop.

I quickly explained that I had arrived to find Iva Jean unexpectedly dead. I skimped on the details, though they both seemed disappointed.

"Poor Iva Jean," Claudia intoned, shaking her head back and forth. "The poor dear was just so upset by Martha Lee's tragic accident. Maybe her poor heart just finally gave out from all the tragedy. Don't you think so, Mayrene?"

Mayrene chimed in that poor Iva Jean had indeed been awful sad lately. I had the feeling that if Claudia claimed that the Pope was actually a black lesbian nun, Mayrene would agree.

I didn't want to argue over the facts of Iva Jean's death. I'd hold my suspicions until later, when I could talk to someone with some actual sense.

"Yes, poor Iva Jean's been having the oddest notions lately. Wouldn't you say so, Mayrene?" Claudia said.

Mayrene allowed as how Iva Jean truly had been having some odd notions lately.

"Such as what?" That lobotomies would raise your collective IQs about a thousand percent, I thought.

Claudia laughed, and Mayrene tittered. "Well, it's not really funny. It's sad, really, but poor Iva Jean! I mean, Mayrene and I were both widowed three months ago when our husbands died tragically and unexpectedly in a boating accident." Claudia managed to look seriously grieved for about three seconds. "And I do swear that poor Iva Jean thought that Mayrene and I had something to do with that ol' boat engine blowing up like that." Claudia fixed me with a gimlet gaze. "Have you ever heard tell of such?"

Noting how underwhelmed with emotion the two ghastly windows seemed to be, I decided I'd have to side with Iva Jean on this one.

Since Claudia was for once expecting a response from

me, rather than from Mayrene, I said wryly, "Imagine that!"

Claudia nodded. "I know, isn't it sad? Poor Iva Jean. When Mayrene and I win our lawsuit against the heinous manufacturers of that engine, we're going on a round-the-world cruise. And we wanted poor Iva Jean to go with us. We would even have paid her way, wouldn't we, Mayrene?" And of course Mayrene nodded emphatically.

If I heard the words *poor Iva Jean* once more out of Claudia's mouth, someone might have to come bail me out of jail. "Well, ladies," I said briskly, "I'm sure you won't mind excusing me. This has all been a terrible strain, and I've got a number of things that I really must do."

Neither Claudia nor Mayrene seemed inclined to offer to help me with any of my tasks, and after casting avid glances around the living room one last time, they wandered back to the front door. I locked the door gratefully behind them.

Gemma looked up at me, and I'd swear the dog grinned. For once we were on the same side. Good riddance to those terrible women, Gemma seemed to say.

I walked back to the kitchen and poured myself another cup of coffee. There were some old friends from Iva Jean's youth whom I needed to call, but no family that I could remember. I put off those calls for the time being. Instead I got out my address book and looked up the phone number of an old flame, who just happened to be the current commissioner of public safety in Mississippi.

Twenty minutes later I had the assurances of my dear friend that the autopsy on Iva Jean would be given top priority, and that I would know the results as soon as pos-

sible. My hand trembled as I hung up the phone. I dreaded
the results. I was sure I was right, that Iva Jean's death was
no accident. But, at the same time, I was puzzled. Who
would have reason to murder her?

I had just fed Gemma when the doorbell rang. Sighing
heavily, I stomped toward the front door, determined to
tell Claudia Hood off, if she had the nerve to bother me
again. I looked out the peephole and recognized, with
gratitude, a friendly face. I opened the door.

"Rosellen, how are you?"

The plump figure standing in the doorway belonged to
Iva Jean's next-door neighbor, Rosellen Martin. Stylishly
dressed, elegant in every way, Rosellen was a delightful
antidote to the two who had been here earlier. She held a
canvas book bag in one hand and flowers in the other.

Rosellen beamed at me as she came inside. "Ernie,
I thought that was your Jeep in the driveway! How are
you? And what a pleasant surprise! I know Iva Jean is
thrilled to have you here." She stepped past me toward the
dining room. "Iva Jean! I've got the flowers you wanted.
Oh, hi, Gemma," she said with a marked decrease in
enthusiasm. "I don't know how she puts up with this creature," Rosellen whispered while I stood stricken.

Finally Rosellen noticed my face. "Oh, dear, Ernie,
whatever is the matter?"

"Rosellen, have you not been at home this afternoon?" I
asked weakly.

"No, dear, I just got back about five minutes ago from
shopping and running some errands. I stopped off to bring
Iva Jean the flowers she wanted. Whatever is the matter?
You're white as a sheet!"

I drew Rosellen back toward the kitchen. "I'm afraid

I've got some bad news." I made her wait until she was sitting at the table before I told her. Her face immediately crumpled, and she started to cry. I reached across the table and clasped her hands in mine. I joined her, and we both cried for a while.

"First my dear sweet Billy, and now Iva Jean. I can't stand this! And I just can't believe she would do that to herself," Rosellen said for the fourth or fifth time, and I agreed with her yet again. Rosellen's husband of forty years, Billy, had died just two months ago. This neighborhood seemed tough on husbands recently. No wonder Iva Jean was suspicious of Claudia and Mayrene.

"But what could it be, otherwise?" Rosellen asked. "Surely it wasn't an accident? I mean, could she have accidentally poison herself?"

"No, I don't think so," I said. "Do you know if she was taking any new medication for anything?"

Rosellen shook her head. "Not as far as I know. You know how she was. She wouldn't even take tranquilizers after Martha Lee died, and she was in such good health. I think she took an aspirin every once in a while, but that was all."

"That's what I thought," I said. "So I don't know what the answer is. Except that I'm afraid someone may have helped her along out of this world."

"Murder!" Rosellen whispered in shock. "Oh, dear Lord! Who would want to murder Iva Jean? And why?"

"I don't know, Rosellen, but I aim to find out."

"If there's anything I can do, you just let me know."

I hesitated. Rosellen's late husband, Billy, had been Iva Jean's lawyer, and if anyone knew much about Iva Jean's new lawyer, Rosellen would. "What can you tell me about Harlan Carr?"

Startled, Rosellen stared at me. "What has he got to do with anything?"

I explained the circumstances of my meeting him today.

Rosellen frowned. "Well, I think, after Billy died, Harlan took on some of his special clients. Harlan only bought into the firm about three months ago. I think Iva Jean said something about needing to amend her will, and she went downtown to the office a couple of days ago." Rosellen shrugged, her face shadowed with sadness. "To tell the truth, since Billy died, I haven't paid much attention to what's going on at the firm. Lately I just don't care." She frowned. "I know Iva Jean was kinda curious about Harlan Carr, but I told her as far as I knew, he was a good lawyer. He used to be with a big firm in Mobile."

I laughed a bit sourly. "I'm glad to know he's who he claims to be. He sure startled me, I can tell you." Frankly, I was more than a bit suspicious of him, but there wouldn't be much purpose in my telling Rosellen that at the moment. I'd bide my time.

Rosellen stood up, blowing her nose on a sodden handkerchief. "Ernie, I really had better get home. I'm still in such shock over poor Iva Jean, I don't know what to do." She looked down at the flowers she had brought in with her, now lying forlornly on the table. "Oh, dear, I brought these for her."

"I'll put them in a vase, don't worry." I assured her. She didn't seem to want to take them with her.

"Oh, and I almost forgot," Rosellen said, stooping down to pick up the canvas bag she'd brought, which she had dumped on the floor beside her chair. She pulled out two medium-size, leather-bound books.

"What are those?" I asked, though I thought I recognized them.

"They're two of Iva Jean's scrapbooks," Rosellen said. She grimaced. "I was over here yesterday, collecting books and other stuff for our church rummage sale, and these somehow got mixed in with the books Iva Jean gave me. I discovered them this afternoon when I dropped my stuff off at the church. I knew Iva Jean would have a fit if something happened to them." Then it hit her all over again, and she started to cry.

I walked her to the door, a consoling arm around her shoulders, trying not to cry myself. I promised to call her the next day, as soon as I had more information about Iva Jean's funeral, and so on. Gemma, who had been amazingly quiet during Rosellen's visit, started whimpering when I closed the door behind my latest visitor.

I knelt down on the floor, and Gemma stared into my face. I know most people would think I was crazy, but I talked to her for a good ten minutes, telling her about Iva Jean's death and promising that someone would look after her. I don't know about the damned dog, but I felt a little better, even though my knees were sore as the dickens by the time I talked myself out.

Back in the kitchen, I picked up Iva Jean's scrapbooks and carried them upstairs to the guest room I always stayed in. Gemma shadowed me. I hadn't wanted to say anything to Rosellen, but I thought I might find a clue to Iva Jean's death in her scrapbooks. She had been keeping them for as long as I'd known her. The oddest things would catch Iva Jean's attention. The world had surely missed an entertaining storyteller in Iva Jean, because she never got around to writing anything. What she might have made of such interesting tidbits as two of the clippings I found on one page: TRUCK DRIVER SUES BANK IN SPERM SCAM and HOUSEWIFE DISCOVERS IMAGE OF JESUS ON HER KITCHEN FLOOR were typical.

Iva Jean had also clipped items about people she knew. I turned a page and found obituaries for Alexander Hood and Clifford Lanier. According to the obituaries, and the accompanying news items I found on subsequent pages, the recently departed husbands of Claudia and Mayrene had been business partners who were both killed in a boating accident on Ross Barnett Reservoir. They had been out fishing on a Sunday afternoon three months ago when an engine malfunction had caused their boat to explode. Another article on the accident mentioned briefly that counsel for the two bereaved widows, Harlan Carr of Martin, Hubble, and Carr, was seeking unspecified damages from the makers of the boat's engine.

Claudia and Mayrene didn't have much about them that bespoke grief when I had seen them earlier. That might be my own antipathy to the two speaking, however. Maybe both men had been jerks and their wives were happy to be shed of them. Nothing odd about that.

But I delighted in speculating that Claudia and Mayrene had somehow helped that boat engine to its timely explosion, ridding the women of two philandering husbands. Maybe the guys had wised up and were getting ready to dump the terrible two, but Claudia and Mayrene struck first. Iva Jean had suspected foul play, Claudia found out somehow, and she had slipped something to Iva Jean, making it look like Iva Jean had killed herself.

Lost in admiration for my theory, I hadn't noticed that Gemma had disappeared from the room. Suddenly the Devil Dog hopped back up on the bed, holding another prize in her mouth.

"What is it this time, you beast?" I held out my hand, and Gemma cocked her head sideways, giving me a self-satisfied grin. "What have you brought me?" I coaxed, and finally Gemma yielded up her prize. This time it was a compact, the shiny plastic surface marred with numerous tooth marks. I opened it cautiously. It was a marvel Gemma hadn't managed to get it open and lick out all the powder inside. Though surely the taste would have discouraged even her.

"Thank you, Gemma," I told her. "Yes, you're a wonderful dog." I laid the compact aside and patted the Devil Dog on the head. "Now settle down, you little idiot, and let me read." Gemma made a circle or two on the bed, and, wonder of wonders, actually curled up for a nap.

I didn't think my luck would hold for long, so I picked up the scrapbook and started where I had left off.

A few pages after the articles on the deceased husbands, I found a clipping of a picture of a newly familiar face from the society pages. Closer scrutiny revealed that Harlan Carr and his lovely wife Antoinette had been the sponsors of a charity ball benefitting the burn unit at the University Hospital. The article was dated two months ago. Harlan Carr certainly had a beautiful wife, and they made a handsome couple. The lawyer's somewhat arrogant visage was softened a bit by the blurred newsprint, but some of his personality came through nevertheless. Out beside the clipping, Iva Jean had scribbled something in her tiny, crabbed handwriting, and I squinted, trying to decipher it. There was a squiggle that could possibly be a question mark, and beside it some numbers: 1970, I thought. What on earth could it mean? There was something about that year I ought to remember, but what was it?

With a sense of dreadful certainty, I laid the scrapbook down and picked up the second one that Rosellen had brought back. I knew, without a doubt, that the answer I wanted was inside. And the memories came flooding back as I opened the book and began looking through its yellowed clippings.

Near the back, I found a brief article: LOCAL YOUTH SOUGHT IN RAPE CASE. The article came from a paper in San Antonio, where Iva Jean and her husband had then lived, just before Jasper Delancey had retired from the air force.

Nineteen seventy was the year in which Iva Jean's only child, Jeannette, had been raped by a boy she had dated once. The boy was the son of a colonel, and he had disappeared shortly after Jeannette had finally decided to talk to the authorities on base. The young man, whose name was Arthur Graham, according to the clipping, had vanished without a trace.

The authorities had never been able to nab Arthur Graham. Jasper and Iva Jean had suspected the boy's father had been the one to help him escape from justice. Jeannette had been brutally treated, and the physical evidence left little question that she had been raped. Jasper retired from the air force, moving his wife and now pregnant daughter back to Mississippi so they could get on with their lives as best they could. Martha Lee, that dear, fatherless child, had appeared nine months after the rape.

There was a grainy photo of young Arthur Graham along with the article. The newsprint had yellowed considerably after twenty-five years, and I sought something familiar in that boyishly handsome face. The hair in the picture looked dirty blonde, and of course there was no telling what color the eyes were, though they looked dark. But there was something about the tilt of the head and the sharpness of the nose that reminded me of someone. Had Iva Jean seen it, too?

I laid the scrapbook down, open to the picture of Arthur Graham, and I picked up the other scrapbook and searched for the photograph of Harlan Carr. Carr's hair was dark, almost black, but that could be the result of dye. The nose and the way he held his head were similar, I decided. It was just possible that Harlan Carr could be Arthur Graham, twenty-five years later. If so, what a shock it must have been for Iva Jean to have recognized her daughter's rapist, after all this time! And for him to have become her lawyer, too.

I couldn't say why, but I knew I had stumbled on the answer, the way Iva Jean must have. Harlan Carr had seemed hauntingly familiar to her, and I know how horrified she must have been when she realized why.

I lay awake a long time that night, trying to figure out what to do. When the phone woke me at seven the next morning, I was bleary-eyed and headachy. But I had a plan but no real evidence. Thanks to my good friend, and his influence over the state crime lab, I knew now that Iva Jean had died from an overdose of digitoxin. I was sure her doctor would tell me that he hadn't prescribed it for her when I called him later.

I looked up from the coffeemaker to see Gemma standing on a chair, snatching a cheese roll from the plate I had just taken out of the microwave.

"Damn dog," I muttered, grabbing the plate away and trying to shoo Gemma down from the chair. Gemma just grinned up at me around the roll in her mouth, and I turned away in disgust to set my slobbery plate out of Gemma's reach in the sink. When I looked back, Gemma was disappearing onto the service porch with a new victim—my address book—in her mouth.

Cussing loudly, I scrambled after her. The dratted animal had disappeared behind the washing machine. There was enough room along one side for Gemma to squeeze by, and from what I could see, there was enough space behind the washing machine for Gemma to have a hidey-hole.

I returned to the kitchen and retrieved a flashlight from the pantry. I shone the light behind the washing machine, and Gemma peered up at me anxiously, her tail stirring up a bit of dust. There was nothing for it but to move the washing machine and get behind it. Gemma wasn't coming out, at least not with my address book, and the good Lord only knew what else Gemma might have squirreled away.

I'm tall and strong, so it took me only a minute or so to move the washing machine far enough out so that I could squeeze behind it and investigate Gemma's hiding place. For once, Gemma had decided that retreat was the order of the day, and she scampered away without taking any of her prizes with her. I picked up my address book, hoping the pages weren't sticking together, wiping the excess dog spit on my jeans. I shone the light on the rest of Gemma's collection.

A pill bottle. Aha! I thought. I fumbled in my pocket for a hanky and used it to pick up the bottle.

My hands trembled as I turned the bottle to read the label. This would tell me one way or another. I started laughing in relief.

Thanks to the Hell Hound, I held in my hand the evidence I'd need to link Harlan Carr to Iva Jean's murder.

I put my plan into action. I made more phone calls, one to another old-and-dear friend, who just happened to be a member of the state Supreme Court and who was well connected enough to get me the information I wanted very quickly. The second call was to Harlan Carr's office. In my best girlishly pleading voice, I persuaded him to come to Iva Jean's house that afternoon to talk to me about the arrangements for Iva Jean's funeral. I promised him some of my famous chocolate cake, and with an audibly patronizing note in his voice, he agreed.

I ran my errands quickly, getting the supplies I needed for my baking, and by lunchtime my friend the Supreme Court judge had given me all the information I needed. Everything was falling neatly into place.

When Harlan Carr rang the doorbell at three o'clock, I was ready. I didn't quite do the Barbara Billingsley "Mrs. Cleaver" routine, but I came damn close. I apologized for my display of ill manners the day before, simpering for all I was worth. And the fool bought every word of it. Sometimes you wonder how men that stupid ever get anywhere in life. But fortunately it works to a woman's advantage sometimes.

Harlan Carr seemed to like my recipe for chocolate cake. He ate three big slices and washed them down with several cups of hot tea. I kept him talking for over half an hour, seeking his opinion on the funeral arrangements, batting my eyelashes a lot, and listening to seemingly endless explanations of my duties as an "executrix," as he insisted on calling me.

Finally, I judged the timing was about right. He was starting to sweat a little. I interrupted yet another pomposity.

"By the way, Harlan," I smiled, "I discovered something terribly interesting about you!"

"And what is that?" he smiled back, those perfect teeth a little stained with chocolate cake. I swear if he'd been a cat he would have been purring with satisfaction.

"I discovered, after talking to an old-and-dear friend"— here I named the Supreme Court judge, and Carr's eyes almost bugged out—"that no one in Jackson knows much about you or where you came from." I smiled as I sipped at my tea. "In fact, no one can trace you any further back than about twenty-five years ago. Say, to about 1970. Now, isn't that interesting?"

His face was flushing, and I could hear his stomach rumbling a bit. Good. I had timed this well after all. He opened his mouth to say something, but I held up a hand.

"And the other thing I find so interesting about you is that such a young and attractive man as you should have to take heart medication." I shook my head pityingly. "That's such a shame, at your age. To have to worry about a dicky heart. And you know, too much digitoxin can really be bad for you, especially when it hasn't been prescribed for you. Right, Arthur?"

By now his face had turned green. He tried to lunge for me, but he decided he'd better head for the bathroom instead. "You know, they say that too many laxatives can put a severe strain on your heart. And with your heart problems, I certainly hope you haven't had too much!" He was in too much of a hurry to do much more than curse in frustration as he fumbled at the door of the bathroom. I'd considered locking it, but that would have been too cruel, I'd decided.

I laughed and picked up my cell phone, which I'd stowed nearby. I punched in 9-1-1 and calmly announced to the operator that I had a murderer in my bathroom and could they please send someone to pick him up.

I couldn't bring Iva Jean back, but I knew she'd appreciate my efforts in nailing her killer. And Gemma would have as much steak to eat as she could manage for the rest of her life.

Like Alpo for Chocolate: A Short Story in Fragrances

Steven Womack

STEVEN WOMACK is the author of the Harry Denton series, the first of which, *Dead Folks' Blues*, won the Edgar Award for best Paperback Original. All the subsequent Harry Denton novels have also been nominated for major crime fiction awards. A screenwriter as well as a novelist, Womack co-wrote the screenplays for *Proudheart*, which was nominated for a Cable Ace Award, and for the ABC-TV movie *Volcano: Fire on the Mountain*. Womack's private eye novels are set in the mean streets of Nashville, but his love of four-pawed creatures—or at least an ailing German shepherd watchdog—permeates "Like Alpo for Chocolate."

Don't get me wrong. I like Alpo.

Really.

I mean, I'm crazy about Alpo. I can't figure out why people don't eat it. But c'mon, let's face it—they don't.

I like chocolate better. I mean, I know it's chocolate because that's what The Thin One calls it. I don't know what it means, but it's good.

Okay, I've heard it all, especially from The Thin One with the long fur the color of dried grass, the one that goes into heat every time the moon changes. Whenever the heat comes on her, she gets crazy for chocolate. I can smell it coming through her, that and a few other things that put me in mind of something, but I can't remember quite what.

Anyway, she's the one that keeps telling me chocolate's not good for me. But I smell it and go into the big room where the fire is and she's sitting on this soft thing that I like to sleep on when no one's looking. And her eyes are all red and she's got the heat smell on her and chocolate, little pieces of it inside this thing on her lap. I can tell she's eaten a lot; it oozes out of her. I can smell it down the hall.

She stares at the big box across the room, the one that has the funny colors inside it and the loud noises I hate. She eats chocolate and stares at the noises, and water runs out of her eyes. All I have to do is sit in front of her and drop my head a little and look at her for a few moments. I'm nearly eye level with her, and she tries to pretend she's looking over my shoulder at the noises.

"Move, Swatch," she says. Then her mouth curls upward and I see her teeth, all shiny with brown water from eating the chocolate.

"C'mon, Swatch," she says. "Move."

Now I know *sit* and *heel* and I think I know *stay*, but I don't know this move stuff. So I focus on the chocolate. And pretty soon, my mouth starts dripping.

"C'mon, baby," she says.

Does this mean I get chocolate? When? Now?

"I know, sweetie," she says. And her eyes puff up and get all redder and more water comes out of them and she reaches over with her paw and scratches behind my ears and something down between my back legs starts jerking and my paw scrapes across the wood floor.

"Even big ol' babies like you need a treat every once in a while," she says. Her nose is running now and her face is all wet and she digs around inside the white thing on her lap and pulls out a brown lump.

"Speak," she says. "C'mon, you big ol' mastiff baby you, speak."

Speak I get, so I pull a great big rumbling one from down deep in my gut and let it roll around for a while and then bring it up and out of me so loud it echoes down the long hallway. And The Thin One's mouth curves up again and this funny, happy sound comes out of her mouth, past the water on her face, and she holds out the chocolate and pops it into my mouth.

It explodes there, sweet chocolate all inside me, running down the sides of my face, in my fur. And my eyes roll back and everything gets real fuzzy and I go limp all over and hit the floor, real hard. Hard enough to shake The Thin One.

"Heavens, Swatch," she says. "You're going to have to lose weight."

By then, I don't even try to figure it out. My left hind leg shakes a little more, the fire behind me is warm on my back, and I drift off.

Life is good.

In the field behind the big house there are clumps of trees, little thickets dotting the rolling hills where the grass grows so high the big metal monster that scares even me has to come in the hot time and cut it all down. And in my dream, I'm a pup again with my three brothers and two sisters that I can't even remember anymore except in my dreams, running over the hills just as the light's going away and there's a small herd of deer just coming out of the largest thicket. And we split up, half of us going around one side of the thicket, half the other. We catch the deer from both sides and they break ahead, their white tails high as they run like crazy, their legs like springs as they head for the fences. And we're right on them, my brothers and sisters and me, and my heart's pounding and my lungs ache and it's glorious. . . .

And then there's a *boom*, a sharp jerking noise that brings me out of the dream and snaps me wide-awake. I spin my head around. I'm alone in the room, except for The Fear. I can smell it, smell it like heat on The Thin One, like chocolate on my paws, like smoldering ashes in the place where they make the fire.

Fear.

Then I see the light's gone outside and I remember: it's The Mean One. Yeah, I remember. Sometimes it's easy to forget, but he always comes back. He smells bad, like fear and sour and sweat all mixed together.

When The Mean One is here, The Thin One shakes a lot and her sounds change. She smells different, too, like all her muscles are tight, like The Fear is practically squirting out of her.

There is bad stuff in the air. I know it before I'm even awake.

So I pull myself up, which when you're my size and my age is quite an achievement. I make sure I've got my balance and trot into the kitchen, where The Mean One is in The Thin One's face.

"Damn it," he yells. "Why not?"

She starts to say something, but his noise jumps on her noise and it goes away, and she brings her paws up to her face and hides it and I see the water coming through. The Thin One makes a lot of water.

The Mean One turns to me and his eyes are fire.

"Didn't I tell you to keep that goddamn thing out in the yard?"

You talking to me? Where's dinner?

He starts toward me and I lower my head and, without my even meaning to, this low rumble comes out of my gut. He stops cold, staring. He knows better. I don't like him; he smells bad and there's no fur on top of his head.

"Stop it, Gene," The Thin One begs. I know begging.

"Don't growl at me, you son-of-a-bitch. I'll shoot your ass deader'n hell."

"Gene, don't!"

"Then get his fat, ugly ass out of here! And make yourself useful. Get me some damn dinner."

The Thin One comes over to me, grabs my collar, starts tugging.

"C'mon, Swatch," she whispers. "C'mon, boy, let's go outside."

So she pulls me until I take my eyes off The Mean One, but I keep my ears perked in case he comes up behind me. The Thin One opens the door and pushes me out onto the deck, the deck that looks out onto the fields. Down in the thickets, I can smell the deer. The wind carries their smell up to the house.

I don't go after them, though. Through the wall you can see through, The Thin One walks up to The Mean One. She says something; he says something. And then his face gets all dark and maybe red and then he reaches out and grabs her. She tries to get away from him, but he's got her around the throat. I jump up on the wall and howl.

He lifts her off the floor, her back legs dancing in the air, then slams her down on the big thing that sits in the middle of the kitchen floor, the thing with the doors and the hole where you get water for the dry stuff she puts in with the Alpo. He's over her now, kind of on top of her, with his paws still around her neck. Her back legs kick out level, banging off the wooden doors on the wall behind her. They're both shaking and bouncing and straining against each other.

And then her kicks get slower and slower, until finally they quit. I lean against the wall, watching them, as The Mean One climbs off her. He stands there looking down at her, the two of them motionless, her back legs hanging limply down. Then he turns and looks at me. My eyes meet his and I roar at him. He turns away.

It gets dark and cold outside. I'm pacing back and forth on the deck, trying to remember why I'm so upset. Something bad's happened and I'm getting hungry. There's a noise around the side of the house and I race around to investigate. The Mean One walks around from the front, the green bottle in his paw like it is every night, a lantern glowing brightly in his other paw, and he goes over to the shed where I sleep when it gets real cold. He goes in, then comes out with this long wooden thing over his shoulder. On the end of the wooden thing, there's dirty metal. He crosses by me, as I stand near the corner of the house, and walks down the incline toward the thicket.

I take a deep breath and let loose with a low rumbling bark. After all, I'm hungry. Guy my size needs his Alpo. The Mean One turns.

"Shut up, you miserable mongrel," he growls back at me. I lift my leg, pee on his favorite deck chair. That'll show him.

I watch as he walks down until he's just a speck of light in the dark. And then he disappears in the thicket.

I turn, look back into the room, searching for The Thin One.

It's okay, he's gone now. You can come out, feed me!

Only The Thin One doesn't hear me. I can't even see her anymore. Where'd she go? Who'll get my Alpo?

I'm suddenly very sad. I settle on the deck and start drifting again, the only distraction the rumbling in my tummy.

I hear a scraping sound away from me and jump up, run to the side of the house. The Mean One's in my shed again, digging around in my stuff. Some nerve. And then he comes out with my blanket wadded up under his arm.

Oh, great, and what am I supposed to sleep on? Not to mention my Alpo. . . . Where's my Alpo, anyway? I mean, who's running this show?

"Out of my way," he mutters as he passes by. I don't know what that means, so he kicks out at me and I back away. I'd tear his head off, except maybe if I'm nice to him, he'll feed me.

The Mean One disappears into the house again and is gone, like forever or something. It doesn't take long to be forever when you're hungry.

Finally, I see him in the big room again. He's got something slung over his shoulder, something all wrapped up. I can't tell what it is, but as he comes into the light I see that it's my blanket it's wrapped up in. I cock my head sideways, trying to figure this out, without much luck.

He slides open the door you can see through and trudges out onto the deck. He's huffing and puffing now and I can smell the sweat coming off him. I step closer to check it out and then, wham, it's like being hit in the nose with something so powerful it nearly knocks you over.

I don't know what The Mean One's carrying, but it's about a dozen different smells all rolled into one powerful slug—chocolate, sweat, fear, pee, dump, the heat smell, and one I haven't felt in a long time, not since I came on the fresh kill the coyotes had taken down way out in the woods. Not this strong anyway. What is it? I take a deeper whiff, steeling myself for the punch, determined to check it out. Then I remember.

Whatever it is, it's not going to move anymore. Pretty soon, it's going to smell real bad.

It might taste pretty good, though. Maybe some possibilities here? It is getting late, you know, and I am hungry.

The Mean One picks up the light again with his free paw and heads down the slope toward the thicket. This time I decide to follow, but I stay behind so he can't kick me. All the time the thing on his shoulder bounces up and down, up and down. . . .

He enters the woods and weaves his way along the deer trail, to a place in the center where water comes bubbling up out of the ground and pools among some rocks. I smell all the things that have been drinking here: deer, other dogs, a bobcat, several skunks, and even my own smell. Somebody's peed in the water recently. Better cover that up, thinks I, so I lift a leg and take care of it.

A few feet beyond the water, The Mean One stops. He

drops the bundle on the ground, then shifts it around and straightens it out. Then he takes his back paw and kicks at the bundle and it rolls over and disappears. I jerk my head, trying to focus. Where'd it go? I mean, it's just gone, like one of my bones.

Then I get it. He's coming back to eat it later. That's it, of course. I should've guessed. I understand now.

Maybe we'll share it. I'm kind of hungry, you know. Been a while since my last Alpo.

The Mean One takes the wooden thing and starts dumping dirt back on his bone. He moves a lot of dirt before he's finished, and then he stomps around packing the dirt down real hard. Then he pulls off a bunch of pine branches and swishes them around on the ground. Finally, he tosses the branches down and walks away past me. I stand there until it's quiet.

So I'm thinking: dinner? Whatever it is, I can probably dig it back up before I get too hungry. On the other hand, Alpo's better than coyote take-down. Think I'll take my chances on The Mean One.

"Swatch! Get up here, boy! Dinnertime!"

That gets my attention. I lope off out of the woods and see him on the deck, holding my bowl. He sets it down in front of me.

"Go ahead, big boy. Eat."

You don't have to tell me twice.

I dig in, my nose pulling in that wonderful Alpo smell. Nothing like fresh Alpo, especially this batch. It's sweet kind of, and a little runnier than usual. I like it. It's not chocolate mind you, but it'll do. I snarf it down like the big dog I am, then trot off to my shed for a good night's sleep.

* * *

It's still dark when I wake up to this terrible rumbling in my gut, like I've got to take the power dump of all time. I scramble up off the floor and fall back down. I don't know what this is, but it's like everything's spinning around. And suddenly, everything in my gut comes out both ends and I'm heaving and coughing and shaking. Then it quiets.

No way I'm sleeping here, thinks I, so I step out into the yard. Everything's quiet, nothing's moving. I gotta pee, so I trot over to the bushes next to the house and lift a leg. Only nothing happens. I squeeze again, lift that leg a little higher.

Nothing.

Later maybe. In the meantime, I ought to be hungry for some Alpo, only the instant I think about it, I'm heaving into the bushes again. There's nothing left inside me, though, just these rib-cracking spasms that go on until I'm exhausted and fall down breathless.

It's light again and I hear something. Something's pounding inside my head and it's kind of hard to breathe. I still have to pee, but nothing's happening. It's starting to hurt, too, like the time I lifted a leg on that bush and got a thorn in me. Talk about embarrassing.

And what's that noise? It's like those noises they make, The Thin One and The Mean One, only the noises are different from any before. There's a strange smell wafting around the corner, too. Something weird.

I pull myself up on my legs and realize I'm sore all over. It hurts to move, but my curiosity's got the better of me. So I limp around the corner and there's another of those damn things I used to chase when I was younger. Only this one's got all kinds of metal and lights on it. And two Thin Ones dressed the same way standing next to it, talking to The Mean One on the porch.

"I don't care what that old biddy said," The Mean One says. "My wife's been gone for days. She must have heard the TV last night. I was watching a movie."

One of the Thin Ones turns my way. I'm limping in his direction, but can barely stay up straight. He smiles, squats down, holds out a paw to me.

"Hey, fella, c'mere." That part I get. I feel a good ear scratch coming.

"Careful," The Mean One says. "He bites."

I look up at him.

Bite? If I bit, you'd be history now, bud.

I stumble over the settle in front of The Thin One. My eyes feel heavy.

"He doesn't look too fierce," The Thin One says, scratching my ears. He's good; he's done this before. In fact, I can smell another me on him.

"Guess he's too old to bite anymore," The Mean One says.

"Doesn't look that old," The Thin Ones says. "He does look kind of sick, though."

"C'mon, partner, can we finish up here?" the other Thin One says.

"Yes, officers," The Mean One answers. "I have to get to work."

Good ear scratching, I'm getting. I try to wag my tail, but it's too heavy.

"A mastiff, isn't he?" the Ear Scratching Thin One says. "Haven't seen one of these in a long time. Noble animal."

"Officer, I really need to get to work."

"Huge appetites, too."

"Part of the reason I need to get to work."

The Thin One scratching my ears cups my jaw and lifts my head. "This animal's very sick," he says.

I have no idea what that means, but this one feels good. And there's something coming off him that smells really good. If I could just place it.

He leans down in my face, gets real close to my eyes. Then he looks up toward the porch.

"What's the matter with this dog?" His noises are lower now, more threatening, almost a growl.

"Nothing, officer, he's just old."

The Thin One runs a finger across my fur, just at my lower jawline, then holds his paw up to his face and sniffs it.

That's when it hit me—chocolate. This one's got chocolate on him somewhere. Wonder if he'll share.

"You let this dog sleep in the garage, sir?"

"Don't have a garage," The Mean One snaps. He's getting tense now; I can smell it.

"Basement? Place where you work on cars?"

The other Thin One looks down at us. "What are you up to, Glenn?"

The Ear Scratching Thin One stands up. "I was just wondering how a dog like this could get into enough antifreeze to make him this sick. Dog this size needs more than a puddle on a garage floor."

The two Thin Ones look at The Mean One.

"What the hell are you talking about?"

"Care to answer my partner's question, sir?"

"Officer, if you're insinuating that I would—"

"Did you feed glycol coolant to this dog, sir?"

I don't know what the noises mean, but suddenly I'm

very thirsty. And if I could get some water down, maybe I could pee.

I pull myself to my feet and turn around, then start stumbling around the edge of the house. Behind me, I hear the Ear Scratching Thin One.

"Hey, boy! Where you going?"

Then pawsteps behind me.

"Swatch! Get back here." It's The Mean One. "Swatch, heel!"

But I'm thirsty and I want good water, not that warm stuff with the dead bugs in it that's been sitting on the deck for as long as I can remember. So I head down the field, ignoring The Mean One.

"Partner, if I didn't know better, I'd say that dog was trying to take us somewhere."

"Swatch! Heel!" There's fear in his noise now. I can smell it.

"Damn you, Swatch! I'm gonna kick your ass, you dumb dog!"

"You're not going to do anything of the sort, sir. And if it turns out you've poisoned that dog, then we're talking cruelty to animals here. That's a misdemeanor in this state."

I neither know nor care what these noises mean. But something inside me is screaming for water, even more than chocolate or Alpo, and I've got to get to that water that comes up out of the ground, that water that's so cold and so good.

And then I want a nap. A nice, long nap in the sun.

I enter the thicket right at the deer trail and wind my way through the woods. Behind me, there is yelling and the crashing of limbs and it feels like some kind of fight's going on. I ain't got a dog in that fight, though, so I head on to the water.

And there it is. . . .

I fall at the water and stick my head in, lapping it up and sucking it down as fast as I can. It's the best thing I've ever put in my mouth, which is saying something. I drink until I can't hold anymore, then turn to the commotion behind me.

The Mean One's sweating and panting and crying now. The Ear Scratching Thin One is down on the ground, squatting over dirt, poking around with his paw. The other Thin One is pulling The Mean One's paws behind him.

"Looks like we got us a freshly dug grave here, partner," the Ear Scratcher says.

"Looks like your buddy here knew where to take us."

The Ear Scratcher looks at me, his lips curling up, showing his teeth. "Smart doggie," he says. "Good doggie."

Then he steps over to me, leans down, does my ears again.

"Good boy," he says. Behind him, The Mean One is making this bubbling, gurgling noise and his face is all wet from his eyes and stuff from his nose and mouth. He's shaking and swaying back and forth. I take a whiff; yep, he's dumped himself.

"You think he'll be okay?" the other Thin One asks.

"Let's get him to the vet and find out." Then he looks down at me. "You want to take a ride, boy? C'mon, let's go see the doc."

I stand up, feeling a little better, and trot over to the closest tree and lift my leg. This time, everything works like it's supposed to.

"Good boy," the Ear Scratcher says. "C'mon, boy. Let's go. Let's take a ride."

I know ride. I know vet. Lots of good ear scratches there.

"C'mon boy," the Ear Scratcher says. I like this one, so I trot along next to him as he walks. I sniff his leg.

Yep, chocolate.

You'll Never Bark in This Town Again

Melissa Cleary

MELISSA CLEARY'S novels, beginning with *A Tail of Two Murders*, feature Jackie Walsh, a college film instructor, and her shepherd (in several senses), Jake. Jake is a former police dog, whose impeccable training is on full display in "You'll Never Bark in This Town Again."

Jackie Walsh stared out the window of Rena Crocker's lavishly appointed Land Rover and thought if she ever became half of a world-famous animal training team for the motion picture industry and could afford a vacation cabin, she'd make sure it was either convenient to an airport or fewer than seven hours' drive from Los Angeles. But then, Jackie supposed, vacationing in a place like that wouldn't exactly fall into the category of getting away from it all.

Jackie wasn't all that keen on getting away in general, preferring the urban Midwestern lifestyle she'd run back to after a stint in the suburbs. Not even her occasional involvement in criminal cases and some close brushes with murder and mayhem had ever made her think she belonged anywhere but downtown Palmer, Ohio.

On the other hand, Rena and Alan Crocker, of Crocker's Critters—a lively crew of trained dogs, cats, pigs, parrots, and assorted exotic animals—owned a forty-foot yacht, a sprawling ranch in the canyons of northeast Los Angeles County, and a two-story chalet at Bass Lake, a few miles from the exact geographic center of California. For them, getting away from it all was a way of life.

Jackie supposed she ought to be a bit more grateful to have been invited along on this minivacation, but the drive was proving long and tedious and the scenery even less interesting than the landscape along a similar Midwestern highway.

Seemingly oblivious to Jackie's boredom, Rena Crocker looked straight ahead through designer sunglasses, hummed along with the radio, and tapped her finger on the car's steering wheel as the big utility vehicle ate up the miles between the brown smudge of LA air in the rearview mirror and the flat plains of California's great central valley ahead.

"How are you doing back there, Jake?" Jackie looked over her shoulder and called back to her German shepherd, who took up most of the space behind the Land Rover's backseat. Jake wuffed softly in reply, and a moment later Jackie heard a high-pitched bark as a small brown-and-white head popped up under Jake's big black-and-tan one.

Any child between the ages of two and twelve would immediately have recognized the Crockers' famous and adored television star, Mack. A pampered but well-behaved Jack Russell terrier, Mack was known to children everywhere as the leading dog of *Mack Attack*, a weekly live-action comedy show now in its second season. He and Rena's husband Alan, a well-known animal trainer and the other human component of Crocker's Critters, had just completed shooting on the show's second season. After deciding that a long weekend at their cabin was called for, Rena had called Jackie in Palmer, Ohio.

"Jackie Walsh? Is that you, Jackie?" The voice on the phone had asked after Jackie picked it up. "This is Rena Crocker in Los Angeles."

"What an amazing coincidence," Jackie remarked. "I was just thinking of you."

"You were? That is amazing."

Jackie shrugged. "Not if you consider that fifteen minutes ago an express courier put an envelope in my hand containing a first-class round-trip plane ticket to LA, and that your name was on the return address portion of the envelope."

"Oh, bother. Alan was supposed to have called you last week and told you that you and Jake were invited to spend the week with us after we wrapped the season's shooting. You know I always promised I'd do something special for the two of you after Jake saved Mack from getting trampled by Bad Bob."

Bad Bob, a retired rodeo bull who lived on the Crockers' ranch, had taken a dislike to Mack during a Texas-style barbecue Alan and Rena had thrown while Jackie was in Hollywood writing a script the year before. Maybe it was the fact that Mack had wandered into his territory while looking for a place to bury a rib bone, or maybe it was only the obvious delight with which he had consumed the barbecued beef that had covered it, but something had raised the old bull's hackles, and he'd come charging across the pasture at the terrier. If Jake hadn't bumped Mack out of his way and gotten badly bruised for his troubles, the star of *Mack Attack* would probably have been little more than a damp spot on the earth of Bad Bob's corral. Bob had been removed to a more remote area of the ranch following the incident, and Jake had been promised a reward for saving Mack's life. As a former police service dog, Jake took this sort of heroism in stride, but the Crockers had insisted he deserved a reward.

"I don't know, Rena," Jackie began. "It's spring break, but I've got so much work to catch up with, and there's Peter . . ."

"Oh, come on, Jackie, your mom will be more than happy to look after Peter for a few days," Rena insisted. "You and Jake come on out and relax with us by the lake. You know I'm not going to take no for an answer."

Jackie had known she wasn't going to get out of this forced vacation, and now that she was here she would have been happy to start relaxing any time now, but they were still three hours out from the lake, somewhere south of Fresno and north of San Bernardino, where one mile of California's Highway 99 looked distressingly like the last and identical to the next.

"I'm sorry Alan wasn't able to make the drive with us," Jackie offered to Rena by way of conversation. Rena had been awfully quiet for Rena, since they had begun the trip that morning at the Crocker ranch.

"Oh, it's always something with Alan," Rena sighed. "I can't tell if he's depressed or just distracted. He hasn't been himself for months. But I'm glad he and Jules are at the meeting with the sponsor and the producers. Maybe they can finally work out those contract details."

Jules Berger was Alan and Rena's agent, or rather the agent who represented Crocker's Critters. Jackie knew him slightly from her days as a television writer in Los

Angeles. Jules was very tall, very blonde, and a very slick Hollywood operator with a reputation for making clients wealthy. Rena had fired their original agent when Jules had come to her with the idea of making a star of the Crockers' Jack Russell terrier and a proposal for *Mack Attack* that cinched them the series contract.

"I don't know what we'd have done without Jules," Rena said with a sigh. "He's completely changed our luck."

Mack's series was coming up for renewal, Alan and Rena had told her over dinner the night before, and Jackie wondered if their luck would hold, with or without Jules Berger. The Crockers wanted a guarantee of three more seasons, with a hefty salary increase for Mack, but the network was threatening to cancel the series. Mack's ratings were better than average, but the toys that had been licensed to accompany the series had been poorly designed, and toy sales had been disappointing.

"Unfortunately for us," Alan had told Jackie as he scratched his canine star behind his little tan ears, "that's where the real money is. Most people think the toys are a sideline item for the show, but the sad fact is that toys are the principal product for a children's series. It's the show that's the sideline. Isn't that right, Mack?"

Mack had barked agreement, sounding none too happy about it.

In addition, a major Hollywood studio was about to make an offer for a feature film, but that deal would be off if *Mack Attack* weren't renewed for a third season.

"Frankly, Jackie, we can't afford for that movie deal to fall through," Rena told her now.

"I've always assumed things were going pretty well for

you guys," Jackie said, a bit surprised at Rena's financial revelations. "I know times were tight for a couple of years there, but Mack's a big star now. . . ." She trailed off, uncertain how to phrase a remark about the terrier's earning power without sounding utterly crass in the process. She had known the Crockers casually for years, but didn't consider herself an intimate friend of the family.

"I'm afraid we're still pretty solidly in debt," Rena informed her. "Mack's salary from the first season went to back taxes, and we couldn't get the best deal on the initial contract. Mack was an unknown two years ago, and nobody expected *Mack Attack* to become such a monster hit with the kiddies. Then after the first season went so well, Alan took out a big insurance policy on Mack's life, and the premiums on that are not exactly small, let me tell you."

"Life insurance for a dog?"

"Well, Mack's not just any dog," Rena reminded her. "We've put a lot of time and expertise into training him to do all those tricks he does on television. Actually, the insurance policy was Jules's brainstorm. If anything happened to Mack, the earning power of Crocker's Critters would be right back in the hole where it was before Mack became successful."

Jackie supposed living the Crockers' Hollywood lifestyle was expensive compared to her own modest life as a film instructor at a private university. Still, she had once been a minor player on the Hollywood scene and had a rough idea what Mack and the rest of Crocker's Critters must be raking in, and she wondered. Well, it was none of her business anyway. Rena and Alan were providing a free vacation for Jackie and Jake, and Jackie's son Peter and

Jackie's mother had stocked Jackie's apartment with enough popcorn, frozen pizzas, and martial arts movies to see them through until Monday. It was time to take Rena's advice and relax.

The Land Rover turned off the two-lane road and up a steep paved driveway that led to a tall, cedar-sided, two-story cabin with chimneys on both ends. Jackie put the dogs outside in the fenced yard that ran around the back of the building, then carried her bag upstairs to one of the guest rooms. She explored the rest of the house at her leisure while Rena paced the living room floor and left message after message with the voicemail service. As Jackie stood in front of a tall window and watched Mack and Jake chasing one another up and down the fence line and rolling on the moist grass, she felt herself beginning to relax for the first time since she had woken up this morning.

A tiny explosion blew bark and dust from a tree not two feet from the dogs, and a fraction of a second later Jackie heard the sound of a gunshot. An instant after that, she realized what had happened and dashed for the door. Mack and Jake ran up and down the fence line, barking furiously. A second shot hit the dirt outside the fence, just inches from both dogs, and Jackie tried to pinpoint the direction of the report, but the sound echoed off the nearby hills, confusing her.

"Jake! Mack! Get in here—now!" Jackie shouted. Mack ran inside. Jake tried to jump the fence, but it was too high. "Jake!" Jackie called again. The big shepherd turned back toward her and, reluctantly, followed the smaller dog into the cabin.

Jackie slammed the door and locked it.

"What the hell was that?" Rena came around the corner into the living room. "It sounded like a gun!"

"I think someone was shooting at the dogs," said Jackie, heart pounding with fear, "and they didn't miss them by much, either."

"I'm calling the sheriff," said Rena.

"I wouldn't worry too much about it, Mrs. Crocker," the sheriff's deputy said, returning his notebook to his shirt pocket. "We get local boys up here trying to poach deer or just fooling around with their rifles sometimes. Fortunately they're not usually very good shots. Mostly they just end up shooting each other."

"That's a relief," said Rena.

"In fact, didn't you call in a similar incident just last summer? I came up here and took your statement. Gunfire close to your house. You know how it is up here, Mrs. Crocker—lots of good old boys who think laws about firearms don't really apply to them personally. They come around here sometimes looking for deer that people have been feeding scraps. Easy pickings."

"With all due respect, Deputy . . . Potter," Jackie said, peeking at the little gold name tag over his left pocket, "unless you have blind poachers in this county, whoever was doing the shooting couldn't possibly have mistaken either Mack or Jake for deer. Besides that, there were only two shots fired, and both of them barely missed the dogs. In my opinion that's too close to be accidental."

The deputy gave Jackie a look that seemed to say he wasn't particularly impressed by her opinion, but was determined to be both patient and professional. "I'll note that in my report, Ms. Walsh." He turned back to Rena.

"You just brought these dogs up here today, is that right, Mrs. Crocker?"

"Not more than two hours ago," Rena supplied.

"And they haven't been outside that fenced yard since you got here?"

"No, but—" Jackie began.

"Then I don't see how they could have made any enemies," said the deputy, the corners of his mouth turning up slightly. "Take my word for it, it was an accident. Don't get me wrong, it's not legal to shoot off firearms in a residential area, and we'll be looking for anyone running around up here with a rifle, but when we find them it'll likely be poachers or target shooters."

"God, I wish Alan were here," Rena sighed as she closed the door behind the deputy. "Well, what now?"

"Our choices seem to be between getting right back in the car and heading back for Los Angeles, or taking Deputy Potter's advice and forgetting the whole thing. I wish I knew what would be the smartest move."

"Alan will be here later tonight, I'm sure," said Rena. "I think the deputy was right about the gunfire being accidental. If you're worried, though, we can keep the dogs inside until dark. You are worried, aren't you?" she said, regarding Jackie with a look of concern. "Do you have a gun?"

"Do I what?" Jackie couldn't hide her surprise. "What would I need a gun for? I'm a college instructor, for God's sake!"

"You're also a detective of sorts. Don't deny it," said Rena. "I've heard all the stories from that ex-cop–ex-boyfriend of yours. He was writing on that police movie project that we supplied the dogs for last year.

When he found out we knew you he had all sorts of tales to tell us."

"Okay, I've been involved in a few criminal investigations, but I'm not a detective. Not really. If you don't believe me, just ask anyone on the Palmer police force."

"Well, it doesn't matter, because I do."

"You do what?" Jackie asked, having lost the point of the whole conversation.

"I do have a gun. Well, don't look so shocked. I live in Los Angeles."

Jackie managed a laugh. "Oh, I forgot you guys take potshots at one another on the freeways. Silly me."

"Well, it's not as bad as the newspapers might have you think, but it's not the safest place in the world, either. Alan's been a marksman since he was in the army years ago. He bought me a gun and insisted I learn how to use it. He took me to his favorite shooting range in West Hollywood, and I got to be quite a good shot. In fact that's where we first met Jules."

"So where's this gun of yours?" Jackie asked.

"It's outside in the glove compartment of the Land Rover."

Jackie wasn't sure whether that made her feel any safer or not, but if she insisted Rena go outside and bring the gun in, she might only make her nervous, and guns in the hands of nervous people definitely did nothing for her sense of security.

"So what are we going to do?" Jackie asked Rena.

"We're going to have dinner and wait for Alan. I'm sure there's nothing to worry about."

"If you say so," Jackie allowed, "but I'd still rather keep the dogs inside."

After a dinner put together from the contents of the well-stocked freezer and pantry, Jackie and Rena shared a bottle of merlot in front of the chalet's two-story stone fireplace. Jake lay at Jackie's feet and picked up his ears now and again at strange noises from outside. Mack curled up on a braided rug not much larger than he was, near the fire, seemingly as uneasy as his shepherd pal. Every few seconds the little terrier raised his head and looked toward the door, whining.

"Come here, Mack," Rena urged the terrier. "Come on over here to Mama." Mack whined again, then put his muzzle back down between his paws, clearly uninterested in leaving his spot.

"He's really Alan's dog," Rena told Jackie, refilling her wineglass from the bottle beside her. "He's the one who's a whiz with the animals. I handle the business end of things, though you could argue that I didn't do such a great job of it before Jules came on the team. I suppose I should have gone to that meeting myself, but I just wanted to get up here and put my feet up for a couple of days. It's been a long season." She put down the bottle and picked up the telephone, stabbing the redial button with a long, polished fingernail.

Jackie looked out the window at the scene outside. In spite of today's scare, she had to give it this: Bass Lake was nothing like Palmer, Ohio, and there were no Film and Society student papers to grade within two thousand miles. There wasn't a trace of automobile exhaust in the scents of pine and fir in the air, and although an occasional car could be heard driving down the road below, the traffic noises Jackie was used to hearing at this time of the evening near her downtown apartment had been replaced by the crackling fire and the sigh of the wind moving through the tops of the trees outside. If people would just stop shooting guns around here, she thought she might actually get to like it.

Rena was visibly anxious depite having drunk most of the bottle of wine. Between leaving messages for her husband and pacing the cabin's hardwood floor, she kept up a running commentary of her financial problems and Alan's moods. Jackie didn't feel their limited acquaintance really called for these kinds of confidences, but maybe Rena just needed to get a lot of stuff off her chest.

"Alan, it's Rena again," Rena was saying into the phone with more than a hint of impatience. "Please call me at the lake when you . . ." She stopped, pulled the phone away from her ear and stared at it. "What the . . . I think the phone's gone dead," she said, turning to Jackie. "Damned nuisance, but it happens around here a lot."

Jake raised his head from the floor and growled. Mack looked up, then left his rug and trotted over to the door that led outside. Jake followed, head up and ears on alert.

"I wonder . . ." Jackie began, rising from her spot on the deep cushioned sofa.

There was a flicker from the lamp beside Rena's chair, and then the house went dark except for the glow of the fire in the fireplace.

"Does this happen a lot around here, too?" Jackie asked her hostess, her voice shaking more than a little.

"Unfortunately, yes," Rena replied.

Just then Jake began barking insistently, running back and forth between the front door and the tall windows near the fireplace, Mack trailing at his heels and echoing his apparent concern.

"I wonder if I should let Jake out to investigate?" Jackie asked.

Rena shook her head. "I wouldn't," she said over the sound of the dogs. "We've had bears down this low before, and even mountain lions. I think they're attracted to the smell of food. It might not be safe for the dogs out there."

A low, roaring sound from outside made Jackie jump nearly out of her skin before she recognized it as the sound of a motor starting up.

"That's the back-up generator," said Rena. "It goes on automatically when the power's interrupted." A moment later the lights in the living room flickered back into life as the generator kicked in and restored power to the chalet. "I wouldn't worry about it. It isn't exactly rare to lose either phone or power up here when the wind's blowing, though I admit we've never lost one right after the other like that."

Jackie thought again about the gun in the glove compartment and wished she'd asked Rena to bring it inside after all. Maybe losing the phone and the power was nothing to worry about, but it was all a bit too much for a day that included bullets fired into the backyard.

Jackie jumped at the sound of a car horn in the distance. A moment later it was repeated.

"I wonder if that's Alan," said Rena, glancing in the direction of the road at the bottom of the hill on which the cabin sat. The horn went off again. "I think maybe we'd better go see."

"Okay," Jackie agreed. "Let's take Jake along. I think Mack should stick to the house, though."

"I'm sure you're right." Rena grabbed a jacket from

the coat tree near the door, and Jackie took her coat and Jake's lead.

"Come here, boy. Let's go for a walk."

Jake never had to be asked twice to go for a walk. He trotted happily across the living room floor and allowed Jackie to clip the lead onto his collar. Mack followed him to the door and sat patiently waiting for Rena.

"Sorry, Mack," said Rena. "This walk isn't for you. You stay inside."

Mack seemed to recognize "stay," which wasn't surprising, given his training, but it was obvious he didn't like it much.

"Okay, let's go," said Rena. She opened the door, and Jackie and Jake stepped out onto the front porch. A moment later, Mack came streaking out the door and ran between Jake's legs. "Damn!" Rena muttered. "Mack, come back here! Mack! Come!"

Mack ignored Rena as usual and ran around to the side of the cabin. He stopped in a rectangle of light cast by the living room lamps and waited, tongue lolling happily. There was a sound of gunfire, and a bit of cedar siding behind him exploded with a pop, sending the little terrier running back toward Jake.

Jake took a moment to decide on his direction, then tore the lead out of Jackie's hand and galloped off into the blackness, down the driveway and across the road. Mack barked once in surprise and followed him, disappearing rapidly among the trees and brush on the hillside on the other side of the two-lane road. Jackie called after her dog, but she could hear him getting farther and farther away.

"Okay, think, Jackie," she said to herself. "What the

hell do you do now?" Then to Rena, "Do you think that was Alan's horn we heard?"

"I couldn't say, really. I just thought it might be since we were expecting him anytime."

"Think about this carefully, Rena. You told me that Alan took out a life insurance policy on Mack. A big one. How big?"

"Two million dollars. Why?"

"Because someone's trying to kill Mack, and it's not you."

"Oh, my God, you think . . ."

"I don't know what I think. That's why I'm asking you. Is Alan capable of something like this? Could he shoot Mack and make it look like an accident? You told me yourself he's a crack shot. And that your business is in financial trouble. And Alan told me last night that the series might be canceled. Maybe Alan knows it already has been, and there won't be any movie deal to pull you out of the hole."

"But someone shot at the dogs this afternoon. Alan wasn't . . ."

"Wasn't here? Who's to say he wasn't? Who told you about the meeting today?"

"Alan did. Are you saying there wasn't really a meeting?"

"I don't know. I'm asking you to think about what you know."

"Absolutely not. Alan would never do such a thing. Detective or not, you're wrong about this. You heard Deputy Potter say this sort of thing happens around here a lot."

"Yeah, well I think three times in one day is more than a lot," said Jackie. "Even in rush hour on the Santa Monica

Freeway on the hottest day of summer, you don't get shot at three times in one day."

From far away, Jackie heard dogs barking, then something that might have been the slamming of a car door. Or it might just have been her heart knocking against her ribs. "I have to go find Jake," she told Rena. "You can stay here if you want to, or come along with me."

"I'm coming," said Rena. They started down the driveway.

"Wait," said Jackie. "Go back and get that gun."

They were almost to the two-lane road when Jackie could see a dark figure coming toward them up the hill. She froze and laid a hand on Rena's arm. Rena stopped. The figure advanced, head down, then stopped and looked up. "Rena? Jackie? What are you doing down here? Was that gunfire I heard a minute ago?" Alan Crocker looked at the gun in his wife's hand.

"Isn't it a little dark for target shooting?"

"Oh, Alan!" Rena cried, rushing forward into his arms. "Something awful has happened! Someone was shooting at Mack, and he ran off with Jake and we don't know where he is!"

At least, Jackie thought to herself, Rena seemed to have abandoned the random gunfire hypothesis. "We were just going to find the dogs," she told Alan. "We brought the gun because there's been someone shooting at them, and it doesn't seem accidental. Where did you come from, anyhow? Why didn't you bring the car up to the house?"

Rena shot her a look, but Jackie wasn't about to abandon her suspicions about Alan just because his wife was relieved to see him.

"Damned thing ran out of gas down the road," he said,

pointing downhill. "I coasted it nearly as far as the driveway, but I couldn't coast it up a steep hill."

Jackie was watching Alan's face closely, but in the almost total darkness it was impossible to see subtleties of expression. What she did see looked like steely determination.

"I'm going after the dogs," he said. "I've got another gun in the car. Or give me yours, Rena—you two should probably go back to the cabin and call the sheriff's substation."

"I think we should all go together," Jackie suggested. She wished she knew a way to insist on carrying the gun, too, but none occurred to her. "The dogs went down the driveway and across the road. That way." She pointed the way. "You didn't see them?"

"They must have run across just before I pulled up," Alan said. "We'll get my gun out of the car on the way."

As they headed into the trees across the road, Alan in the lead with his semiautomatic pistol at the ready, Jackie wished someone had thought of a flashlight. She wasn't sure whether it was safe to be seen, but then they weren't exactly proceeding quietly at any rate, crashing through the scrub oak and manzanita on the hill. "Alan, slow down!" she called in the loudest whisper she could manage. He didn't seem to hear her, but hurried on.

"Ow!" Rena yelped, and Jackie heard the crack of branches and a loud thump. She turned around to see Rena lying on the ground holding one of her ankles in both hands. Jackie went back to help her up, then looked around for Alan, but he was completely out of sight.

"Maybe we should wait here for Alan to come back," Rena suggested, testing her weight on the injured ankle and wincing visibly. Jackie picked up Rena's pistol from the ground and handed it to her. Rena put it into her coat pocket and leaned against a fir tree. Jackie looked into the blackness. She could still hear the dogs barking, closer now, and a distant sound that might have been Alan stumbling through the brush, but she could see almost nothing.

After what seemed like forever, but was probably only a couple of minutes, Jackie could hear someone coming closer. She looked at Rena. Rena took the pistol from her pocket and pointed it into the featureless darkness. A few moments later Alan emerged from the shadow of the trees with Jules Berger walking in front of him, hands on his head in a position Jackie recognized from having once held a couple of murder suspects at gunpoint in a forest not unlike this one.

"I found him back there," Alan said grimly. "He's got to be the one who was shooting at Mack. The dogs are locked in his motor home. After the sheriff takes him away, I'll let them out."

"Rena, don't believe him!" Jules begged, his voice breaking. "He's the one with the gun!"

Rena looked back and forth between the two men, the pistol wavering in her grip.

Jackie had to admit Jules had a point. "If he was doing the shooting, where's his gun?" she asked Alan.

"I think he locked it in the motor home with the dogs," said Alan. "He could have lured them into the back door and sneaked out the driver's side and closed both doors before they could turn around and get out again. And he might have been in too much of a hurry to remember to bring his rifle with him, especially with Jake snarling down his neck."

"Rena, Alan's the one who's been trying to kill Mack!" Jules insisted. "He found out the series had been canceled and the movie deal was never going to happen. Without Mack's insurance policy, he'd be flat broke!"

"Canceled?" said Alan. "How could you know that? The meeting was postponed, and they weren't supposed to make a decision until after we'd talked to them again."

Rena was shaking all over and having difficulty standing on her bad foot. The gun she held moved back and forth uncertainly between the two men in front of her. "I don't know what to do!" she wailed.

"Hold the gun on Jules," Jackie told her, "and I'll go back to the cabin and call the sheriff."

"Why Jules?" Rena asked.

"Because he'd be the first to know if Mack's series was canceled, not Alan," Jackie told her. "He's the agent. The producers would notify him and have him tell you. Besides, you said yourself it was his idea to take out the insurance policy in the first place. Second, or maybe third, why would he bring a motor home up here if he could just stay in the cabin? Because he was camped out waiting for a good shot at your dog and didn't want to muss his Armani suit, that's why. Why would he even come up here at all without notifying one of you? It's your cabin. Jules is your bad guy. Trust me. Help Alan hold him, and I'll go make that call."

Rena looked at Jules, tears trembling on her lower eyelids. "Jules?" she whimpered. "What should I do?"

Jules sighed with weary impatience. "Rena, darling, do I have to tell you everything? Shoot these two and let's get out of here. I'm covered with mosquito bites, and I think I ran into some poison oak back there."

"Rena?" Alan's voice was freighted with shock and disbelief.

Rena pointed her pistol at Jackie. Jackie remembered her earlier desire to take control of the pistol and wished heartily she'd had the guts to be possibly rude then instead of possibly dead in the next few minutes. If she lived through this, not a foregone conclusion by any means, it was going to be a relief to get back home where the only people she knew who carried guns were police officers.

"What an idiot I am!" she exclaimed. "Of course he wouldn't be doing this alone! You're the one who handles the finances, and you've made a hash of it, haven't you? You needed that two million dollars to get back in the black, and you were willing to kill Mack to get it."

"Rena?" Alan was repeating himself, but Jackie figured he wasn't capable of much else right now. She felt awfully sorry for him, but hoped he could keep his wits about him for just a big longer. "Rena, you need to call a halt to this right now. If you do it Jules's way you'll have to kill both Alan and me. Do you really think you can get away with that?"

"Why wouldn't we?" Jules answered for her. "There must be millions of acres up here in which to bury two people and two dogs. By the time anything could be proved against us we'd have the insurance money, and we could be anywhere in the world with brand-new identities."

"Listen to him, Rena. He's been planning for this all along. I guess your original plan was to make Mack's death seem like an accidental shooting—you already knew that fools have been known to fire rifles at anything that moves or doesn't up here, and if the sheriff determined that Mack was killed by random gunfire you'd have no trouble

collecting on the insurance. Of course Jules wasn't counting on moving targets and a side-wind. Not exactly a rifle
range out here, is it, Jules?"

Jules glared.

"Then you had to turn off the power to try to get another
shot at Mack if we were lured outside. Only you didn't
know about the back-up generator, did you? You even had
me along to witness the accident, only I wasn't being too
cooperative, was I?"

"I told you not to bring her up here," Jules snapped
at Rena.

"Shut up!" Rena snapped back. "The dogs are locked in
the motor home?"

"That's right."

"Did you roll up the windows? Mack can get out of a
pretty small space, you know."

"For God's sake, Rena, that shepherd was going to rip
my throat out! I couldn't stop to check whether the windows were completely rolled up! Now are you going to
shoot them or not?"

"I guess I am," said Rena, though Jackie had to admit
she didn't seem all that happy about it. "I'm sorry, Alan. I
know you well enough to know you won't be able to use a
gun on either Jules or me. You're deadly against a target,
but you could never take a life." She pointed the pistol at
her husband and tightened her finger on the trigger.

Alan fell forward, arms out in front of him, pistol flying,
and a split second later Jackie saw why. A black form
vaulted over him and crashed into Rena, taking her gun
hand in jaws powerful enough to snap bone—Jake.

Rena screamed and dropped the gun. Jules dove for it,
but Jackie had anticipated him and got there first, launch-

ing herself under Jake and covering the weapon with her body. Jules landed on top of her and tried to roll her off the pistol. Jake let go of Rena and advanced on Jules, growling deep in his throat. His jaws closed around Jules's shoulder, tearing holes in Giorgio Armani's exquisite handiwork. Jules squealed, whether for his suit or his shoulder, Jackie wasn't entirely sure.

"Looks like your dog has this situation under control," said a voice from somewhere over her head. Jackie looked up to see Deputy Potter pointing his revolver at Jules's head. "Let's all go down to the station and talk over the details."

Jake recognized the deputy's authority and backed away, still growling. A second deputy cuffed Jules's hands behind his back and lifted him from the ground. Jackie raised herself to her knees and hugged her dog. "How did you get out of that motor home?" she asked him.

"I let him out," said Deputy Potter. "After that little dog came up to my patrol car and practically dragged me over there. Looks like the little guy got out through the window."

Jules moaned. Rena dissolved into tears. Jackie and Deputy Potter looked at Mack, who was jumping up and down with joy to see Alan. Alan held out his arms and Mack jumped into them, licking his master's face with abandon.

Jackie got up and dusted off the worst of the dirt and leaves from her clothes. Her hands were a little scraped, but it was a whole lot better than being shot.

"I was investigating some gunfire I heard," Deputy Potter continued. "I thought it might be whoever had been shooting around here this afternoon. Guess I was right about that, huh, Ms. Walsh?" He gave Jules and Rena a look of disgust. "And here I was looking forward to another boring night on patrol duty. Now I'm going to be filling out forms and writing incident reports for the rest of my shift." He smiled at his own joke as he took Rena's arm and led her toward the patrol car. "Then they'll go to trial and I'll have to go to court, probably more than once. This is going to be no end of bother for me."

"Sorry we won't be able to help you out, Deputy Potter," Jackie told him. "Jake and I are going back to Ohio for a vacation."

If you enjoyed the stories in
CANINE CRIMES,
we invite you to investigate further:

Turn the page for more mysteries from
the contributors to
CANINE CRIMES . . .

THE PUZZLED HEART
by
AMANDA CROSS

Kate Fansler's husband, Reed, has been kidnapped—and will be killed unless Kate obeys the carefully delineated directives of a ransom note.

Tormented by her own puzzled heart, Kate seeks solace and wise counsel from friends both old and new. But who precisely is the enemy? Is he or she a vengeful colleague? A hostile student? A political terrorist?

The questions mount as Kate searches for Reed—accompanied by her trusty new companion, a Saint Bernard puppy named Bancroft. Hovering near Kate and Bancroft are rampant cruelties and calculated menace. The moment is ripe for murder . . .

Published by Ballantine Books.
Available at your local bookstore.

Veterinary Mysteries
by (Lillian M. Roberts)

RIDING FOR A FALL

The return of Ross McRoberts—an old flame from vet school—spells trouble for Andi Pauling's fledgling Palm Springs veterinarian clinic. First his horses become the targets of malicious sabotage, and then a popular Argentine polo player turns up dead. . . .

THE HAND THAT FEEDS YOU

Andi Pauling fears the worst when a client brings a severely battered pit bull to her for treatment. Even more disturbing is the mute, withdrawn little girl accompanying him. When the dog's owner is murdered and the child vanishes, Andi infiltrates the illegal dogfight circuit to find the girl—and is targeted by a vicious pack of very human predators.

ALMOST HUMAN

Andi Pauling is accustomed to putting pets to sleep when their condition is hopeless—a sad but necessary procedure. But she is unprepared for a pet owner's request to do the same for her. When the woman dies under suspicious circumstances, Andi finds herself in deep trouble—suspected of murder.

Published by Fawcett Books.
Available at your local bookstore.

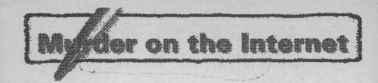